"Who is the Maid of Lorne and what does she desire?"

"I am a woman with no father and no family and no home to call her own. I am a woman who gave herself to her enemy. I am the Maid of Lorne no more." Her voice shook in its desolation.

Sebastien walked up behind her. Reaching out, he slipped his arm around her shoulders and pulled her back against him. Lara did not pull away. He whispered in her ear.

"Do not despair, Lara." The emptiness in her gaze unsettled him, and he acknowledged that he would rather face her anger or her confusion than this melancholy.

"You asked me once what I want. What does Sebastien of Cleish want? I want you, Lara. I want to hold you and feel your body as it heats to my touch. I want you to open to me and I want to fill you with myself."

He took a step closer and she took one back. Finally he pulled her into his arms and kissed her the way he'd wanted to all night. Indeed, the way he'd wanted to since the night they were wed.

* * *

The Maid of Lorne
Harlequin Historical #786—January 2006

TERRI BRISBIN

THE MAID OF LORNE

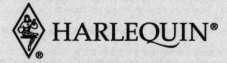

HARLEQUIN®

TORONTO • NEW YORK • LONDON
AMSTERDAM • PARIS • SYDNEY • HAMBURG
STOCKHOLM • ATHENS • TOKYO • MILAN • MADRID
PRAGUE • WARSAW • BUDAPEST • AUCKLAND

ISBN 0-373-29386-0

THE MAID OF LORNE

Copyright © 2006 by Theresa S. Brisbin

All rights reserved. Except for use in any review, the reproduction or
utilization of this work in whole or in part in any form by any electronic,
mechanical or other means, now known or hereafter invented, including
xerography, photocopying and recording, or in any information storage
or retrieval system, is forbidden without the written permission of the
publisher, Harlequin Enterprises Limited, 225 Duncan Mill Road,
Don Mills, Ontario, Canada M3B 3K9.

All characters in this book have no existence outside the imagination of
the author and have no relation whatsoever to anyone bearing the same
name or names. They are not even distantly inspired by any individual
known or unknown to the author, and all incidents are pure invention.

This edition published by arrangement with Harlequin Books S.A.

® and TM are trademarks of the publisher. Trademarks indicated with
® are registered in the United States Patent and Trademark Office, the
Canadian Trade Marks Office and in other countries.

www.eHarlequin.com

Printed in U.S.A.

**DON'T MISS THESE OTHER
NOVELS AVAILABLE NOW:**

Please address questions and book requests to:
Harlequin Reader Service
U.S.: 3010 Walden Ave., P.O. Box 1325, Buffalo, NY 14269
Canadian: P.O. Box 609, Fort Erie, Ont. L2A 5X3

This book is dedicated to my travel companions,
Sue-Ellen Welfonder and Lisa Trumbauer, who said,
on that fateful day in May 2002 as we drove down the
western coast of Scotland, "Turn here and check out this
castle—it's called Dunstaffnage and Robert the Bruce
took it from the MacDougalls." Thank you for being a
part of my magical first trip to the Scottish Highlands
and for introducing me to the special place that
would inspire this story. *Slainte!*

I would also like to dedicate this book to my former
agent, Linda Kruger of the Fogelman Agency. She retired
from the business in February 2005 to tend to her family
and, although I am not happy for me as I write this, I am
very happy for her and those important people in her life.
Linda—thanks for your support through seven
and a half years and twelve books!

My thanks to Sue-Ellen Welfonder, an expert on
Robert the Bruce's life and exploits, and to the
writers on the WOWResearch e-mail list for
always knowing the answers or knowing where
to find them. I bow to your wisdom!

Prologue

The 11th day of August
In the Year of Our Lord, 1308

The stench of blood and sweat and death permeated the air around the field. The victory here had assured Scotland's embattled king that he would gain the foothold he needed in the west, and break the power of some of the more dangerous "lords of the isles." Thinking to ambush his troops as they made their way toward the coast, the MacDougalls had underestimated his abilities and those of his supporters.

As he stood before the man who had handed him victory at the battle of Brander Pass that morning, the Bruce was covered in not a little blood. Robert smiled grimly.

"You have your orders, Sebastien. Carry them out. Those who will accompany you to Dunstaffnage know their duties and will support anything you do there in my name."

His most trusted warrior and spy simply nodded as he always did, and turned to leave. Sebastien of Cleish had presented him with their enemy's ambush plans and a clever strategy in response to it.

"Wed or dead by nightfall, Sebastien, and I'll be wanting proof of either one."

"Aye, sire. Wed or dead." The warrior bowed to him and was already on his way out of the tent when he spoke the words.

Robert took a deep breath before calling his squire to help him undress. Dunstaffnage Castle, the MacDougall's lands and his eldest daughter, the Maid of Lorne, would be within his grasp before the sun set this evening.

Chapter One

She'd closed the gates against him.

In spite of the messenger sent with the news of the Bruce's victory over her father, she refused him entrance into Dunstaffnage Castle. Sebastien was definitely leaning toward the "dead" portion of his orders from the king as he sat outside the main gate. Letting out an exasperated breath, he motioned to one of the men surrounding the three sides of the castle facing the land, and nodded.

Peering up to the battlements, he could see the eldest daughter of John MacDougall watching his every move. He pushed the helm and mail off his head and waited for their weapon to be brought forward. His horse danced beneath him, probably feeling the strain of the battle of wills going on around it. Sebastien was certainly feeling it. With the glare of the sun behind her, he could not quite get a clear look at his adversary.

Hearing the noises behind him, he moved over a few paces so that their hostages were clearly visible to all watching from the upper levels of the castle. The commotion behind him increased and he watched as Lara MacDougall drew nearer to the edge of the crenellated wall and looked over. She grabbed hold of the stone as though she needed support.

If he'd been the one watching his younger siblings wrapped in chains and dragged by the heavily armed warriors of their deadliest enemy, he might react badly, too. The young boy and girl were also screeching loud enough to be heard by anyone within miles.

His quarry stepped back from the wall and he lost sight of her for a minute before she leaned out again. Sebastien could hear the argument going on, but could not make out the words. The only thing he could tell was that not everyone was in agreement with whatever she planned to do. He realized that he had not heard her voice yet, for earlier her steward had called out her responses to his demands.

"What are your terms?" she called now.

Sebastien laughed aloud before answering. "Terms? I will not kill these two if you open the gates immediately. Delay and I will not even promise that." He dismounted and his squire ran forward to take control of the horse from him. "I am tired and not in good humor, lady. If you make me fight my way in, I also promise that *you* will bear the consequences."

The air was filled with expectation as everyone waited. Sebastien had no doubt that she would order the gates open. Her brother and sister had told him that much on the ride here. They'd revealed that she'd always stood between them and danger, but this time, in trying to send them away from danger, she'd inadvertently placed them in the path of it.

Sebastien had been honest, though; he was tired and wanted to bring this to an end. He wanted nothing so much as a hot bath to rid himself of the odors and filth of battle and blood, and the sooner he got inside, the sooner he might have exactly that. Of course, depending on her actions, he might have one more messy task to accomplish for his king before he bathed.

She disappeared from the battlements and he heard her calling out orders as she ran. He put his helmet back on and mounted again, for it was better to face enemies well-armed and from the back of a horse than on the ground. With a wave of his hand, his men regrouped around him and the children were moved to the back, out of danger from misfired arrows or misguided men.

Would she feel humiliated when she discovered the truth of his treatment of her siblings? How would she react when he offered her the choice that Robert had demanded only hours ago—wed or dead? Now, after seeing her valiant efforts to defend her home, he was certain it would not be an easy thing to carry out her execution. He would, of course, if she did not consent to the marriage, but it would be more difficult than following other orders from the Bruce.

The scraping of wood and metal filled the air as the portcullis was raised and the gates pulled open. Then, with loud squealing, the drawbridge was lowered to the ground. Two guards marched forward with one woman between them. Sebastien was tempted to laugh again, but spared his adversary the humiliation. As if these two men could protect her against anything he wanted to do… The small group stopped after crossing the bridge and stepping onto the rocky ground surrounding the MacDougall fortress.

"Secure the castle," Sebastien called out without ever lifting his gaze from her face. A troop of his men rode forward, the hooves of their horses clattering on the wood of the drawbridge.

She looked as though she wanted to say something, but hesitated. Now that he could see her features, he realized she was younger than he'd first thought. She wore a plain gown and had her blond hair pulled back and woven into a long thick braid. But the hautiness and arrogance of the MacDougall was etched on her face.

Sebastien dismounted once more and approached her. Her expression displayed a hint of fear as he drew near, and then she seemed to control it.

"How many years have you?" He scrutinized her face and form as he asked. 'Twas difficult to tell from just looking. He reached up and removed the helmet he wore and pushed his hair and the mail over it back off his head.

"Enough to know that only one of the Bruce's minions would use children as his shield…."

Her words drifted off as he dropped his helm and reached out to take hold of her face. Pulling her by her chin, he dragged her close enough so that only she could hear his words. Staring directly into her cold blue eyes, he clarified her new position so there would be no mistake.

"Speak carefully, lady. To insult me is to insult the Bruce. And he now rules Dunstaffnage—and you."

Her face blanched and she reached up to pull his

hand away. Although her touch sent shivers down his spine, the look of hatred in her eyes shocked him. Was it meant for him or for Robert? Sebastien released her and sent her stumbling back a few paces.

"I would see my brother and sister." It was a demand, with no acceptance in her tone that he was the victor here.

"I think not." They had business to conclude before he would surrender his leverage.

"You think to keep them prisoner? Will you throw them in the cell that opens to the ocean's winds? Will you keep them wrapped in chains…?"

He grabbed her once more. She challenged him with every word she spoke and, in spite of a certain exhilaration he felt because of it, he could not allow that to happen. This time he used both hands to take her by the shoulders.

"Until we finish our business, you will go nowhere but where I take you, and do nothing that I do not tell you to do."

He drew her closer until only inches separated their faces. Suddenly he was fighting an urge to kiss her instead of threaten her. Tamping down that desire, he gritted his teeth and forced out the words of his orders from the Bruce.

"The Bruce has taken your father prisoner and I hold your siblings and this castle for Robert. You have the choice of what happens to them."

"I have the choice?" Her voice came out as a stuttering whisper. He could see the fear in her eyes now.

"You will be wed or dead by nightfall—it is up to you."

All the color left her face and she looked as though she might faint. After a few moments, she spoke.

"Wed or dead? Who will carry out this sentence?"

"You will wed me or be dead by my hand, lady. Choose now."

Lara MacDougall could not speak. As most of those living at Dunstaffnage knew, that did not happen often. She stared up at the face of her enemy and could not believe the words he had just said. Wed him or die? Today?

She shook her head, simply not able to comprehend the reasons behind his supposed orders from the Bruce. Pah! The Bruce? How dare he think he had the right to rule Scotland and especially this area! Her father had held power here for so long she could not remember it ever being any different. And who was this Sebastien of Cleish to think that he was deserving of the hand of the Maid of Lorne? Blinking, she shook her head again.

"Is that your answer? You would choose to die?"

He released her and she watched in horror as he stepped back and pulled a long sword from its sheath. His brows gathered in a mighty frown, but his intent was clear—her death. Before she could protest or say anything, the sounds of screaming emanated from the castle. Lara reacted as she always did when her family or people were threatened—she turned to run back inside to determine the reason. Could the Bruce's men be killing those within? Her young maid and some cousins had remained inside when she'd left. Were they being attacked?

Her captor's arm wrapped around her waist and

pulled her back against his body. She tore at his hands and called out her maid's name, trying to get free, but the brute's strength was impressive. He hardly even moved as she struggled. When she stopped for a moment, intending to try again, he took her braid in his fist and pulled her head toward his. His breath was hot against her neck and his words were just as heated.

"You will get back inside either as my wife or in a wooden box. No other way. Until you decide, you stay here." She finally realized he meant what he said. She shivered in fear as the words sank in. Before she could think about her own situation, she must get his agreement to keep those inside safe during his stay here.

"But the women inside…? What is happening to them?" She almost feared asking the question, knowing what men in battle did to their enemies' women afterward.

"They will not be harmed as long as they do not resist my control over the keep. That is more than I can say for your father's methods of occupation."

They stayed in this position for a few moments as she considered his words. At least alive she could continue to fight for her family. Alive, she could find a way to get her brother and sister away from Dunstaffnage and to the safety of her uncle's lands. Alive, she would…have to marry a man who cared not if he took her as wife or took her head for the Bruce.

But she would be alive, and that was all that mattered now.

"I choose…" She struggled to get the words out. In her wildest imaginings and worst nightmares she had never pictured this as her future—married on the orders of her father's bitterest enemy. What kind of life would she have to endure as this man's wife?

He eased his hold of her and she turned to face him. Her gaze moved over his face and body. He was well-formed, with a warrior's build. Although he was covered with sweat and blood, she could not see any signs of disfigurement or disease.

"I see no other way than to choose marriage to you."

Lara did not know what she had expected as a response to her words, but the grunt and nod, followed by him walking off toward the chapel, was not it. He called out orders to those under his command who stood nearby as he strode away. When he realized that she remained where he had left her, he turned back to her.

"Come, lady. The priest awaits us in the chapel." With barely a pause and a wave at her, he continued down the worn path toward the stone building set off some distance from the castle.

"Priest?" she called out. "Surely you do not mean to carry out the wedding ceremony *now*." Lara put her fists on her hips and waited for him to answer.

Her question did stop his progress, for he turned back and walked to her. His long strides made her feel like a stalked animal. Lara forced herself to remain upright and to stay where she was. In a moment, he was towering over her.

"The priest is waiting now, and prepared for wedding or funeral."

"You jest!"

"Nay, lady. If you walk in, we wed. If I carry your body, he says the Mass for the Dead. Now, does your choice stand?"

She would marry now, without family or friends to stand with her? Lara had envisioned a nicer ceremony and celebration to mark the occasion for the daughter of the MacDougall. Now, she would marry in her worn work gown, to a man covered in the blood of her clan.

"I said I would wed and I stand by my word."

"Come, then. Father Connaughty will be pleased to see you walk in."

The barbarian then had the nerve to hold out his arm to her. Looking about, seeing the soldiers surrounding her and noting that her people watched from some of the windows of the towers and from the gate, she pulled her courage around her and placed her hand on his arm. With her head held high, she walked at his side to her fate.

She had never believed that marrying for love was an option for her. In her position as the eldest daughter, she knew her marriage would be an alliance, but she had never considered that it would be a punishment.

Chapter Two

Like a pig destined for slaughter, she had been washed and seasoned and dressed. And all at the explicit orders of her husband. She had not, however, been fatted yet, for his orders were for the bedding to occur before the meal. In shock over hearing of the agreement between her father and the Bruce for her settlements and the disposition of the castle and the wealth she inherited from her mother, she'd listened to the rest of it with little interest.

Now, she stood staring into the fire in her chamber's brazier, trying not to think about what would happen next. Oh, she knew about coupling with a man. Nothing much that happened between men and women was secret in clan life. But to have to do *that* with a complete stranger, a man who had barged into her life and who held in his grasp not only her life, but also the lives of her family and people, was difficult to contemplate.

But, it was out of her hands now. He held all the power. Whatever he ordered was done, either by those men who accompanied him here, or by her people,

who had been told of his orders and his marriage to
their laird's daughter. Part of her, deep inside, would
remain quiet and wait for a better time to fight back.
And fight back she would.

The Bruce might hold Dunstaffnage for now, but
there were ways to make certain that his possession was
a temporary thing. Allies of her father were no doubt
already planning how to recapture the castle and to free
him. As the wife of the Bruce's man here, she could get
access to information that might help the fight against
him and hasten the MacDougall's return to his center
of power.

"You look quite formidable when you frown like
that, lady."

His voice was deep and rich and it caused waves of
unease to pass through her. Did her guilt show on her
face? Clearing her thoughts, she turned to face her
stranger husband.

Gone was the bloodied warrior she'd exchanged
vows with in the chapel but an hour before. In his place
was a handsome nobleman with his long brown hair
pulled back from his face. Clothed in a long dressing
robe as he was, she could see the long gash on his neck,
now cleaned and sewn. Lara had noted his height when
he had taken hold of her, so that was no surprise, but his
piercing green eyes and strong chin and even smile were.

She looked up and realized that she had been gawk-
ing…and he had noticed. Taking a deep breath, she
wiped her sweaty palms over her own robe.

"Although your maid said you preferred ale, I
brought this wine to share with you. 'Tis a gift from
the Bruce to honor our marriage."

The man walked toward her, carrying two goblets. Lara's first instinct was to knock the cups from his hands, for drinking the Bruce's wine would be an insult to those in her clan who had died this day. From the firm set of his chin, she knew that Sebastien would not tolerate that behavior from her. He had promised retribution against those she loved if she did not do as he told her, and she believed that he would seek it.

"I admire self-control." He made a mock salute after handing her one of the goblets.

"I do not know what you mean, sir." She lowered her gaze to the cup she now held.

"You wished to knock the wine from my hands at the mention of the Bruce. I am pleased that you exercised control over that wayward plan."

"Am I so easy to discern?"

"Nay, lady. But as one who struggles with the same weakness, I recognize it quickly in others." He stepped closer and guided her cup to her lips. "Try the wine before condemning it for its giver."

Lara sniffed at the goblet, wondering if he had drugged it with some herb to make her more compliant for what he planned.

"Does the wine smell turned?" He sniffed at his own and frowned, then sipped it. "What think you wrong with it?" He gazed into her eyes, and then he nodded as he seem to read her thoughts once more. "You think I have drugged yours? To what purpose?"

Sebastien stepped back and took her wine. He drank deeply from it and then handed it back to her.

"If I want you dead or intend to strike at you, wife, you will see it coming. I do not hide behind the cow-

ardly art of poison. You will know if…when you are
my target."

He turned from her and walked to the window in her
chamber. Leaning an elbow on the frame, he stared out
at the gathering dusk and drank the rest of his wine.
Lara knew he was angry now. She saw it in his stance
and in the way that the muscles of his neck tightened
as he gritted his teeth.

"Sir, I meant no insult."

He laughed and looked at her. "You think I would
drug you into submission, and then say you insult me
not?" His laugh turned sarcastic. "Lady, your barbs are
like weapons and you wield them with amazing accu-
racy."

Their gazes held this time and he moved closer to
her. She knew that her actions determined his treatment
of so many of her people. She could live through whatever he planned for her. She was a MacDougall and
would not shirk from what needed to be done. If lying
with this man was the price for her life and those of her
siblings and father, she could do it.

Lifting her goblet to her mouth, she tilted it and
drank the contents in one long swallow. Drops of wine
collected on her lips when she lowered the cup, and she
thought to lick them off, but his mouth was there first.
Warm and firm, he pressed his lips to hers. As she felt
the tip of his tongue slide over her mouth, and a heated
pulsing begin to move through her, she pulled away.

"I know my duty, sir. I do not need your wine to ease
my way in this." If he did not like subterfuge, he would
get none from her in this matter. The quicker done the
better; once bedded and their vows sealed, she would

finally see her brother and sister…if he kept his word. "I will not fight you."

Lara handed him back the goblet and walked to the side of her bed. At first, she thought to climb on top. But, if they lay on the thick woolen covers, the sign needed to prove consummation would not be apparent. So she tugged the blankets out of the way and climbed on the fine linen sheets that covered her bed. Careful to gather her robe about her, she lay down and closed her eyes.

And she waited.

No sound filled the chamber except the crackling of the wood in the brazier. She was certain he could hear her heart pounding in her chest. Still, he made no move or any sounds. Lara felt the tension grow inside of her. It was difficult to breathe and her skin tingled as the coolness of the room penetrated the thin material of the dressing gown she wore. She longed to pull the thick layer of blankets over her, but she did not.

And still she waited.

She was beautiful and intelligent and proud. She was loyal to her people and she was a skilled tactician in her own right. And she was his now.

And she was terrified.

Oh, his wife would never admit to it, but he could read that in her gaze and in her stance when he entered the room. It was obvious to him until she gathered her self-control and banished the fleeting glimpse of terror within those deep blue eyes. Then, to his surprise, she climbed onto the bed and placed herself like the sacrifice she was on the pristine white sheets. Although what he must do would embarrass her, he would rather not have to humiliate her before her people and the Bruce's men.

He liked the challenges that she presented to him at every step of the way. Sebastien could not let them go unmet, but he learned more about her and the way her mind worked every time she resisted him and his orders.

Sebastien walked the few steps to the bed and gazed down at Lara. Her form was certainly pleasing to him. The dressing gown hid little from his eyes, and her position offered an enticing view of her lush breasts and shapely legs. Her blond hair spilled around her like waves, on the pillows and the bedcovers, tempting him to feel it and smell it. Bedding her would be no hardship to him. Catching a glimpse out the window at the sun as it moved toward the sea, he knew he had little time to dawdle at the task.

Sebastien untied his robe and let it drop to the floor. He sat next to her on the bed, forcing her to move.

"Sir, you may use the other side," she squeaked as she looked through lowered lashes at him. "You are naked!"

"I will take the side nearest the door, Lara. Move now."

He did laugh as she scrambled across the bed and positioned herself as far away from him as possible, all without looking directly at him. He granted her the reprieve of pulling up a sheet to cover them, and then he reached over and grabbed her hand.

"Now, wife, come closer."

He slowly pulled her nearer to him until she lay

next to him, her soft robe touching his leg. Sebastien reached down and untied the belt holding it together and tugged it free. She began to struggle as she realized his intent, but he paused.

"I intend no ravishment this evening, Lara. If you follow my lead, you may find the joy that exists in the joining of a man and a woman."

"I have no choice in this, sir. You are stronger than I and can force your will on me whenever you choose to. You hold my family as prisoners and use my actions to decide their fates. And you say this is not taking me against my will?"

Her voice shook as she spoke the words. She was correct—she had no choice. But then, neither did he. He had never forced himself on any woman, and doing it now would surely make her his enemy. But, more important to him at this moment, he had never disobeyed an order from the Bruce. Preserving her dignity was one thing, but his orders were not for discussion.

"If you let me begin, I will give you as much choice in this as I can."

She leaned away and looked at him, suspicion in every part of her expression and emanating from the depths of her ice-blue eyes.

"Then I choose to go down to dinner now."

Sebastien laughed and pulled her into his arms. He tucked her head under his chin and held her still. "There will be time for eating when we finish here."

When she lifted her head to reply, he stopped her with a kiss. Sebastien slid his hands down to her hips and pulled her against him, allowing her to feel the reaction of his body to her nearness. He tasted her surprise, but continued to caress her back and bottom even as he deepened the kiss. With smooth movements, he spread her long hair out over them. Then he slipped her robe off her shoulders and pushed it away.

The shock of her heated skin against his made him harden even more. He knew that she felt him and his readiness and knew it for what it was. He slid his hands up and held her mouth on his, moving his tongue over her lips and then inside, touching the tip of hers. He imitated what the other part of his body would do soon, and was pleased at the sound of her breathlessness.

She had made no move of her own, so he guided her arms around his neck. Her breasts now pressed against his chest and her hips cradled his erection. He paused to let her become familiar with the feeling of body touching body. His skin was on fire and the need to touch her more intimately grew until he could no longer resist it.

Sebastien turned them over until she was on her back, and he stroked her face and then her neck. Lara tensed as his hands moved lower. Her breasts tingled and ached as his fingers glided over her skin, moving ever downward from her neck to her breasts and stomach and lower still.

She really wanted to push him off and make him stop, but part of her was enticed by his touch. And that part of her shamed the rest of her for her compliance in her own seduction. He lifted her chin until their gazes met, and then he stared with a frightening intensity at her as his touch became more and more insistent. When his hand reached the curls at the juncture of her thighs, her body reacted on its own, tightening and arching against his hand.

Heat and wetness poured from the aching place between her legs, but she wanted to beg him to remove his hand. As though he sensed her doubts, he leaned over her once more and kissed her until she nearly forgot the truth between them. She was the Maid of Lorne, eldest daughter of the MacDougall. She had duties to her clan and this seducer could not sway her from them.

Her resistance lasted but a moment, until his fingers slid into the place that ached for his touch. Her legs opened to him and he used his hand to tease and ready her for more. Throbbing waves pulsed throughout her body until she thought she might burst. The groan that escaped her seemed to encourage him, for he knelt between her thighs and used his mouth and hands to ensorcell her more.

When his mouth covered the taut tip of her breast, even as his hand moved inside her to touch someplace unknown to her, she did moan. He suckled on her harder and rubbed the engorged fullness between her legs faster until she did begin to scream. Covering her mouth with his and capturing her sounds, he placed himself over the throbbing place and pushed his hardness into her. A moment of stretching was followed by one of stinging and then she was simply filled with him.

He stopped and she forced her eyes to open and look at him. Sweat covered his brow and his upper lip and she could feel the moist weeping where he lay between her thighs.

"Wife," he whispered as he began to move again, pushing in to stretch her with his fullness, and then withdrawing. Some new tension built within her; the need to arch against him and to scream out his name increased with every one of his thrusts. Lara fought not to surrender, but her body betrayed her. Under his expert control, he drew her moans and took her to the height of excitement. She felt him grow larger and harder and then, as his body tensed over her, she lost any ability to think at all. She could only feel—feel him filling her, feel herself thrumming with pleasure, feel her loss of control as she reached for what he offered. Matching his groan, she let go and followed where he led. He filled her with his seed and then they collapsed together, out of breath and covered in the sweat and smell of passion.

Minutes passed and neither spoke as their breathing returned to what it should be. Unsure now of what to do or say, Lara simply waited for him to move off her. It was the knock on her door that spurred him into action.

"Sebastien, 'tis time." A man's deep voice carried through the door to them.

Sebastien said nothing in response, but he rolled away from her and stood next to the bed. He tugged the ends of the top sheet from under the thick mattress and wiped himself off on it. Lara felt the heat of a blush in her cheeks at the sight of her blood on his member, but his next action completely surprised her.

He eased her legs apart and cleaned up the maiden's blood and spent seed from between her thighs. He would not meet her gaze. Mayhap he was sparing her embarrassment of such a task? Once he finished wiping her, he held out her robe to her and helped her from the bed. Pulling his own robe back on, he tugged on the sheet until it came free, and carried it to the door of her chamber. She watched in horror as he opened the door halfway and handed the bloodied sheet to the man outside.

"Show this downstairs to those who must see it and then take it immediately to the Bruce. Tell him it is the Maid of Lorne's blood, shed by me as he ordered."

Shock and humiliation filled her even as she still felt the remnants of pleasure's grip. She had not mattered to him. Even as he worked her body for the desired response, he had not been thinking of her, but of his king and his orders. As she betrayed her clan with her surrender to passion in his arms, he had used her to complete a mission from his king.

The gentleness he had shown her was simply a means to an end, and she had been beguiled by his soft words and touches. Pulling herself to stand, she wrapped her robe around her and picked up the belt from the ground where it lay. He stood near the door watching her, but he refused to meet her gaze. Finally, his words broke the silence.

"I will wait dinner for you in the hall. Get dressed and join me there."

Then he was gone and the sound of the door closing released her from her reverie. Even as she collapsed on the floor and sobbed for all that had been lost that day, she vowed to herself that she would not fail her people again.

Chapter Three

Not one to prevaricate once he'd made a decision, Sebastien surprised himself by standing outside the bedchamber door and wondering if he'd handled things well enough. Orders, especially from his king, were orders, in spite of the fact that many times the Bruce allowed him to decide the method of implementation.

When innocents were involved, Sebastien preferred guile over bloodshed, seduction over force and negotiations over murder. When facing his enemies, there were no such alternatives. When dealing with women outside his bed, no rules or reason seemed to work.

Now, listening to the sobbing inside the chamber, Sebastien knew he would not be able to handle his wife in the same manner as he had handled everyone in his life before this day.

Leaning back against the cold stone wall, he remembered the moment of her surrender. In an instant he'd felt her resistance melt away and her stiff body soften under his hands and mouth. Knowing she was untried and nervous, he'd used his experience against her innocence, and bedded her without force. Consummating the marriage was no chore and had brought both of them pleasure, so why did it weigh on his mind so much now?

Shaking off this introspection, Sebastien nodded to the guard posted at the door and walked back toward the chamber that he was using on a temporary basis. A form separated from the shadows in the corner of the corridor and he tensed for a moment. Then he recognized the red-haired young woman as Lara's maid.

"Sir," she said, nodding her head in an unsuccessful attempt at obeisance. Anger flashed in her dark eyes as she met his gaze, and showed in the set of her chin. Anger?

"What is your name?" He stepped closer, forcing her to look up at him. He was a master at this game.

"Margaret," she said. No "sir" this time.

Did she not realize the precarious position she was in? He held her life and the lives of everyone in this keep in his hands and could order her death at any moment. Then he noticed that her own hands, clasped tightly before her, trembled slightly. Good. She was worried.

"What do you want, Margaret?"

Before she could speak, an older woman reached her side and then moved to stand in front of her, as if to protect the maid from him. The sound of running followed, and a moment later, his man François rounded the corner and stopped before him.

"Your pardon, sir," he began, out of breath from hurrying. "I did not realize this one had slipped from the hall."

François took hold of Margaret's arm and tugged her away, obviously intent on dragging her back to where Sebastien had ordered all of Lara's people to stay. Another guard arrived, took hold of the other woman and awaited his orders.

"I would see my lady," Margaret called out to him, struggling with François and slipping from his grasp. "Sir, I beg you...."

Somehow he knew the cost of her words, and he held up his hand to halt his men. The two women moved closer and Sebastien waited for their explanation.

"I would see my lady," Margaret repeated.

"You will see her, girl. She will arrive in the hall for the meal in a short time."

He had not thought that faces could pale as quickly as theirs did then. All of the color in their cheeks drained and they looked at each other in dread.

"Who are you and why are you here against my orders?" he asked, pointing at the older one.

"I am called Gara, sir." She showed the wisdom of her age and bowed her head to him. "I served the Mac-Dougalls as a healer, sir." She raised her head and gazed at him, but did not challenge him as the maid had.

A healer? Now he saw their purpose and their mistake.

"The lady needs no healer, Gara. Go back and take this one with you to await Lara's arrival in the hall."

Margaret broke free at that moment and ran to him. Slamming her fists ineffectually against his chest, she cried out, "Is it not enough that you have shamed her before her people? Must you now add to her humiliation by forcing her to face them before her blood on that sheet is even dried?"

François reached her before she could say anything else, grabbed her by her hair and forced her to her knees on the floor. Sebastien looked at Gara and knew now what they thought had happened. Startled by Margaret's words and her vehemence, he first thought to explain, but realized he owed them nothing. He was the victor here, not they.

"Release her," he ordered. "Go back to the hall now."

When the maid looked as though she would argue, Gara grabbed her arm and pulled her along the corridor, whispering harshly as they moved.

"I want no other MacDougalls in this tower, François. Not without my orders."

His men bowed and retraced their path away from him. Alone once more, he turned back to his chamber and entered it. It took no more than a few minutes for him to ready himself for the meal—his only clean surcoat and mail replaced the robe, which had been a gift from the Bruce. A warrior did not have many wardrobe choices and his trunks had not yet caught up to him. His squire, Philippe, fretted over him and then followed him down the corridor and stairs, into the hall and up to the chair set in the middle of the table on the dais.

Sebastien noticed the silence in the room. Then he observed the divide among those present—the few remaining MacDougalls off to one side, restricted to sharing one long table, and his men spread out through the rest of the hall. The MacDougalls watched him with open suspicion, while his men toasted him and his accomplishments openly.

He did not expect it to be a comfortable first night in his newly conquered keep, but he had not anticipated the overt and palpable mood of anger and uncertainty. When a few of his soldiers called out bawdy comments about his bedding of the Maid of Lorne, and the rumbling began to bubble up among the crowd, he knew he had underestimated the situation, after all. From the belligerent expressions on the faces of the MacDougalls he knew that war would break out anew if he brought Lara here now.

Motioning to one of the guards, he gave new orders about visitations to his wife and sent the man off. Then, with a word to Philippe, he climbed the dais and sat at the table that had so recently hosted his enemy.

Security was his first concern, and seeing the keep and those in it under his firm control his first priority. It mattered not to him if some here thought he saved their lady some embarrassment. If it helped gain their compliance, all the better.

Guile over bloodshed.

Without the distraction of his wife in the hall, Sebastien finished his meal quickly and then called his commanders to make plans for holding Dunstaffnage and moving forward with the Bruce's battle plans to take the west of Scotland.

Her nose itched.

Lara ignored it for as long as she could before opening her eyes to face this new day. Untangling the lay-

ers of her cloak from over her arms, she could finally
reach up and rub the irritation away. It would not be so
easy to rid herself and her clan of the invaders who now
held her home and her siblings in their grasp.

Light poured in through the opening in the wall, and
she tried to loosen muscles that were stiff from sitting rig-
idly through the night. After Margaret and Gara's short
but welcomed visit, she'd dragged her father's chair to
the farthest corner of the chamber and fallen asleep there.

She would not lie waiting for him in the bed where
he had…they had… And she would not face him in any
manner but fully dressed and ready to defend herself
from anything else he'd planned. The necessary re-
quirements for him to prove his claim had been made,
and she did not intend to share his bed again.

From Margaret, Lara had discovered that her sister
and brother were being held, apparently safely for the
moment, in a chamber with several of the younger
women who had remained in the keep. On Lord Sebastien's orders, no one had been accosted or harmed.

Pushing off her cloak, Lara stretched out her arms
and tried to release the tightness between her shoulders. Looking around the room, she saw so many re-
minders of her father.

No word of his end had reached her. Neither of the
other women had news of it, nor had they heard Sebastien's soldiers talk of it. Had he died in battle? Had
it been at the Bruce's hands, or at those of the man who
had gone on to spill her blood, as well? A shudder
racked her at the thought of her actions in the arms of
this enemy. Pray God, her father had not learned of
how she'd lost the castle and her honor to this man.

The growing noises in the corridor drew her from her thoughts, and she took up a position against the wall where the shadows hid her from anyone entering the room. The door opened with a bang as two men and then another two carried in large wooden chests and placed them along one wall.

The procession continued, with furniture and trunks being brought in and others being taken out, all without even a single man glancing in her direction. In a short time, the room had been transformed from her father's into someone else's. After the servants left, she peeked inside the storage boxes to see what kind of possessions Sebastien carried with him, and was surprised to find some of her own belongings in the unfamiliar chests.

Searching through to discover what was there, she never heard him enter.

"Fear not. Your belongings are all present."

Lara stood and backed away from the trunks. The nobleman was gone; the warrior stood before her now in his battle armor, with his sword at his side and his helm under his arm.

"I did not accuse you of stealing my gowns," she began. The thought had crossed her mind, but common sense held back any words of blame.

"This is our chamber now and your things have been brought here. I ordered your belongings searched for any weapons first, so that is the cause for the disarray."

He pointed at the one nearest her, the one she'd been searching, and she realized that Margaret's neat work was completely undone. Anger grew within Lara, but the cold look on his face and the set of his chin stopped her from protesting.

"Did he die at your hands?"

She blurted out the words before she had even thought of asking him. Lara clasped her hands together and prepared for the news.

"I would not kill a child," he whispered through clenched teeth. His own hand moved to the hilt of his sword and grasped it. Now, both horror and anger shone from his eyes at the misunderstood accusation. "Your brother is safe, as is your sister. They will be brought to you soon."

"No, no," she stuttered, shaking her head. "I did not mean Malcolm. I was speaking of… I would know my father's fate." Lara held her breath, wondering if his words would give her any measure of comfort at all.

"Your father lives, Lara. Although he dishonored himself and all of you by breaking his truce, his life has been spared."

She let out a shaky breath and shook her head. "I did not think the Bruce would let him live. I did not think any of us would survive if the Bruce took the Pass."

"Ah, so you know of the battle then?" Sebastien took a few steps toward her and she realized she had erred in bringing up yesterday's battle. "Did you know of your father's plans to ambush our forces while still under the flag of truce?" Another step and she was forced to tilt her head back. "Did you know of his negotiations with Edward of England to hold this place in that king's name?"

Lara swallowed and then swallowed again, the lump in her throat tightening and preventing her from speaking, which may have been a good thing since she did know all of those things. She knew almost everything about her father's battle plans and his intention to rule in this area on behalf of the English king. Her father had no faith that the Bruce was rightful king of Scotland, or of his abilities to gather all of the clans under one banner.

This man would use that information against her and her family. She knew that from nothing more than the hardened gaze of his eyes.

"I am but a mere woman, sir," she said, tilting her head in what she hoped was an appropriate manner when acquiescing.

Silence filled the space between them for a moment that stretched on and on, finally broken by his sarcastic laugh. Startled, she met his gaze now and found no humor there.

"Others may believe that tale, but they did not face you on the battlements. Believe this, lady—I will keep my back protected when it comes to dealing with you."

Though secretly pleased at his words, she reacted to the insult within them. "As will I when dealing with you."

He examined her from the top of her head to the tips of her toes and then met her gaze. She thought his lips might twitch into a smile, but they turned downward into a grimace instead.

"Just so, lady."

He stepped away now and she felt the moment of confrontation end. He switched his helm to his other hand and pointed at one of the trunks.

"The Bruce will be here shortly. Prepare yourself

and come to the hall so that you can be presented to him."

"I would rather not meet that…" There were so many ways she could describe the man Sebastien followed—worm, despoiler, murderer—that she could not choose which to say. Settling on a simple one, she pushed it through clenched teeth. "…bastard."

Sebastien's move was so swift, she did not see him until their faces were inches apart and he held her chin in his hand, his tight grip becoming painful as she fought against it.

"You will meet the king when he calls for you," he whispered in an ominous voice. "And you will do nothing but bow your head and hear his words. Do not speak to anyone. Do not dare to address him other than to answer a question, and take care when you select your words."

"I…" She tried to argue with his pronouncement, but his next statement not only stopped her but chilled her heart.

"The Bruce may hold your father responsible for your actions, but I will hold you and your siblings hostage for your good behavior. Disobey me in this and you will all suffer the consequences."

The part of her that could not believe he would harm a child was not so certain when hearing his menacing tone of voice. Her gaze met his and she nodded slightly.

"He will be here anon. Ready yourself."

This time he did not wait for her answer, turning abruptly and leaving the room. The now ever-present guard reached for the door and pulled it closed.

A clamor in the yard gained her attention and she

looked out to see what was happening. A large contingent of armed men, led by the only man it could have been—the Bruce—entered through the gates in the wall, to the boisterous cheering of those watching. Lara shivered at what this man represented.

An end to her family's dominance in Lorne. An end to her family itself, since she knew that the Bruce would not allow her father to remain here. An end to everything she had done and to the person she was.

Shaking herself from such thoughts, Lara knew that her behavior this day would determine her brother and sister's fate. Not ready to trust Sebastien of Cleish's words or his actions, she decided to comply with his orders. Once she learned her family's fate, she could make plans to escape.

Chapter Four

"Sire!"

Lara heard Sebastien's deep voice call out as she reached the doorway of the keep, and as she watched, he went down on one knee before the Bruce. Everyone in the yard stopped their actions and followed Sebastien's lead, all except for her. Clutching the cold stone at her back, she tried to calm the growing terror within her about what was to come.

Robert the Bruce slid off his horse and approached Sebastien, grasping him by the shoulders and pulling him to his feet. After the customary kiss, the Bruce whispered words only Sebastien could hear. Unease pricked her as they both turned to face her. More whispered words took place between them and then the Bruce held up his hand and waved to the guard at the gate.

'Twas lucky for her that she stood against the stone doorway, for when her father was brought forward, beaten bloody and in chains, she nearly fell to her knees. The steely look in his eyes, a look that spoke of control and unbowed resistance, warned her to do nothing. The Bruce, Sebastien and her father climbed to the top of the stairway and faced those gathered before them.

Strangers filled the place. Lara recognized only a handful of the men and a very few women, those from the kitchen and a few villagers, there among the Bruce's soldiers. Lara now clenched her hands in front of her to keep from trembling as she waited to hear her father's, and her own, fate.

"I give thanks to God Almighty for having delivered us from our enemies," the Bruce called out in a booming voice. "With His intervention, the perfidy of the MacDougalls did not succeed."

Loud yelling and clapping followed his words, and Lara felt the soldiers' anger at her clan wash over her as though it were something tangible. She began to stumble, until an armored hand slid under her elbow to steady her. Sebastien stood at her side.

"The MacDougalls have been scattered. Their castle and lands are now ours in the name of Scotland!"

Lara's stomach began to churn as the Bruce turned and looked at her. In his cold gaze, she could read his satisfaction at being in control here and now. A shiver tore down her spine and fear at what was about to happen drew a tight grip around her throat.

"The Maid of Lorne has been claimed and the blood shed in her claiming declares that she, too, is ours." The Bruce nodded to one of the soldiers near him, and the sheet proclaiming her surrender was unfurled and displayed for all to see. The cheering was unbearable for her.

She wanted to shrivel up and die at that moment. If her father had not known, now he did, as did everyone listening. Her chest tightened and her eyes burned as she fought to stay on her feet. Had Sebastien told of how she'd given in instead of fighting him off? If her father knew that she had indeed surrendered body and soul to the enemy, he would kill her himself. If the Bruce knew, he would use it against her and to humiliate her father even more than his presence and condition did now.

The moment while she waited to hear the words that would damn her in her clan's eyes stretched on forever. Gathering her courage from deep within, she looked at the Bruce. She was a MacDougall and would face her fate and not cringe from it.

"To prevent any resistance to our claims on this land, the children of the MacDougall will be held hostage for his behavior. The MacDougall swore a sacred oath to leave this land for England, never to return, and his children's lives were pledged as a surety on that oath."

She could not have prevented her gasp from escaping if she'd tried. News of this oath, this new truce that would protect her father's life at the cost of hers and her brother's and sister's, shocked her to her core. Although she could feel herself trembling, she could not stop it. He could not have given them over with no effort to free them, could he?

Two soldiers took her father's arms and dragged him down the steps to a horse that had been led forward. Realizing that she would most likely not see him again, she escaped Sebastien's grasp, rushed down the steps and clutched at her father's leg as he now sat astride the horse.

"Papa?" she cried out. "Papa!"

Part of her felt the terror of a small child being abandoned. Horror filled another part of her at his willingness to barter his children for his own safety. But the larger part of her simply wanted to know why.

Her father leaned down and loosened her fingers from where they encircled his leg. Under his breath, he whispered a few words to her. "Look to your uncle now."

Lara leaned back and stared at him, hoping for something more, but he used his foot to push her away. Stumbling back, she landed in the dirt, and she could only watch in horror and humiliation as her father denied her before their foe.

"You opened the gates to our enemy and then gave yourself and your brother and sister into their hands. They could never have *taken* the castle, girl," he said through clenched teeth, his voice sharp and biting. Then he spat on the ground next to where she lay and turned his face and gaze away from her as though she did not merit his attention.

Sebastien swore under his breath at his own stupidity. He should have foreseen the MacDougall's reaction when faced with his daughter's fate. The old man was hard, harder and colder than anyone else he knew, so his act of rejection against Lara should have not have caught him unawares. Sebastien strode down the steps and grasped her by the arm, lifting her to her feet. Obviously in shock, she did nothing to help or hinder his efforts to raise her up and bring her to his side.

She made no sound, although tears streamed down her cheeks. He was tempted to wipe them away, but he had other matters to handle. The MacDougall and his armed guards galloped through the gates toward the south, and Sebastien turned his attentions back to his king.

"Sebastien of Cleish will hold this fortress until I decide the fate of Dunstaffnage and the lands surrounding it." Sebastien had been prepared for that assignment, but clenched his teeth as he thought on the Bruce's most effective means of controlling an area— destruction of the castle and scattering the people. So the next words surprised him. "He will also serve as commander of my troops in this area, answering only to me."

The cheers began with his own men and spread throughout the soldiers in the yard, on the battlements and near the gate. Sebastien had earned his way through the ranks, not inheriting titles or honors or command by his name, and not being held back due to the lack of one, either. His success meant much to the average soldier about the opportunities in serving the Bruce.

"Come, Sebastien. We have much to discuss before I leave this day."

Sebastien could sense how unsteady Lara was, and felt reluctant to release her. Nodding to the Bruce, he turned to find Lara's serving woman. The King's next words rang out before he could find her.

"And assign someone to ready the MacDougall's heir to leave with me."

Sebastien had not yet told Lara of the Bruce's plan

to take her brother and sister from Dunstaffnage. Although he could not argue it here, he opposed the king's plan. Lara's scream and her lunge at the king limited his options.

Tightening his grip on her arm until she gasped, he drew her close and warned her in low tones, "Do nothing to anger the king or your siblings will pay the cost."

She looked at him, and such hatred poured from her gaze that he nearly let her slip from his hold. Nearly. "Do nothing but what I tell you," he whispered harshly while releasing her and pushing her toward the guard who approached from behind her. "See to your lady," he ordered.

She regained her feet as the guard caught up to her, and she looked as though she would disobey his orders. For a moment, he waited. Then she became a different person before his eyes. Straightening her back and shoulders, Lara shook off the guard's hand and nodded to Sebastien. When her maid reached her side, they walked into the keep with the guard trailing their steps.

Sebastien let out a silent but relieved sigh, knowing the battle he'd just won. And then he took in a deep breath as he faced the next one, this time with his king. Gathering his wits about him, Sebastien led the way into the hall, where food and drink awaited them and where he would try to prevail upon the king in the matter of the children.

Lara tried to take no notice of the pitying glances from some of those standing in the corridors of the keep as she walked by them. Margaret grumbled and fretted all the way along the stone passageway, and it only made Lara feel worse. Powerless in the same hallways where just a day ago she'd given the orders, she forced herself to focus on the most important of her problems— the Bruce's plan to take her brother and sister from the castle.

A shiver chilled her bones as the realization of what usually became of hostages struck her. The Bruce's own wife and daughter were paying the cost of his sins. What would he do now that he controlled the MacDougall's heir—both in name and body?

She stopped halfway up the stairs leading to her— *their*—chambers, and knew she must first discover more and then make plans to get her siblings out of Dun- staffnage to safety. It was imperative that their position as hostages be nullified if her clan was to act against the Bruce.

"Milady?" Margaret asked, stepping between Lara and the guards. "Are you well?"

Lara paused and decided that she needed to hear any discussions between Sebastien of Cleish and his king. The best place for that was in the small chamber next to the stairs leading to the kitchens below. Every un- guarded word could be heard there.

In as haughty a tone as she dared, she looked down her nose at the guards and her maid. "I have forgotten my needles in the steward's closet, Margaret. I will get them before we retire to my chambers."

With a glare that spoke much, she stopped any ar- guments or offers Margaret might have made, and turned back down the steps. One of the guards began to argue with her and she glared at him as well.

"Did your lord say that I was a prisoner to be kept in my chambers? Did he say I could not come and go as I pleased?" Not giving the young man time to think on it, she pushed her way around him and strode confidently toward the kitchen stairs.

They followed her, of course, and when they arrived outside the room, she waved her maid off. "I will find them myself, Margaret. Wait here with the guards."

To his credit, one of the soldiers insisted on peering into the room, most likely looking for other ways out. Once satisfied with his findings, he stepped back and allowed her to enter. Lara closed the door and then climbed around the trunks stored there to reach the farthest wall—the one made of wood, through which sounds could pass.

"It is not like you to argue with me, Sebastien. Especially on something so inconsequential as these children."

"And it is not like you, sire, to take children as hostages. After…" He paused, probably hesitant to mention the treatment of the Bruce's kith and kin. "You swore that you would not answer in kind against the innocent what has been done to your own. This boy has not even reached the same age as—"

A loud bang, like her father's fist on the table, interrupted Sebastien's words. "Do not think to tell me how to act!" The Bruce's voice deepened. "Lorne has forsworn his oath before. I will take no chances—"

To her surprise, Sebastien interrupted his king again. "Sire, hear me before you decide."

Lara pressed her ear to the wall so as to not miss anything said. The fate of her half brother and sister lay in the argument in the next room, and she needed to hear it.

"You will be riding hard, and those two, with maids and escorts, will be a distraction to you. Let them stay here, where I will keep them secure until you send for them or until you need them no more. Keeping them here might make the MacDougall think before attacking the castle."

Lara heard someone pacing across the dais, heavy footsteps moving back and forth. Her heart raced, yet she could not breathe, waiting for the decision about her siblings.

"It might make this castle a target for attack if he thinks he can free them and then be free of his oath and truce with me."

"Ah, but sire, Dunstaffnage is impregnable, as we both know."

The rumbling of male laughter unnerved her and she stepped away from the wall. 'Twas true. Dunstaffnage had never fallen in battle or in siege—its position high on the rock cliffs gave it a great advantage, with the sea guarding its back. That same rock under its foundations made it impossible for tunnels to be dug to undermine its walls. So it had stood against all enemies…until she had opened the gates. Her stomach churned as she realized that only through her stupidity was Dunstaffnage in the Bruce's control now. Shaking her head in denial, she stumbled back, landing hard against the wooden crates near her.

Her father had given her instructions to keep everyone inside and not open the gates to anyone. In attempting to get Malcolm and Catriona to safety, she had failed him. They had been captured, giving the enemy the key to the castle, and turning them all over to the Scots rebels. She had lost their home and their clan to the Bruce.

"Milady?" Margaret knocked lightly on the door as she opened it a bit. "Have you found them?"

Shaking herself from the remorse now threatening to overwhelm her, Lara moved around the trunks to the center of the room. Margaret opened the door fully, and the guards stepped to either side of the entrance.

"I did not. Mayhap they are in my chambers, after all."

Without even a glance at Margaret or the guards, Lara strode down the corridor to the stairway that led to her chambers. She needed to be alone to face the awesome mistake she'd made. A guard rushed ahead to open her door, and once more leaned into the room to check for...she knew not what. The keep was secured and completely under the control of the Bruce's followers. The only ones left of her clan were herself, the children and, from what she'd witnessed in the yard, a few servants in the keep and stables. Certainly no threat to the Bruce or to his new warden, her husband.

The guard offered a slight bow, more a tilt of his head, and then he retreated into the corridor to join the other man. When Margaret began to enter, Lara waved her off. She needed to be alone before the staggering consequences of her actions overtook her.

Margaret backed out, uncertainty filling her expression, and then the door closed. Lara lunged to the shuttered window and pushed it open. The breeze off the sea poured in, and what had once soothed her fears and restlessness now taunted her. Her childhood home was in the hands of the enemy, her father exiled and hating her for it. Her brother and sister were alive for the moment, but their fate now rested with the usurper king and his minions.

As if her thoughts had conjured them, she watched the two men—Robert the Bruce and Sebastien of Cleish—walk down the steps and mount their horses. What were they about? What decision had they made about the children? Standing on her toes and looking through the yard, she saw no sign that the king was taking them. Mayhap he had changed his mind?

Tempted to call out, Lara found her gaze captured by the sight of Sebastien on his horse. Just as he neared the gate, he turned back and his eyes met hers. Even from this far she could see his nod to her, and she puzzled over the meaning of it. Then he put his helmet on and followed the Bruce through the gate and out of Dunstaffnage.

If only it were as easy for her to leave.

"They will be your prisoners then, until I summon them."

"My thanks, sire," Sebastien said, nodding at the Bruce.

"I still do not comprehend why you would want their custody. From what I have seen and heard, both from you and from her father, controlling your new wife will be task enough for you."

Had the king read his thoughts? Sebastien met

Bruce's gaze and saw the teasing within it. Robert did not take Lorne's daughter seriously, but Sebastien would not make that same mistake. After speaking to most of the prisoners and those servants who remained behind, he knew that Lara MacDougall had managed the castle in her father's stead many times. She knew the defenses, the provisions, the number of soldiers needed to hold it and how long it could stand under siege.

"Is that why you gave her to me? A challenge to keep me busy while you have fun cavorting all over Scotland?"

Surely the king knew he would chafe under these new restrictions, staying here instead of being in Robert's vanguard of warriors during the important campaigns of the next months and year. The battles they faced, to claim the west of Scotland, while the Bruce's allies took and held the east, would determine the fate of them all. And staying here, tied in one place, was not how Sebastien saw himself and his battle skills being best used.

"It is imperative that this castle and this coast be held, Sebastien. I can trust very few to see to that. I know you view this as some kind of limitation, but you have my utmost confidence in this."

When said thusly, how could he argue or second-guess the king? Knowing when to hold his tongue, he simply nodded once more and watched the Bruce dismount. Sebastien had won the argument he'd wanted to this day—the children would remain. Accepting that it would be the only one, he nodded in agreement.

"I also need you to make arrangements for the gathering at Kilcrenan next week," Robert said quietly. He looked from side to side to make certain his words could not be heard, then he continued, "I need the counsel of all of my best men before embarking on what I hope is the final campaign to take Scotland back from our enemies."

"I understand, sire," Sebastien answered.

Robert had chosen a village to the south as the site of his "parliament," where his nobles would plan the next offensives. Its location was a secret closely guarded by a very few. If the Bruce's enemies knew of it, it could be devastating to those who fought for him.

"Well, you had best return to the castle," the king said, walking to him and extending his arm. Sebastien leaned over the horse's side and returned the gesture.

"I still think you should stay in Dunstaffnage, Sire. 'Twould be safer for you than out in the open." Sebastien surveyed the area around the camp. He supposed that the king was safe as long as he was surrounded by his army.

"Sebastien," the Bruce said as he leaned closer. "You must exert yourself there, and my presence will interfere with that. Make that place and those people yours, so that none can doubt you."

On the face of it, it sounded much like a warning about his men, and even about the MacDougalls who remained behind. But Sebastien knew better. Questions had been raised about his position within the hierarchy of the Bruce's forces. There was always some nobleman who felt slighted by the rewards or the rank given to Sebastien, or the esteem in which the king held him. Although Sebastien knew that every honor had been earned with the sweat and blood of him or his men, others chose to think differently. When adversity should have united them, it turned small cracks of jealousy and intrigue into major crevasses of greed and mistrust.

"As you wish, sire," he replied, bowing his head.

"Go now, Sebastien. A newly wedded man should not tarry long."

Thoughts jumbled together in his mind at the king's words. He certainly did not feel wedded, or at least not the way he'd always thought he would feel when married. He'd believed that when Scotland was in the hands of the Bruce, he would settle down with a quiet girl and have a home and bairns. If the king gave him some manor or lands…well, Sebastien had never thought of or craved something as grand or as important as Dunstaffnage.

Now, he held that castle and the enemy's daughter in his grasp, and faced challenges he'd never dreamt of. The weariness, unnoticed before, crept up on him now. He'd not slept the previous night, handling all sorts of duties and details, and now the lack of rest weighed him down.

After watching the king safely enter his tent, Sebastien turned his mount and began the short ride back to the castle. A small part of him wondered about the woman waiting there. Amidst all the bloodshed and war, she stood out in his thoughts like the first blossom of spring, somehow fresh and untouched by the coldness surrounding it. When he remembered her expression as her father had denounced her, and then her strength as she'd pulled herself under control, he knew she would survive whatever came her way.

For the first time since he began fighting in the Bruce's cause, Sebastien allowed himself to think on what it could be like with a home and a wife. After years of killing and watching comrades die, after marching endlessly from one end of Scotland to the other, after facing odds that foretold their defeat and death, he permitted a small dream to take hold in his heart.

He and the Maid of Lorne were wed in name and deed. Could it not be in truth? Many other women were joined against their wills, to seal bargains, so theirs was not so unusual a beginning. They were from different sides of this conflict, but again, that was not so different from other unions. Coming from the Lowlands, he did not have a clan, as she did. His father did not even know of Sebastien's existence, but others like himself had risen in importance to found their own dynasties.

He reached up and wiped the exhaustion from his face. His small troop rode over the last hill and approached Dunstaffnage Castle from the south. Its rugged stone walls and jagged appearance against the clear August sky declared that it would stand long after he was dead and buried. He only prayed that Scotland would stand as long as the walls of Dunstaffnage.

Chapter Five

❧❧❧

Within the space of a day, Dunstaffnage was an armed camp. As the home of the MacDougalls, it had always been filled with warriors and battle plans, but now it was an enemy camp. Lara watched for most of the afternoon as soldiers poured in and out of the gates, carrying all sorts of provisions and weapons into the yard and keep.

After her humiliation this morning and Sebastien's departure, she felt safer staying in her chambers in the north tower. She could observe all who came and went, but did not have to face them. Knowing it was simply a temporary reprieve, she took what it offered her.

"My lady?" Margaret's worried voice accompanied the knock on her door. "My lady, he…"

"I cannot hear you, Margaret." Not hearing her words clearly, Lara walked to the door and tugged on it. Expecting to find her maid, instead she faced the armor-covered chest of her new husband.

"She is warning you that I am on my way here."

Blunt, if nothing else, he stood before her, helm

under his arm, much like the first time she'd looked upon his face. Could it have been just a day ago? Margaret stood a little distance away, worry etched on her features. Lara stepped back and opened the door. Better to meet the devil head-on, if you had to meet him.

"Come in, sir."

The frown he gifted her with was worth the effort it took to gather her pride around her. After handing his helmet to one of the guards, he walked into the room and turned to face her, uncertainty in his eyes. Examining her from head to toe and back again, his gaze grew intense as it moved over her. When he was finished, he nodded and stood, arms crossed and chin raised.

"You look…well," he said in a quiet voice.

Lara closed the door and walked over to the window. Facing him, she nodded. "Considering that in the last day my family has been destroyed and taken prisoner, I have been married against my will, taken against my will and now shunned by my own father for it, I *am* well, sir."

She did not even try to mask the cynicism and sarcasm in her tone. Actually, when she thought on it, she had described quite accurately the events that had changed her life. Meeting his dark expression, she guessed that he did not agree. Once more his reaction surprised her.

"I would disagree with your interpretation of the events, my lady. Your family is alive—your brother and sister and yourself—here in your own home, and your father alive in his chosen exile in England. You chose marriage, and sealed the choice in this bed." Sebastien paused and laid his hand on the bed next to them, sliding it over the woolen blankets that covered the place where he had taken her virtue. His frown deepened as though he thought on his words. "And repudiation by a man willing to bargain his own children away for his life and his freedom is not something to be mourned."

Was he trying to soothe her ravaged feelings? It seemed to her that he was. Searching his eyes for the truth, she saw only honesty there. She opened her mouth to retort, but realized that his words spoke of her siblings. "They stay here?" she asked, offering a prayer to the Almighty that it was true.

"The king has agreed to allow Malcolm and Catriona to remain here in my custody."

Lara felt tears fill her eyes at his words. She had not heard the king's decision while listening through the wall. She'd become so overwrought at the revelation that she had surrendered the castle without cause that she'd not stayed to hear the rest. Now that she knew he had counseled his king to leave the children behind, she accepted that she must make some gesture.

"Thank you, sir, for that. I know you petitioned your king and I am grateful."

She bowed her head in honest gratitude. He could have let the Bruce take the children. Many other men would not choose the side of captured enemies before their sovereign—the risk to their own reputation and safety was too great. But this man had, and had secured their custody.

"Why? Why did you do it?" The question was out before she could decide the wisdom of asking it. And at what cost? She truly wanted to know. Lara raised her eyes now to meet his gaze.

"Too many innocents have died in this fight between kings and countries. I simply did not wish to see your siblings pay the price that another should bear."

"And now, sir? What is to become of us now?" She clasped her hands before her to stop the shaking. Her fate was in his control. He could put her aside, imprison her, beat her, kill her even, and she had no say in the matter. "What expectations do you have of me and the children?"

"I know that this is difficult for you, lady. One day in charge of this keep and castle, and the next its pris...guest. Many things will change for you in the coming weeks and months, and I cannot give you all the answers you seek. For now," he said, looking around the room, "I ask that you remain in these chambers unless I accompany you."

"A prisoner in truth, then?" she asked, using the word that he avoided.

"If it were only my men in control here, I would not restrict you so. But there are others here whose behavior I cannot vouch for. So, until the king moves on, the only way I can ensure your safety and that of your family and servants is to isolate you here. The children, your cousins and other servants have been moved into the chambers on the first level of this tower. The level below this one will serve as your solar, and they may join you there as you wish."

No mention was made of where he would sleep, and Lara did not ask. Glancing at the bed, she could not bring herself to speak of it. He cleared his throat and gained her attention.

"My obligations to the king will take me from here often. I have appointed a man called Etienne as steward to oversee the running of the estate, and he will act in my name in my absence. He should arrive in a day or two to begin his duties."

"And Callum? What has become of him?" She steeled herself for the inevitable word of the old man's death. The new conqueror would surely have executed those he could not trust in the keep, especially if he had placed his own in command.

"He, and the others left behind by your father, are being held…for now. You know there is a matter of trust, Lara. And I cannot trust those who were in charge when I took Dunstaffnage."

Like a slap across her face, the words stung her. As though he sensed her pain, he reached out to take her hand. Lara pulled away and stepped back. She could read the pity in his eyes now and she would not accept it from him.

"As you wish, sir."

He moved closer and lifted her chin so she could not look away. "'Tis not as I wish, lady, but it is as it must be."

He must have delivered the message he wanted her to know, for he dropped his hand and walked to the door. "If there is aught you need or want, tell my squire and he will see to it or come to me. His name is Philippe, and he will report to you anon."

Sebastien tugged open the door, and she saw only Margaret standing in the corridor. Before he crossed the threshold, he looked back at her and spoke in a voice so low only she could hear it. "Are you…well?"

His voice deepened with the huskiness she'd heard the night before, in his ardent whispers. The sound of it, and the heat in his voice and his gaze, were so strong that she could not mistake his meaning. Since he'd left the chambers last evening, they had not spoken of what had happened between them. Not certain she wished to speak of it now or ever, she simply nodded, feeling a burning flush rise in her cheeks.

"I am well, sir. I will survive."

"Of that I have no doubt, lady." Stepping to the door once more, he left the chamber and allowed Margaret entrance. "I will return later."

With a slight bow, he strode down the stairs. Her maid rushed to her side, but Lara waved her away and told her to see to Malcolm and Catriona. Once she was alone, Lara pondered his words and his actions. He behaved as no one else she had ever met. She could sense an honorable heart within him; indeed, honor seemed to guide his every action. How had such a man come to be a supporter of the Bruce?

As she paced the length and breadth of the room, the true question formed in her mind. The one that had bothered her since the king's words claimed her a vanquished enemy.

How would Sebastien of Cleish respond when his wife denied him? Would he abandon her and her siblings? Would he banish her to a convent, as so many noblewomen were when they were obstinate or inconvenient?

Or would he simply force her to his will and desires?

A shiver coursed through her, one filled with dread and anticipation. Always one to face a problem straight on, rather than dissembling over it endlessly, Lara formulated plans to make her position to the new warden of Dunstaffnage quite clear. Unfortunately, he did not return for four nights, and caught her unaware when he did.

Sebastien struggled up the steps to the top floor of the tower, as quietly as he could in armor and mail. He paused at the landing and walked into the smaller first room. With a nod, he allowed Philippe to remove the accoutrements of war from his body for the first time in days. These last four had been spent on horseback, surveying the surrounding lands and searching for pockets of resistance that would be useful to his enemies, and dangerous to those he served. He ached in places he'd forgotten he could feel.

Standing and stretching his arms up to touch the ceiling of the smaller chamber, he thought on the woman inside the next room. Was she asleep or had his movements awakened her? Would she be welcoming or as defiant as her people were? So tired that he did not care, he opened the door slowly and as quietly as he could.

A wry smile tugged at his mouth as he spied her across the room, in the farthest corner, sitting in the hard chair she'd called her father's. And she was sleeping soundly. He motioned for Philippe to remain without, and closed the door. Crossing the room, he stood over her and watched her sleep.

The daft woman had wrapped herself in several cloaks before wedging herself into the chair. If she sought warmth, the best place was in the bed, under its

layers of heavy woolen blankets, or closer to the fire
that burned, low but steady, in the hearth. Then the reason for this cocoon struck him, and he held his laugh
inside. Did she realize that even a layer of armor would
not stop him if his quest was to have her naked and
under him once more?

At this moment, though, he wanted nothing so much
as a few hours of sleep, and he hesitated to move her—
waking her would bring on a torrent of questions or accusations that he did not want to face now. Crouching
down, he slid his arms behind her back and under her
legs, and lifted her from the chair. He placed her sleeping, snoring form on the far side of the bed and then,
after hiding his dagger beneath his pillow and arranging his sword on the floor within reach, Sebastien
climbed in on the side closest the door.

His body was ready for sleep, but his mind kept
throwing problems at him. One by one, he analyzed
them, sought solutions and came up with methods to
overcome them. Finally, just as he felt the pull of sleep
dragging him down, Lara sighed and mumbled his
name, bringing him back to alertness. Turning on his
side, he watched the movement of her mouth and the
frown that spread across her forehead.

Was she cursing him in her sleep? Fighting him?
When she turned her head and he glimpsed the side of
her neck, he frowned as well. Clear on her skin were
the marks of his armored gauntlets in the places where
he had grabbed her chin. Though fading, the marks of
purple and blue and green taunted him. If he'd done this
with one hand, what did her arm look like where he had
grabbed and held on when she'd tried to accost Robert?

He had the chance to discover the truth when she turned, or tried to turn, onto her side. As she moved, he eased the layers of cloak and gown down her shoulder until he could see the damning evidence for himself.

How had she kept silent when he'd injured her thusly? Although now a week old, the bruises were angry and swollen, a red handprint still visible, among other colors. He guessed that her other shoulder matched this one, and clenched his teeth.

Reaching out, he outlined the bruises with the tip of one finger, sliding around the worst of them. Her skin was soft and smooth, and the urge to follow his finger with his tongue and to taste the fairness of his wife grew within him. He struggled against it, knowing nothing good would come of such desires, and drew the gown back up over her shoulder, careful not to press on the injuries.

They were not the worst he had ever inflicted on someone, not even the worst he'd done to a woman, but they tried the limits of his self-control. Awake, she goaded him with barbed words and taunted him with her quick mind and fairness. Asleep, she tempted him to a weakness that could be deadly to him and to the king he fought to protect.

He shifted to the edge of the bed, as far from her as he could move, and closed his eyes. It would take months before this area was safe and free of the Mac-Dougall clan and their influences. Until her uncle and the rest could be defeated and the Bruce become king in fact, she would remain as she was—a prisoner and a hostage.

His man woke him as ordered just before dawn's light, and Sebastien dressed quickly without help. Philippe, he knew, would be waiting outside the door with his mail and armor. Looking around the room, he realized that the fire had burned down to almost to ashes during the night. In spite of it being August, the thick castle walls held in the chill and dampness. Using some kindling next to the hearth, he sparked it to life and threw a few pieces of wood on it.

Turning back, he found Lara watching his every move. As she came awake, she seem to realize where she was, and began to struggle with the covers. Before he could reach her, she tumbled off the bed and landed on the floor with a groan. He walked to that side of the bed, but she scrambled away, pushing the cloaks off as she gained her feet. 'Twas his turn to groan when he spied the small dagger in her hands, pointed at him.

"Lady, put that away. You are in no danger here."

"I will not...." she whispered. Then her gaze found the crumpled bedclothes and her own disarray. "You cannot..."

When words failed her again, Sebastien took a step closer. She was against the wall in the corner now, with no place to move. He shook his head and waved at her. The dagger wobbled in her grasp. Seizing his chance, he quickly grabbed for her hand and twisted her wrist, causing the knife to fall to the floor. He kicked it away and released her hand before he could do any true harm to it.

"Sir," she began as she met his gaze. Her sleep-filled eyes were now clear, and he saw that she was completely awake.

"Lady, you were startled from sleep and fell off the bed." He picked up the dagger from the floor and held it out to her. Such a weapon was truly no danger to him.

"I was in the chair," she said, accepting it and sliding it back into the small leather hilt on her belt. With trembling hands she pushed her hair back from her face and over her shoulders. "What do you want here?"

A myriad of wants passed through his thoughts in that moment, but none were of a nature that he could speak of now. He retrieved his sword and his own deadly dagger, and opened the door, handing them to his squire.

"I but sought a few hours of sleep here. Now I must go."

"You slept here?" The confusion in her expression was a sort of reward to him. "'Tis morning?" She'd been so deeply asleep that she had not realized he'd shared her bed. What liberties could he have taken before she woke? His body reacted to the possibilities even as he knew his honor would never permit it.

"Aye, lady." Philippe stood at the door, so Sebastien bowed and turned to leave.

"Sir? Wait, I pray thee," she said, walking a few steps closer to him. "I have a request of you."

He stopped and waited for her words. She had not asked much of him yet and he was intrigued.

"May I visit the chapel?" She took another step toward him as she asked. "I would like to pray there."

The chapel was a few hundred yards away, between the main camp of the Bruce's forces and the castle itself. As it had been the site of their wedding, he was surprised she wished to return there at all.

"I could send Father Connaughty to you here if you require his counsel." It was safer for her than leaving the tower right now. Too many soldiers being cared for in the yard had been injured by her family, and the sight of her might give rise to trouble.

"It is the place that gives me comfort, sir. My mother is buried there and I've spent hours praying there. But I understand, sir. I would do the same if I were the victor here."

Sebastien was not certain at first if her understanding amused, comforted or bewildered him. Then the glint in her eyes gave away her actions. Most women he had met would be moaning and crying, crumpled into a heap after the last days that she'd faced. Yet here she stood, offering him a not-so-obvious challenge to his authority that she dressed up prettily as acquiescence to his rule.

"If my duties permit, mayhap I could take you there before the evening meal."

"As you wish, sir." She bowed her head this time, but not quickly enough to disguise the satisfied smile that lifted the corners of her mouth.

In spite of knowing she was manipulating him, and in spite of knowing that she did not return his desires, that small needful part of him hidden deep inside reveled at the chance of sparring with her. Of drawing her back from her fear and hurt into the person she must have been when her father still ruled here. Of such…possibilities.

Chapter Six

Despite the heavily armed guards and Sebastien's second-in-command making the offer in his stead, Lara accepted the gesture and the opportunity it presented. It was the first time in nearly a week that she'd been allowed out of the north tower, or anywhere else in the keep but the two floors she was permitted. There had been a moment when she'd almost decided not to go, but she took a deep breath and straightened her shoulders and followed the guard through the courtyard.

From the window in her bedchamber, she could see the yard, but at a distance. Walking among the Bruce's men, some injured, some not, unnerved her. Disgusting insults were spoken just loud enough for her to hear. They called her names—despicable variations of the honorable one given her as the MacDougall's eldest daughter, with none of the respect it carried among her own.

One curse threatening her and Catriona was so vulgar that Sebastien's man, apparently one high in his esteem, kicked the fellow who said it hard enough to

render him unconscious. She stumbled away at the
sight, and only the knight's hand under her elbow kept
her from hitting the ground.

He was completely opposite in appearance from his
commander, with short-cropped black hair and a dark
complexion, but he had the tall, muscular physique of
an accomplished warrior. His grim expression warned
one and all that further interference would not be tol-
erated. With a nod, the man led Lara through the gate
and down the path, which was lighted by the fires of
many small groups huddled around them preparing for
the coming night.

Now, the chapel stood a few yards away, and she
tried to shake off hatred that was aimed at her. The
knight stood silently at her side as his men searched it
before they would allow her entrance, and then the
commander moved to follow her in. Stopping just inside the door, she faced him.

"Am I permitted privacy at prayer, sir?" she asked
the one called Hugh. She needed time alone to think.

"Aye, my lady, if you wish," he said with a bow. She
nodded in pleasure and waited for him to leave before
walking toward the front of the chapel.

The place was dark, lit only by candles on the altar
and a torch sitting high in a sconce on the wall near the
door. She could walk from back to front in only twenty
paces, the chapel was so small. Two windows cut into
the stone walls opened on each side. Her mother was
buried just off to the right of the entrance, and Lara
paused to say a prayer for her soul. Then she knelt before the altar and took in a deep breath.

At first, she thought the shadows moved. Lara controlled her surprise and watched as a form soundlessly detached itself from the farthest corner and moved toward her. Wrapped as it was in a long, dark cloak, she could not see it clearly, but the voice was one she recognized.

"How be ye faring, dear cousin?" it asked in a whisper that made her skin itch. "My da has been fretting night and day about ye being held prisoner here."

"I am well, Eachann. When did you arrive here?" She peered into the darkness and saw no place of entry. "And how did you get in without being seen?" She stayed on her knees so that, if one of the guards opened the door of the chapel, it would appear that she was praying.

"Never ye mind about the how of it, sweetling. I have been watching for ye for more than four days, Lara. 'Tis a pity to see ye kept so. Has he beaten ye?"

Lara shivered at the question. Her cousin's constant fascination with pain terrified her. She shook her head in answer. His dark eyes took on a mean shine, but his voice softened to an ominous whisper. "'Tis a good thing then. I would not have ye mistreated."

She sensed more to his answer, but resisted the urge to ask about it. Her time here was not unlimited, and she could almost hear the pacing of Sebastien's man outside the door. "Why are you here?"

"Da wants you to listen to them and report anything that may tell us their plans. The word is that with the fall of Dunstaffnage, the Bruce moves north from here, but we must know before launching our attack."

"But I am isolated, Eachann. No one speaks to me, not even *him*." Lara sat back on her heels and thought of how to accomplish this task. If she could give them some knowledge of the Bruce's plans, it could gain her forgiveness in her clan's eyes.

"The servants hear everything. Let them gather what they can, and you bring it to me. Let Da decide if 'tis important or no'."

Before she could respond, Eachann held up his hand and stepped back into the shadows. Still on her knees, she straightened up and bowed her head, waiting for his word.

"Go say a prayer for your mother's soul," he ordered in a low voice.

"I did that, Eachann."

He shook a fisted hand at her. "Lara, do what I tell ye. Go say a prayer for your ma…and listen well while you pray."

Shrugging, Lara stood and walked back to the stone that lay over her mother's grave. In the quiet of the chapel, she could hear voices outside the window. She glanced back at Eachann in the darkness near the altar. How had he known? Now, standing as silently as she could, she listened.

"When do you leave, then?" Hugh asked.

"In three days. I go and Robert will meet all of us in Kilcrenan." It was Sebastien's voice. "'Twill be just over a week before I return."

He was leaving?

"How many go with you? Or should I say, how many do you leave with me?" Hugh laughed lightly.

"I take three score of Robert's men with me," Sebastien answered. "My men remain with you for the safety of all we've gained."

Something moved in the woods next to the church, and the men stopped talking abruptly. Lara saw her cousin motioning to her, and she crept back to the altar.

"What did they say?"

"The Bruce goes to Kilcrenan. Sebastien leaves in three days."

"Good, Lara. We might make a good spy out of you yet," he whispered.

"Spy?" she asked. The dishonor of it struck her sharply. "I am no spy."

"Ye have turned whore, why not spy as well?" Eachann laughed bitterly. "Men spill secrets in the heat of passion, and if ye spy as well as we've heard ye whore for the Bruce's man, ye might earn your way back into the clan."

Lara reeled back at the horrible accusation, but Eachann grabbed her arm and drew her so close that his rancid breath burned her cheek. "I will be visiting this place every five days to meet with ye. If I canna', I will have someone come in my stead. Be here."

Then, before she could argue, her cousin released her and stepped back into the shadows with a harsh, whispered curse. Falling to her knees once more, she heard the door pulled open and approaching steps behind her on the stone floor.

She tried to catch her breath, but the dread and the shame of her cousin's accusations made it difficult. What kind of rumors had gotten back to her uncle? *Whore?* She had been forced on threat of death to marry the man, and had been taken. And yet they believed the worst.

Lara knew Sebastien stood behind her now, but she

did not dare face him. Would the guilt show on her face? Would he know what she'd just done?

"Lady?" he said. "Are you ready to return?"

He leaned over and held his hand out to her, to help her stand. She did not take it, but rose on her own and then, with a deep breath forced in and out, turned to him.

"I know about what happened in the yard, Lara." His voice, softer now and filled with concern, poured over her. "As I told you before, they are not my men."

She sensed that this was as much of an apology as she would receive, and more would make her uncomfortable. She did not know if her cousin stood watching or not; however, she did not want to stay here now.

"I am ready to go back."

He held out his arm and waited. Finally, she placed her hand on his and walked down the center of the chapel. Just as she reached the door, a wind blew into the church and the candles and torch went out. Sebastien stepped out first and, as Lara followed, a single whispered word echoed through the stone building. *Whore.*

Something was wrong. She was stiff as she walked by his side, and he could not discern if it was anger or fear or something else that made her behave so. Sebastien suspected that most of it was due to the coarse names expressed by the soldiers in the yard. Hugh had sent word to him and he'd come directly to the chapel.

He would feel better when these men were gone. He knew the warriors in his command, knew whom he could trust and those he could not. He knew what they were capable of and what their limitations were. But the bulk of the Bruce's forces were unknown to him and unpredictable. And, as this evening's actions had shown, they would turn on anyone weaker in a moment.

In three days, he would lead a force away from Dunstaffnage to the shores of Loch Awe and the meeting of the Bruce's allies from all over Scotland. Robert had promised to decide Dunstaffnage's fate at that meeting.

Lara was silent as they walked through the woods, to the drawbridge and over it. He felt her hand trembling on his, though he guided her along a path already cleared of soldiers. The wind whipped around them and he knew it foretold of a change in the weather. Lara did not react when her hair was loosened by the force of it and tore around her madly. She did not slow her steps or pull away.

Soon they reached the hall, and he escorted her in and to the entrance of the tower. He wanted to say something to her, something more, but words failed him. Her maid stood waiting there and he relinquished his hold on her. As Lara climbed the steps to her chambers, he turned back to Hugh.

"She may have the freedom of the keep once I leave."

"I understand, Sebastien." His friend of many years nodded. "And the chapel?"

"Only at your command and with your presence."

Sebastien's stomach growled and he nodded toward the hall. Joined by Hugh and his other commanders, he sat at the table and ate his meal. But with every bite, he thought about the distress in Lara's face as she'd turned to him in the chapel. She had not looked that upset on the day they were married, indeed, not even when her father had repudiated her. And the fair skin around her eyes was still marred with the darkish coloring of sleepless nights.

Was it what Hugh had revealed to him? The threats that could never be carried out as long as he was in charge? Or was there something more at work? After assigning tasks for the morrow and deciding which of his commanders would oversee various duties while he was on the king's business, Sebastien trudged up the stairs to the chamber.

Before even reaching it, he was stopped by a guard with a message to meet Hugh near the stables. Sebastien dismissed the men that followed him and made his way there. Entering with no torch to light his way, he found the place they'd designated to meet, and was not surprised to see another man present as well. They greeted each other as the kin they were.

"I trailed him here a few days ago and lost him just over a mile away," Munro reported. "I do not think he entered the castle, but he may still be nearby."

Sebastien nodded. Munro served in his network of spies and had been following the MacDougall's nephew, whose father now led the clan. A vicious, unmerciful man, Eachann liked to terrorize and torment his victims before killing them.

"Have there been any signs of him?"

"Nothing reported yet, Sebastien," Hugh said. "I will send out more soldiers and make our control a bit more visible, to see if that discourages him."

"Anything else, Munro? Any words in the wind?" His cousin looked as though he would say something and then stopped himself and stared at him intently. "What is it?"

"Tread carefully, Sebastien. If Eachann is here, then he has spies of his own. Guard your back." Munro looked at Hugh and frowned. "Guard *his* back."

Hugh nodded in reply.

They clasped arms and parted, with Munro drifting into the darkness to leave the castle in his own way, while Sebastien and Hugh walked back toward the keep.

"So, the game is under way then." It was a statement, not a question, and Sebastien nodded in agreement.

"'Twas always under way, Hugh. Until the Comyns are destroyed and the throne his, Robert is not safe."

Sebastien stopped and turned to his friend. Lowering his voice, he shared the plan with Hugh. "Robert thinks to use Dunstaffnage as a launching point for his movements up the coast. We must root out any enemies or spies here."

Hugh whistled lightly. "He will not raze the castle then?"

"Nay, this one will stand, but it must be held. That will be your duty while I see to the king."

Hugh straightened to his full height, towering over him by several inches. "I understand, Sebastien."

"And keep her safe while I am gone," Sebastien added. He need mention no name. "She will be her own worst enemy at times."

They reached the keep and parted in the hall, Hugh

heading for his quarters with the other commanders and Sebastien climbing the steps to the tower rooms.

The game has indeed begun, he thought as he crossed to the door to his chambers. May the best man win.

Chapter Seven

Although she knew she had not slept, Lara somehow woke up in the bed again. She'd paced for hours after her return from the chapel, the tension inside her gripping her stomach. Refusing the meal sent up for her and the children, she chose to go back over everything her cousin had said during their encounter. Then she'd wrapped herself in her cloak once more and propped herself in her father's chair and tried unsuccessfully to sleep.

Now here she was, under the thick covers on one side of an obviously used bed. Pushing her hair back, she peered around the room, looking for telltale signs that Sebastien had indeed shared the bed through the night. The trunk where he kept his clothing was open. The other pillow bore his imprint. Indeed, the other side of the bed still bore his warmth as well. Sliding her hand over it, she thought on how he continued to move her each night without her waking.

As soon as she climbed off the bed, Margaret entered with water for washing. Another servant followed with a covered tray.

"I know you did not eat last even, or much of anything of substance for the whole of the day, milady," Margaret said as Lara directed the kitchen maid to the table. "But on such days as these, everyone is off their usual customs."

"I fear it will continue for some time, Margaret," she answered, sharing only a small measure of her unease with the woman who'd grown up at her side.

Lara's stomach now reminded her of its emptiness. She completed her ablutions and then, sitting in her chair with the tray on her lap, tore the loaf of steaming bread apart and ate one piece after another until it was gone.

"My lady," Margaret said. "Has he said what is to become of us? I was terrified when I heard that the bairns might be taken from us."

"As was I, Margaret. Apparently, keeping them here fits into the Bruce's plans more than taking them with him. For now, they would seem safe."

"And you? Now that you are married to the Bruce's man? What's to become of you?" Margaret's fingers twisted together even as her brow knitted in a frown of worry. "And of me?"

"The knight assured me that we are safe. Prisoners, although not called that, but safe in our tower. More than that, I know not.

"Margaret, I have a boon to ask of you," Lara added, broaching a subject that she had lost sleep over since Eachann's demands. "You make your way through the castle and keep. Tell me who remains here from our clan. I worry that some have not escaped to safety."

"Milady," Margaret began, "I fear I have not taken

notice of much other than you or the children in these last days."

Lara reached over and patted the maid's hand, trying to ease her worry. "There will, I think, be time to sort these things out. For now, are the children below?"

"Yes, milady." The young girl who had brought the tray answered from across the chamber. She was one of those who'd remained behind, who were now pressed into services they did not usually provide. With so many gone from Dunstaffnage, fewer hands carried out many tasks.

"Milady?" Margaret cleared her throat and glanced to the other side of the room, nodding slightly at the young girl waiting to take the tray back to the kitchens. Realizing the message to caution, Lara nodded and drank deeply from the cup of ale. She needed to have a care to be discreet in her attempts to gather information. There would be time.

"Milady?" Margaret asked again, gaining her attention once more.

Looking up, Lara discovered Sebastien watching her. As was his usual custom, he stood dressed in his mail and parts of his armor, but no helmet on his head. That meant he was staying close to the castle. She smiled as she realized this pattern of behavior in the man now her husband.

She held the tray out to the girl and stood in greeting. His gaze was intent and it made her nervous. Through the last two weeks, although married, they'd had very little contact at all. He'd taken over her home and her people, and she'd been banished as effectively as her father had been. Etienne now ran the keep, and Lara's opinions were not sought by anyone.

She smoothed her gown with nervous palms and waited for him to speak first.

"Good morrow, lady." His lips curved at the corners, not quite a smile.

"Sir," she replied, nodding.

"I did not intend to disturb your meal. Pray thee, sit and eat." He motioned toward the tray now held by Margaret, but Lara shook her head.

"I have broken my fast already, sir. My appetite is less than my maid hopes, and for far less than she brings me each morn," she said.

"I have come to ask you to sup with me this evening." He paused and his expression was one of puzzlement. "If your appetite returns, of course."

Lara looked at him and tried to discern a reason for this invitation. "Where do you wish to eat? In the solar below?"

"I would wish to eat here for some measure of privacy, but I am certain that you would wish a measure of freedom." He turned and, in a quiet voice, told both Margaret and the kitchen maid to leave. He waited for the door to close and then faced Lara once more.

Here was her chance. The one that she'd missed because of his absences or other duties that kept him so busy.

"What would you like to discuss that requires privacy, sir? We could accomplish it now, if it pleases you?"

He frowned at her; his eyes narrowed and he squared his shoulders. "I have no specific topic, lady.

I just had hoped for…" He stopped. "We have much…" Another start and stop. "We are married and…" His frown deepened and he shook his head.

Now it was his turn to look lost and confused, as confused as she usually felt around him. He walked to the window and peered out onto the dreary day. Lara waited, fear filling her heart, since she knew his words would be about their marriage, and therefore something she did not want to hear.

"Our marriage was precipitous and unexpected," he said finally, still staring out into the rain. "I would like to discuss with you the expectations I do have for our union."

She swallowed and then swallowed again, her mouth suddenly dry and unable to form words. This was exactly her concern, too, but she had not anticipated his raising the topic. He had not turned to face her yet, so she took a deeper breath and tried to stay calm. She had few rights and little recourse against him as her husband, so she prepared herself for the worst.

"Too many things are uncertain at this time," he said as he finally did face her. "There are too many arrangements that cannot be confirmed yet to make any bold declarations to you about our future. But, there is time to become accustomed to each other before any decisions are made."

"Decisions, sir? What kind of decisions are being made about me?" Would she ever be able to face life as a pawn of her enemy? She placed her fisted hands on her hips. "I thought everything was settled. You took my virtue. You took my family. You stole my future."

She tried so very hard to use anger as her shield against this uncertainty. However, the naked longing she spied in his gaze, longing for she knew not what, was so strong that it nonetheless unnerved her. He could not simply want her in a carnal sense—a man as handsome as he could surely have any woman he wooed to his bed, so there was no need to take an unwilling one.

"What more do you want from me?"

Oh, God help her. She should never have asked the question, for she did not want to hear the answer. Truly, it was one of the stupidest things she'd ever done, and now there was nothing for her to do but await his answer.

He cleared his throat and smiled, a smile tinged with sadness. "I simply want to share a meal with you. No more, no less than that."

When put so plainly, how could she refuse? But something deep within told her she must. "And whom do you threaten if I refuse this *request?*"

He let out an exasperated breath and muttered something too low for her to hear. Lara took a step back, afraid she'd pushed him too far with her obstinacy.

"Since that is how I have sought to control your behavior these last weeks, I can understand how you would expect that to be the course for every action I take. Your pardon, lady, for asking you to do something so distasteful."

Surprising her completely, he bowed and turned away without another word, opening the door and leaving before she could comprehend his intentions. Blinking and expecting to see him still there, Lara shook her head and tried to clear her thoughts. Staring at the closed door, she searched for an explanation of how she felt.

He had just held out some offer to her, one made from a man to a woman, not enemy to enemy. He had attempted to ease her fears, and she had rejected whatever he made an effort to do. Tempted to follow him and accept his invitation, Lara heard her cousin's words come back to her, and the accusation he'd made stopped her from any foolish softness.

Sebastien was the enemy. His words and other ploys to soften her were meant to remove her as a threat to his assuming the role that belonged to her father and to Malcolm after him—Laird of Dunstaffnage. Lara wrapped her arms around her waist and shuddered at how close she'd come to betraying them all again, for the hope of some kind words and treatment.

But wait. She stared at the door again. He was not the only one who could gain knowledge through such an exchange. Had not Eachann ordered her to gather such information about their enemy and share it with him? She could ask her own questions of this knight in the service of the Bruce, and help her clan's allies in their continuing battles against them.

Examining it in that perspective, she realized she must accept this invitation. Pulling open the door and hastening past both her maid and his astonished squire, who stood holding Sebastien's helmet and sword, she ran down the steps after him. She stopped at each floor to see if he were there, but she did not find him in the solar nor on the first level. Reaching the entrance to the hall, she stumbled to a stop as two guards blocked her path.

Lara struggled to catch her breath as she called out to him. "Sir?" He was at the far end of the hall and walking briskly away. With the noise of dozens of soldiers and servants in the hall, there was no way for her voice to reach him. Instead, his second-in-command stepped in front of her.

"My lady? Is there something you need?" he asked her in a formal tone that served to remind her of her position and her heritage. Standing back, she waited a moment until she could speak without effort.

"Sir Hugh." With his nod, she continued, "I had thought to speak to your commander, but he left."

"Aye, my lady. He has many duties to be about here." There was some measure of sanction in his voice, as though she somehow took Sebastien from such tasks. Lara looked at Hugh to see if his eyes betrayed him, showing the disdain she heard in his voice, but there was none. Still, she could not resist the urge to remind him of his place, as well.

"Then you must also have some that you should be about. You are dismissed." She began to turn away when she noticed the glances of the guards. 'Twas almost as though they waited for him to reprimand her in some way. No hand gripped her to stop her, so she climbed the first step.

"As you wish, my lady," Sir Hugh said.

Lara did not dare to stop and look back. She continued her ascent until she'd reached the solar, and called for Margaret. Would Sir Hugh tell Sebastien that she had dismissed him, and done it disrespectfully in front of their guards? What would his reaction be?

She decided that she needed to prepare for their next encounter, so she called for her needles and thread and went to the solar to join Malcolm and Catriona there. Embroidery always soothed her nerves. She would work on the tapestry for a bit and sort her thoughts as she moved the threads, connecting and weaving colors and patterns into shapes and designs.

As it had been since the knight's arrival, her brother's subject of discussion was Sebastien of Cleish and everything about him. After Malcolm praised the new conqueror of Dunstaffnage for too many minutes, Lara cut off further gushing with a warning for the boy to consider his own clan and his own allegiances. Malcolm's scowl matched her own as the solar finally grew silent. Catriona climbed off Lara's lap and onto Margaret's, reacting to the tension.

Lara took a deep breath, trying to sort out her own thoughts and feelings.

Two hours and many skeins of jumbled thread later, her thoughts were as muddled as ever.

He cursed himself for the fool he was a thousand times as he circled the perimeter of Dunstaffnage for the fifth time. The rain had lessened, but not the winds, which tore at him. He was alone now that he had ordered the guards to remain at the gate, near the stone wall that led away from the castle and into the woods where the chapel stood.

The castle was an imposing sight, especially when viewed from this close. Its sheer rock walls and base would convince attackers of the futility of such action. With rain and wind bashing against it from the firth, it stood as a testament to the wisdom of those who'd planned its design and its location.

Those damn MacDougalls, he thought as he stared through the rain at the two towers facing him now.

He should be grateful that they saved Robert the time, efforts and expense of building such a guard tower for Loch Etive and farther upriver at the narrow pass of Brander, Loch Awe and its rich, fertile lands and castles. For now, Sebastien felt like a target, his men assigned to guard this castle as the main forces of the king moved north.

Slowed by their lack of provisions, Robert had decided to stock this place and use it during the next months to shore up his hold over these lands controlled, for now, by allies of the powerful Comyns. Not many were privy to his plans, but Robert had shared them with Sebastien, and intended to announce them to his noble supporters at the gathering in Kilcrenan.

Sebastien could only imagine the resistance that would explode there at the news that he, an illegitimate soldier from largely unknown origins, would receive the wardenship of the captured MacDougall lands and titles permanently. Sebastien of Cleish would stand as guardian to the MacDougall's heir and control this crucial part of the coastline of western Scotland in reward for his service to the Bruce and his promise of allegiance for the future.

Robert had revealed that once the war was done, Sebastien was to receive a large grant of land here that he could pass on to any sons of his own. And, so long as Malcolm would swear allegiance and be counseled by Sebastien, the boy would regain Dunstaffnage once he was old enough to control the men who served the MacDougalls.

Of course, Sebastien knew that through all of this, Lara would be an overwhelming influence on the boy and on the path to peace in this area. Malcolm had revealed some of Lara's warnings against betraying his clan. Sebastien would need to gain her support and trust in order to gain the boy's.

For someone who had never truly dreamed of home and hearth, he was surprised how those dreams now invaded his thoughts and, nightly, invaded his sleep. This invitation to sit and sup with him sprang forth from the odd longings he'd developed since marrying the Maid of Lorne and learning of the king's plans.

Not that she gave Sebastien any encouragement. She fought him with words or with silence at every step. She exerted pressure on her brother to make him resistant to any argument for a true truce, or to any offers to continue his training. She refused to share a meal with Sebastien.

Foolish thoughts again! Here he stood, one of the Bruce's most able commanders of men, twisted in complete confusion over a mere woman. He turned his face into the rain, allowing its chill to infuse him once more. He'd been so rattled by her accusations that he'd left without his helmet, his sword, or his damn cloak, which would have protected his armor from this onslaught of rain.

Even more frustrating, he found himself standing on the shore of the firth, staring up at the north tower where she was. Not sure of how much time had passed, he wiped his face and decided to go back to his duties.

Since he would be leaving in another two days, there was much to see to, and wasting his time like this was not his usual behavior. Shrugging off this nonsensical worrying over Lara and her part in his future, indeed in Scotland's future, he turned and nearly walked into Hugh.

"A good fight would rid you of this restlessness," his friend said. "Or is it a good lay you need?" he asked with a raised eyebrow and a wary expression in his dark eyes.

"Either? Both? Neither?" he answered flatly.

"If 'tis a good fight you want, I can provide that to you," Hugh replied, smacking him on the back. "It's been nigh to a month since I faced a real challenge on the field."

"A month? Have you forgotten Brander Pass?"

"Nay, Sebastien, I have not. But fighting Mac-Dougalls is not really a challenge…not when they run from you."

Sebastien shook his head over Hugh's attempt at an insulting jest.

"Speaking of running away, the lady followed you from her tower." Hugh crossed his arms over his chest. "But you were running from the hall so fast that you did not hear her call."

"Did she tell you why?" He tried to dampen the interest in his voice, but it was obvious even to his own ears.

"Nay, but she did not delay in reminding me of my proper place." His friend laughed now as though remembering what had occurred. "She has spirit, that one. But, in spite of her clear intent, I did not accept her challenge and tell her that the two places I belong are in battle or between the warm and welcoming thighs of a fair wench." Hugh laughed louder this time, and Sebastien chuckled because he knew that his friend usually would not hesitate to enter a battle of words.

Sebastien sobered then, daring to ask the one person he trusted with his life the question that had been tormenting him for the last hours and days. "Do you ever wish for more than this soldier's life? Do you ever crave living in one place with one woman?"

"Is that what has you in such a state?" Hugh stepped back and looked him over from head to toe as though he did not know him. "Sebastien, for mercenaries such as us, there is only the battle. I cannot see myself in one place even when the Bruce controls the whole of Scotland. And I cannot think that you would be happy in such a life."

He shrugged, trying to consider his friend's words. Hugh did not yet know of the Bruce's decision, which gave Sebastien an option he'd never had before. The fact that he'd been ordered to marry or kill Lara was the first step, and Sebastien was certain that Robert had never meant for him to kill her. The Bruce was excellent at making people believe they had a choice, when none truly existed.

Robert wanted Sebastien in place and in control when he presented his counselors with his plans. It would be much more difficult for those within Robert's forces who opposed him to stop him once he actually held Dunstaffnage, the Maid of Lorne and the heir to the clan.

But now what?

The castle, he could hold.

The heir, he could protect and train.

The woman? Wed and consummated. Their marriage was a fact, but Lara refused to accept it. Could he change her mind and exert the same control over her that he did over his other responsibilities? He shook his head.

Hugh misunderstood the gesture. "So, you see the wisdom of my words. Though this marriage accomplishes some feat for the Bruce, he will no doubt assist you in nullifying it when his enemies are no more. Dunstaffnage is simply a stop along our path as soldiers, and she is simply a diversion for you while we are here. Accept her as such and do not allow her this power over you."

Sebastien's thoughts warred in his mind. Part of him, the part that had lived the same life as Hugh for years, accepted the truth in his friend's words. Unfortunately, that other part, the part that knew much more about the Bruce and about his plans and about the truth of Sebastien's background, did not wish to acknowledge it for the harsh description of his life that it was.

His delay in arguing his friend's assumption made Hugh believe he agreed. "Come then. Let us find that worthless lad you call squire and give him your mail and armor so that he can clean off the results of this rain."

Sebastien nodded and walked with Hugh back toward the drawbridge. Philippe could indeed clean his mail and armor and begin teaching Malcolm to, as well. Sebastien's skin itched for him to remove it, but he hesitated while outside the keep.

"Then I will fight you man-to-man and truly give you something to worry about," Hugh added the challenge very casually.

Thinking that just might take his mind off these unsettling questions and considerations, Sebastien nodded. As they crossed the yard and he called for Philippe, intending to give him instructions, the rain stopped and the winds died down. Most of the men who'd been staying in the yard had been moved, those still injured into the hall, and the rest to Robert's camp. Still, a crowd began gathering as word spread of their plan.

Philippe helped him off with his mail and the hauberk beneath it, and then handed him his sword. Asking permission for both him and Malcolm to stay and watch, he yelled happily when Sebastien granted it. Philippe moved off to one side of the yard and pulled Malcolm, who'd just arrived at Sebastien's orders, along with him. At his nod, the guard he'd assigned stood behind the boys.

"Well, Sebastien, are you feeling confident?" Hugh taunted him, swinging his weapon very close and motioning for him to strike first.

Sebastien laughed out loud and directed an insult at his friend. With that, the fight was on. Though thoroughly soaked by the rain, Sebastien was able to move more easily without the heavy mail encasing him. Hugh met him blow for blow, feint for feint and move for move. Their footwork was not the best or smoothest—the heavy rain had turned the yard into a muddy quagmire and they both slipped and fell several times.

But the fight continued until they were so covered

in mud they could no longer see each other. They tossed their swords down and continued to fight hand to hand until they could no longer take hold of their opponent. Although the onlookers grumbled about the fight being a draw, Sebastien and Hugh promised a better one once the yard dried out. As they strode out to use the water of the firth to remove the mud, Philippe and Malcolm ran after them, talking excitedly about the fight. Sebastien would work against the quiet resistance that Malcolm's sister offered by including the lad in Phillippe's assignments and introducing him to knightly training. The boy was quite interested in swordplay.

As though the thought of her had conjured her up, Sebastien glanced up at the tower and spied Lara gazing from a window in their chambers. He raised his sword to her and watched as she stepped back until he could see her no more. Shaking his head, he turned to Hugh and the boys, and went out to clean up before entering the hall.

Chapter Eight

The door opened and he stood before her, looking much the same as he had the night of their wedding. Not the brutish soldier she'd watched fight in the mud earlier this day. Nay, this was a man whose bearing cried out of noble blood coursing through his veins. A man who defined good breeding. Yet, as far as she could discover, he was simply a knight, one of unknown or at least questionable origins, who had risen in favor with his king as a direct result of his skills.

She shuddered as she remembered seeing his strength displayed in the yard. Both men had removed their hauberks and mail and fought in only their trews and boots. That same strength was now hidden beneath his raiment.

"Are you chilled, lady?" he asked as he held out his arm to her. "There is a fire in the solar to take away the coolness."

"I am not cold, just a bit tired."

"Then I will not keep you long from your…bed."

She heard the smile in his voice as he spoke of her

resting place. Lara could still not figure out how he moved her each night to the bed, and not once had she awakened. She walked at his side, down the steps to the solar, and was surprised by what she found there. The room had been transformed, a small table now in the center, covered with linen and plates and goblets for their use, with a chair on each side. Candles were lit and a fire did indeed burn in the hearth, chasing away the dampness of the day.

Her stomach warned her by its tenseness that this would be no simple meal. Why had she thought this a good idea? When Malcolm returned safely to their rooms, she had decided to accept Sebastien's invitation. After sending word through Philippe, Lara had worried the rest of the day about how to gain the information she needed from this enigmatic man.

They paused for a moment, not entering the room, and then he continued to walk down the steps, guiding her to the entrance to the hall.

"Sir? Do we not eat in the solar?" she asked.

"I thought after being closed up inside these last days, that you might enjoy a walk along the battlements? The sky has cleared and the evening is actually quite pleasant and we have some time before our meal is ready."

He spoke in a voice that could tempt an angel into sin. Did he know how unsettled she'd been by her walk to the chapel? Both the path there and then meeting her cousin had terrified her. She wanted desperately to walk; truly, she wanted to run to release the tension within her.

"I confess, sir, that you have discovered my weakness. I detest the uselessness and inactivity of these last days. I would indeed like to take a walk."

Although she knew the route in the dark with her eyes closed, she allowed him to lead her out of the hall and up the stairs near the south tower, to the battlements. There was a path around the entire perimeter of the castle, and from it, when the weather cooperated, one could see the best views of the firth to the west and south and Loch Linnhe to the north. Reaching the top, Lara let go of his arm and walked to the crenellated edge of one of the stone walls. Leaning forward, she looked out at the woods where the chapel lay, and toward the open expanses of land to the southeast, where the Bruce's forces camped.

"I have something to discuss with the guards, Lara. Walk ahead if you'd like." He waited for her answer and when she nodded, he turned and approached the guards patrolling the walls.

A taste of a freedom she no longer had, she thought as she walked away as fast as she could without appearing to be running. Not that she could escape him if she wanted to, but being alone here was a relief. She held the crispinette that covered her braided hair in place as she turned into the wind, but not even that slowed her pace. Breathing deeply, she allowed the winds that swept over these heights to push against her until she turned a corner and the winds were at her back.

Laughing, Lara continued her brisk speed, returning to where she'd left Sebastien much sooner than she wished. He was still speaking with the guards, so she resumed her path, not stopping until she reached the place farthest from him. There she stood and leaned over, looking at the boats that could be used to cross the firth or the loch. Many more than her father usually had, this was a small fleet at the ready for some use. Guards circled, protecting the boats from any attack—or sabotage?

Soon, as the sun dropped lower to the west, the winds turned colder and she began to shiver. Still, she would rather be cold than inside, so she did not leave the spot. Instead, she sat between two of the crenellations and closed her eyes.

"You are making my men nervous, lady."

She opened her eyes and found Sebastien standing before her, holding a cloak. "How so, sir?"

"Your hurried pace and the way you dare to hang over the side of the walls."

"This is my home, sir. I have climbed these walls from the time I was a child." She realized it sounded as though she could climb down the two-score-and-five-feet-tall walls of stone. Well, she could, but that was not something he needed to know.

"Mayhap that was something better left unsaid?"

"Ah, you mistook my words, sir. I mean that I have walked this path all my life. I am quite comfortable moving around on these battlements." She stood and stepped away from the edge, an action that placed her nearer to him.

"You are shivering now," he said, moving closer still. "I brought this for you."

He did not offer the cloak to her, instead reaching out to drape it around her shoulders. Tugging the ends together, he gathered them under her chin. That pulled her closer to him than she'd expected, but with such a hold, she could not move away. His nearness overwhelmed her and as he leaned his head down and gazed into her eyes, she knew he would kiss her.

When his lips were a scant inch from hers, he stopped and did not come any closer. She held her breath, knowing from their night together how this would feel, and trying to make her body not react to what it knew could happen. And from the way her heart pounded in her chest and the way her mouth went dry, apparently her body wanted it to happen again. Lara closed her eyes and fought the urge to cross the empty space and press her mouth to his. She remembered the touch of his lips on her…mouth and on other… Her traitorous body tightened in places better not thought about, and she shivered once more.

Then, Sebastien stepped away, allowing the ends of the cloak to dangle loosely. Lara searched his face for some explanation and fought the wayward desire that now spiraled within her. She stumbled a few steps back and turned away from his gaze. Did he know what his nearness did to her? Was seduction his plan all along? And she could not stop the errant and most dangerous thought of all—why had he stopped?

"My pardon, lady," he said from behind her. "I did not mean to…" His words ceased, as though he did not know what to say. Lara turned back to him and the look of confusion in his expression calmed her somehow.

"I had sought to ease your fears and anxiety about our meal together, and now I can see I have simply made it worse with my lack of control." He glanced over at the men near the stairway and then at her. "I have not finished my instructions to the guards. If you would join me in the solar when you are finished walking, I will give you some time here."

Without waiting for her consent, he did indeed leave her there…alone. Lara pulled the cloak around her more tightly and walked back to the edge. Trying not to think about what had almost happened between them, she allowed the wind to soothe her before facing their next encounter.

Sebastien counted off each step he took away from her, clenching his fists against the urge to pull her into his arms and kiss her until she was breathless. Although he could deny the wisdom in doing such a thing, he could not deny how much he wanted to do exactly that…and more. Much, much more.

He truly had nothing else to speak to the guards about, so he left the battlements after indicating that the lady was to be allowed there. He ran down the steps, crossed through the hall and made his way to the solar. Everything was ready now and the servants, and Lara's maid, met him with expectant gazes when he entered the room.

Sebastien sat down and asked for wine while he waited. Would she drag this out? Would she come back as he'd directed? Taking the first swallow of the wine, he hoped it would settle *his* stomach. Only a few minutes passed before he heard footsteps coming up the stairs toward the solar. Then she was there. He stood as she entered, and watched silently as she handed the cloak to her maid.

"Sir? If you please, I have need to return to my chambers for a brief time before we eat."

He tried to discern if there was guile in this request,

but could see nothing that indicated more or less than she'd asked for. Nodding his assent, he was curious when she whispered something to her maid before leaving. Whatever words she'd said caused the girl to blush and look away.

True to her words, Lara returned a few minutes later and, after sharing a glance with her maid, walked over and sat next to him at the table. Once she'd been served wine, he gestured to the servants and they began placing platters of roasted meats and fish before them. Sebastien had explained to them the foods he wanted served and how he wanted the meal to be done. As he'd ordered, the table was filled with a selection of her favorites, ones revealed to him by the old cook, whom he had kept on in the kitchens.

If she recognized them, she did not say, but her gaze moved from dish to dish, and every so often he noticed a smile on her lips. Once everything was in place, the servants bowed and left. Lara turned and seemed to stare at the closed door for a minute. He waited for her to turn back and face him.

"I hear that you have not been eating lately," he began. "Your cook said these were some of your favorite dishes and I thought to entice you with them."

"Thank you for your thoughtfulness, sir, but there is more than needed for only the two of us. Should we not invite Malcolm and Catriona to sup with us? I am certain Malcolm would be interested in discussing the fight he witnessed earlier."

Sebastien could not help it—the laugh escaped before he could stop it. "They are eating elsewhere and are well cared for, lady."

She worried her lower lip between her teeth and gazed at the dishes again. He lifted a platter of thick slices of beef to her. The succulent aroma made his own stomach grumble. He thought she might refuse, but then nodded in agreement. Placing a slice on the plate in front of him, he cut it into smaller pieces and offered them to her.

Sebastien watched as she scooped some onto her own plate and then skewered one with her eating dagger. There was a moment when she bit into the well-cooked and well-spiced meat that a look of satisfaction crossed her face. He wondered what that was about, but did not ask. Instead, he took samples from most of the dishes and placed them on her plate. She began to eat with enthusiasm, so he considered how he could begin their talk.

He waited for her to eat a substantial amount before starting. From watching her these last few weeks and from the questions he asked of those closest to her, he knew that when she was upset, she did not eat. So he knew that her visit to the chapel had not soothed her at all, and he wondered why not. Had it only been the incident in the yard that had distressed her?

Sebastien reached over and refilled the goblet in front of her. "There is ale, if you prefer it."

"Nay, the wine is quite good." She sipped it. "Another gift from the Bruce?"

"The same. He gave us a keg of his favorite to…"

"To mark our wedding." She finished the statement when he paused.

Now it was his turn to swallow deeply from his own

cup. She'd mentioned it in a matter-of-fact manner. "Aye."

"What else did he give you for marrying me? What honors were heaped on you for taking the enemy's daughter as your wife? Or should I ask what offense you committed to be sentenced to such an arrangement?" Her blue eyes narrowed as she asked.

The sharp edge of sarcasm filled her voice and he answered in kind. "I gained no rich rewards or honors by our marriage. I but obeyed my king's orders. We needed to secure the castle and the claim to the Mac-Dougall's lands and you were the means of that." If such things were to come from the king, so be it; he need not confirm it to her yet.

She lost all color from her cheeks and he regretted immediately the harshness in his tone. Why did he allow her to goad him into this kind of exchange? He read her pattern of behavior clearly—that was one advantage of his years as a spy. Sebastien could watch individuals over a period of time and learn their secrets by what they did and how they did it.

Lara would be even more upset when she realized this about him. In spite of her efforts not to give away anything about herself, he'd already discovered many things about her.

She had an incredible amount of vigor and needed to have that force of life directed into usefulness or she got herself in trouble. She knew much more about her father and her clan's battle plans than she wanted Sebastien to realize. And although she put on a brave and confident face, she suffered from an intense insecurity when it came to her own worth. Tales of how she constantly tried to achieve more than would be expected of a daughter, even the esteemed Maid of Lorne, had been shared with him.

The most important thing he'd discovered about her was something she'd revealed during their last few encounters. Lara used her anger as a shield when her fears were touched. When something or someone threatened to expose that timidity that she kept under tight control, she struck out like an angry bee—stinging the one who came too close. He'd learned that after feeling the stab himself.

"Come now, Lara. If you have questions, simply ask them of me and do not try to bait me to strike out at you in words or with my hands."

He watched as she cleared her throat and thought on his words. Good, she was thinking before striking out again. He could teach her to trust him—it would just take time.

"What will you do with me now that I am not breeding?"

A momentary pang of regret filled him at this news. Ah, so that was what required her to visit her chambers before coming here, and what caused her maid to blush. "Your courses are…"

"Aye." She glanced away and would not meet his gaze.

"Things will not always be as they are now, Lara. This place will not be your prison for much longer."

"What do you mean? Will you put me aside, then? Or will your king intercede to end this marriage?"

"We face many uncertainties in these next months and years. The king has not yet announced his decision for the final disposition of MacDougall lands. I think it best to wait for his word in this."

He knew so much more, but could not share it with her or anyone yet. Within a week, all would be made clear and everyone would know that their marriage was not some temporary arrangement to be cast aside when the king moved on from here in pursuit of his kingdom.

She stood and walked to the hearth, leaning over it silently for a short time. Then, she looked at him. "I am certain I know what your king wants in this, but tell me of Sebastien of Cleish and what he wants?"

He needed no time to think on his words. "First, I am a faithful vassal of my king, and second, a man who sometimes wants too much too quickly. But 'tis the Bruce's wishes that will decide the matter."

Her eyes were haunted now, with some intangible emotion that he could not name. "You know your place. What is to become of me now that you and your king are here?"

"Mayhap if we begin by asking who is the Maid of Lorne and what does she desire?" He asked the question to her now and waited to hear the description she would choose—it would say much about her.

"I am a woman with no father and no family and no home to call her own. I am a woman who gave herself to her enemy. I am the Maid of Lorne no more." Her voice shook in its desolation.

He stood and walked up behind her. Reaching out, he slipped his arm around her shoulders and drew her back against him. She stilled in his embrace, but did not pull away. Sebastien whispered in her ear.

"Do not despair, Lara. Many others have been in similar circumstances and survived, even made good lives of bad beginnings. The Bruce is a fair man and I trust his judgment in this matter."

She did not move or acknowledge his words at all, so he released her and stepped back. "I must go on a mission for the king soon and will leave Hugh in charge of Dunstaffnage. No harm will come to you while he is in command here."

The emptiness in her gaze unsettled him, and he acknowledged that he would rather face her anger or her confusion or any other emotion she could feel rather than this melancholy. How could he draw forth her anger?

"You asked what I want, Lara. What does Sebastien of Cleish want? I want you, Lara. I want to hold you and feel your body as it heats to my touch. I want you to open to me and I want to fill you with myself."

She met his eyes and hers widened as she recognized the pure lust and wanting he was feeling at that moment. He took a step closer and she took one back. Finally, he reached across the gap between them, pulled her into his arms and kissed her the way he'd wanted to all night. Indeed, the way he'd wanted to since the night they were wed.

He slid his hands to each side of her head and held her still as his mouth claimed hers. He took advantage of her surprise to taste her deeply, to touch his tongue to hers and to press his mouth to hers, over and over again. He stared into her eyes until she closed them. Sebastien felt her hands come up onto his wrists as though she would stop him, but she did not.

And she did not pull away from him or his kisses.

Soon they were both out of breath from the intensity of his plundering. He leaned away and slid his hands down her neck and over her shoulders. He grazed her breasts with the backs of his fingers as they moved down to grasp hers. The shudder that moved through her stirred him even more.

"We do not have to be enemies, Lara. We can be husband and wife, man and woman."

As though opening the shutters in a dark room, his words pierced through the seduction he wove around her, and brought her to herself. Not even a day had passed since her cousin had accused her of whoring with the enemy, and she stood her ready to give herself over to his passions.

"If you die in the service of your king, I will be wife to the enemy no more," she said, wiping her hand over her mouth to remove any taste of him. "As you said, things will not always be as they are now, but I will always be a MacDougall, while you remain a nameless bastard serving an upstart who thinks he should be king."

Lara threw out the insult and waited for his reaction, dreading it and yet praying for it at the same time. She had listened to the gossip of the servants since their capture. She had discovered this weakness even as he probed for hers. Now, when she felt unable to resist him and his appeal, she had ruthlessly used it to force some room between them.

And it worked.

As she watched, his face transformed into the warrior she'd faced from the battlements that first day. His green eyes grew cold and distant, and she could see him wrapping his control around himself even as she pushed her righteous anger forward as her shield.

"I think it would be best if you retired, lady," he said, breaking the silence. "Seek your chambers now." He strode to the door and pulled it open with such force that it crashed against the wall after slipping from his grasp.

Margaret and his man Hugh jumped to their feet and stared in at them. Surprised to see them together and obviously in each other's company, Lara censured her maid with a warning glance. Apparently, Margaret was suffering from the same weakness that her lady was damned by—an attraction to the enemy. Taking her arm, Lara pulled her away and up the stairs to her room to safety.

"I cannot tell if you are feeling victorious or not."

Sebastien stood back and allowed Hugh entrance to the solar. His friend immediately sat at the table and began picking food off the plates still there. Although the dishes were now chilled, Hugh did not hesitate to taste all he could. Too many days and nights without food trained warriors to eat when food was available.

After allowing his anger to dissipate, Sebastien closed the door and joined Hugh at the table. Choosing a joint of rabbit that had been braised in a rich broth, he tore off and passed to his friend a chunk of bread to use on the juices. They dipped the bread, chewed it thoroughly and swallowed, almost in unison.

"Indeed, Hugh. I do feel the victor in this."

"From the expression on her face, the lady does not

feel the same way." Hugh poured wine into both goblets and drank from the nearest one. "I would hide my sword, if I were you, and not leave it within her reach. You might be missing some body parts that are best kept, if you take my meaning?"

Sebastien laughed then, confident in the results of the encounter with his wife. "As you will be if she discovers your attentions to her maid." Hugh flinched at his words. "There is not much that goes on here that I do not know about, friend. Have a care if you only dally with the lass."

Holding out the goblet, Hugh offered a mock salute. "So what did you learn?"

"She wants me."

"That was the purpose of this whole escapade, then?" Hugh asked, looking over the remnants of the supper and the room. "To see if you could make her desire you? You may need my counsel if that was your aim."

"That would have been too simply done," he said with a laugh, knowing it for the boast it was. "Her world has been torn down around her and she has been left to pick up the shattered remains."

Hugh shrugged. "This is war."

"Ah, but she is mine now."

"And this changes everything?" Hugh frowned as he thought on what Sebastien said. "Please do not say that you plan to keep her after all? A wife, Sebastien?"

"Aye, *my* wife."

Hugh let out a loud exasperated breath. "So, pray tell me, sir knight, what is this plan of yours?" He slammed down the food in his hands and wiped his palms across the cloth on the table in a deliberate move to aggravate him and remind them both of their origins.

"She handles challenges best when angry, so I angered her."

"And that will accomplish what?" Hugh stood and sought another pitcher of wine. Finding only ale, he poured that in his goblet this time. Sitting back down, he drank from the cup.

"It will make your life more difficult while I am away." Sebastien nodded a salute to him. "And it will give her the backbone needed these next days while I am with the king."

"My thanks for your kind consideration, friend."

"Ah...come now, Hugh. Surely you can manage one angry woman? So long as she never discovers what you and her maid are up to, you should probably remain safe. Well, at least alive."

"As you wish, Sebastien. Although I confess I do wish you'd change your thinking on this matter and ask the king's permission to dissolve this union when you have his ear."

"I will consider your words," Sebastien said, ending the discussion. "Now, has Etienne met with the old man yet?"

"He has and not gotten too far, I fear. Callum is just as obstinate as his lady."

"That is another of your duties then while I see to the king."

"Sebastien," Hugh whined. "This is conveniently timed for you."

"Come now, Hugh. Use your skills as a negotiator and have this in place before I return. Do not fail me in this." Sebastien stood and gestured for Hugh to come along. "The lady is agitated and will take some time to fall asleep. I want to show you my plans for a new building along the south wall."

Chapter Nine

He left a day earlier than planned, and led his men under cover of night and by boat rather than marching the entire distance. Sebastien felt confident that the change in location for the meeting was warranted. If Eachann was indeed in the area, his spies were watching every move made by the king's forces, and he would know of the plans to meet in Kilcrenan. At the last moment possible, Sebastien had moved the king's gathering to the priory of St. Modan's in Ardchattan and sent out trusted messengers to inform those involved of the change.

Pleased by the obvious insult to the MacDougalls' honor that it was—Ardchattan had been founded and long supported by the clan—Sebastien longed to see both Eachann's and his father's expressions when they discovered the ruse and the truth of it. Since that would not be possible, he contented himself that he had once again protected Robert from danger.

As all of Robert's allies gathered to discuss the future of his kingdom, Sebastien prepared himself for the

fight. Robert assured him that it would not undermine
the support, both in fighting men and money, that they
gave to his campaigns, but Sebastien worried. Now
that the nobles were gathering, the king's plans would
be known to all.

As was his custom, Sebastien did not claim a place
near the king, preferring to be with his back against a
wall—a sturdy wall—where he could see everyone's
movements and the way in which the gathering would
progress. And where he could keep watch out the door
to make certain his guards missed nothing.

Most of the principals were present by midday and
the king called for their attention. Sebastien smiled at
the Bruce's use of the old Gaelic. Diplomat and plan-
ner that he was, this demonstrated Robert's Scottish
character at a time when Norman, French, English and
even Irish loyalties pulled many in different directions.

Sebastien caught the eye of James Douglas and nodded. The Black Douglas had, at Robert's specific orders, recently razed his own castle to keep the English
from it, and must be perplexed by Robert's decision
over Dunstaffnage. Sebastien glanced around the large
chamber and saw all of the king's closest friends, ad-
visors and allies. Neil Campbell, Edward Bruce,
Gilbert de la Haye, Robert Boyd, even the recently returned to grace Thomas Randolph was present.

Realizing the importance of safety for these men,
Sebastien slipped from the chamber to walk the
grounds once more and to speak with each of his sen-
tries. Checking the church, where they'd detained all
of the monks as well as any who worked for the priory, he found all as it should be. At the gates, his own

men stood watch. Each noble had traveled lightly to avoid detection, and brought with him only a small number of warriors. Those men were now deployed in the woods and valleys that surrounded the priory to prevent an attack. Convinced that all safeguards were in place, Sebastien returned to the meeting chamber and to his position by the door.

"You cannot give this to him!"

He shook his head as the first words he heard were yelled at the king. Robert had made his wishes known. Crossing his arms over his chest, Sebastien leaned against the wall, ready for Robert's summons. The rest argued about him as though he were not present.

"He has no family ties," shouted the Earl of Lennox.

"All the better to serve me with unquestioning loyalty," Robert replied. "Family ties sometimes force our hand in ways we regret."

Silence reigned for a moment. So many families had been split apart by the battle for the Scottish throne. No doubt many men were remembering that now.

"He is only a soldier, sire. Not fit to hold such an important post," someone called out. Sebastien did not recognize the voice and did not wish to.

"He was knighted the morning of our battle in the pass. By my decree and my own sword. Would any of you argue that his accomplishments are not worthy of knighthood?"

Robert was sly; he ignored the general practice that knighthood was reserved for men of good background and only those who had trained for years. Sebastien had been trained, of course, on the true battlefields, where success meant life and failure meant death. There could be no better teacher.

"His spies and information have saved my arse more than once," the Douglas shouted, and most there laughed. "If Dunstaffnage must stand…" he paused and spat on the ground "…and I ken Robert's need for this one…" he looked at many of the men and met their gazes "…then Sebastien of Cleish has my support to hold it."

Sebastien had not realized he was holding his breath. At the Douglas's declaration, he let it out and began to think this would work out for the best. Robert waved him forward, and Sebastien left his place by the door and walked to the king.

"'Tis settled then this day. Sebastien of Cleish is now laird and royal warden of Dunstaffnage and guardian to the children of John of Lorne. Malcolm Mac-Dougall is in your charge until he can pledge for himself before me. Train him well, Sebastien, for we will need more warriors for the battles to come."

"And the other MacDougalls, sire?" Sebastien asked, for their future had not been disclosed.

"The same as the rest—they pledge their support or they are exiled. Make it so within the next month, for I want the area secure."

"As you order, sire," he answered, with a bow. He regained his place in the back before Robert's words made sense. He'd been named Laird—Lord—of Dunstaffnage. No longer a simple soldier or even a knight, he was now, by the king's decree, a lord of the realm.

After years of practice, he was not so enamored by the pronouncement that he missed the discontent and grumbling of some present there. The Campbell contingent seemed the most unhappy by this move. Their lands lay all around the MacDougalls' in Argyll, and they had certainly hoped that the land and castle would be annexed to their properties.

They approached the king immediately to make their case, but he waved them off. "Come, we have much to discuss about our enemies. Rather than wasting our time with arguments between friends, we must decide about moving north."

Any further discussion was squashed and the subject of the Earl of Ross was raised then. The earl's part in the capture of Robert's wife, daughter and sister, along with others, made Robert ripe to consider a decisive action against the man. Now, with the east and south mostly secured, they could move against their few remaining Scottish opponents before turning their efforts on ridding the country of the English.

In spite of the importance of such a discussion, all Sebastien could think about was Lara. Now he could offer her a place, a home and family, and the security of being his wife in truth. But, how would she react to this news?

No matter how he convinced himself that he had goaded her into her insults, the ones she'd made about him being a bastard stung. It was the truth, but she knew not all the facts surrounding his birth and his parentage. No one did, save Hugh.

One night after Sebastien had been wounded in a battle and was delirious from the ensuing fever, he'd revealed to his friend details he'd sworn would never be spoken of. Hugh had vowed to never let the truth be known, and the two had become the best of friends, fighting and wenching their way across Scotland in the service of the Bruce.

Now, Sebastien had risen to this new honor. Would Lara accept him as equal in rank to her? Deep in his heart, he hoped they could have a life together. Mayhap once she knew of his duties and of his guardianship of her brother and sister, she would realize the chance before them.

The meeting dragged on for two days, and then, after seeing the Bruce's forces reunited with the king on the road that led to the shores of Loch Linnhe and the Glenmor, Sebastien took his men back to Dunstaffnage.

For the first time in his life, he allowed another word to enter his thoughts.

Home.

He was going home.

When she realized she'd been duped, or at least lied to, Lara asked permission to visit the chapel. She waited as long as she possibly could for Eachann's man to show up. As her cousin had suggested, she'd spoken with others in the keep to gather information about the Bruce's plans. One man overheard "Kilcrenan," while another heard soldiers discussing a move north, over Loch Etive. A serving maid now on good terms with one of the guards told her about some talk of St. Modan's.

Eachann's man listened, cursed under his breath and then left without saying a word to her, so she did not know if she'd helped or not. She hoped that they

were watching the castle, and knew that Sebastien had
left early for whatever his mission was. If what she'd
overheard was true, he would be back in another day
or so.

Once they'd entered the castle, the guards dropped
away from her side and she was permitted to walk
freely there. A surprise from *her husband,* Sir Hugh
had announced the morning after he'd gone. Still furious over Sebastien's attempts to seduce her, she'd
awakened to find his place in the bed marked but cold,
and him and his soldiers already on their way. When
Sir Hugh had appeared, to explain the new rules regard-
ing her restrictions, or lessening of them, Etienne and
old Callum had stood at his side.

Another change wrought by *her husband.* Callum
now served Etienne in his duties as steward of Dunstaffnage. She wanted to rush to his side and ask Callum about his new position, but he warned her off with
a look. Mayhap the old man was not so changed then
in his ways.

So, she accepted the new rules about where she
could and could not go, and then set off to discover the
changes since her husband took control.

The storerooms beneath the hall were filled now
with all manner of foodstuffs and provisions. Instead
of coming from surrounding farms belonging to her
family, supplies began to arrive from all different
places. A new smithy was being constructed off the
kitchens, as was another storehouse. The yard was
filled with the sounds of renovations from morning
until dark. Lara found the best place to watch was from
the battlements, so she spent most of the next days

there. Margaret would stay with her for a time and then she would beg off and leave.

Malcolm and Philippe had also managed to become fast friends in a short time. Sebastien had assigned them to duties in the stables and in the smithy, and they were anything but quiet when together. Although Philippe was older by four years, he accepted the difference and kept her brother close. Largely ignored by their father, Malcolm now began to thrive under the attention of these other men.

Catriona, who had been so close to Lara since her birth, and especially these last weeks, now clung to Margaret, or sometimes, with childish affection, shadowed Phillippe's movements while he was inside the keep.

Lara stood looking over the wall into the yard, wondering if she was seeing the new Dunstaffnage. And if it were, where did she fit in? By the seventh day of Sebastien's absence, she was no closer to discovering it. And on the eighth day, when he rode back into the yard, she knew her world had changed once more.

He dismounted and Sir Hugh approached him quickly. They put their heads together for a few minutes and she could tell even from her distance that Hugh was thoroughly questioning Sebastien about something. Then, Hugh stepped back and shook his head—clearly not believing whatever Sebastien had said. Both men laughed loudly and then embraced each other.

Clearly good news. For someone.

More words were exchanged and several orders called out to men close by. More gathered, and she watched as the news spread across the yard, among his soldiers, even to the MacDougall servants and anyone else present. Then she noticed that Sir Hugh was pointing in her direction, and Sebastien headed for the stairway.

Lara stood back and waited, wanting but not wanting to go and meet him. Curious about what news he brought, she found her hands trembled. Clasping them, she took a deep breath and let it out. He paused to speak to the guards along the perimeter, then reached her side quickly.

"Lady," he said with a bow. "How do you fare?" She felt the heat of his gaze as it moved over her.

"Well, sir." Except that her hands still shook. Then Lara noticed the blood on his leg and his arm. Fresh blood, from its appearance. "You had some trouble?"

"A minor skirmish a few miles from here. I assure you, I am none the worse for it." He stepped closer and, without warning, kissed her on the forehead. "I am glad you are well then, lady. I fear we separated on less than ideal terms at our last encounter." His face flushed as though he had admitted more than he wished to, and he cleared his throat before speaking again. "I have missed you, Lara."

Surprised by his words and his forthright, even bold, manner, she could not answer. Before either of them could say anything more, a guard approached rapidly and called out to him.

"My lord, Sir Hugh said to tell you that everyone is gathering as you ordered."

My lord? The guard called him lord? She stared at him, waiting for his explanation...or his correction of the guard's address.

"Tell Hugh that we shall be there momentarily," he replied without looking away from her, and then he waited for the guard to leave. "There is news I would share with you before we go to the hall."

"I suspected as much. And, if it was good news for me, you would not be hesitating and wanting to give it to me in private," she said.

"It could be, if you let it be, Lara."

Her mouth went dry as he spoke her name in that low voice, and the tremors spread through her. Could he see what his voice alone did to her? "What has happened?"

"The king has announced his decision about Dunstaffnage." *And about you…* He did not say it, but she knew. "I have been appointed royal warden and guardian of both Malcolm and Catriona."

"There is more. I can see how you guard your words and give me this news of great import piece by piece. Come, sir, tell me the rest." She tried to imagine the worst and could not, most likely a testament to the last month of her life.

"He has made me Laird of Dunstaffnage and has awarded me these lands and the title until Malcolm is of an age to pledge for himself."

Lara thought herself prepared, but hearing it said, she reeled from all it meant. "So, everyone is taken care of then, but for me."

"Do you not understand, Lara? This is what you wanted. A home, your home, and a prison no longer to you and your family. A place to be needed. A husband, not of your choosing, but one who stands high in favor with the king and one who can protect you from those who are your enemies." He held out his hand to her.

Sebastien stood before her, offering so much with his words and his simple gesture that she feared her total capitulation to him. All she need do was reach out her hand. He waited a minute, then another, and then he lowered his own. His eyes showed no sign of how or even if her rejection affected him, but he turned away and began walking toward the stairway.

Lara's stomach knotted within her. She knew she must do something, but what? He went to tell the rest about his new position and his new responsibilities, and her absence from his side would cause gossip and problems. He had tried to accommodate her. He had listened when he could have ignored her pleas and her deepest needs.

"My lord? Pray thee, I would come with you to the hall."

Sebastien stopped and, without facing her, waited for her to catch up to him. When she'd reached his side, they walked to the stairs, down to the yard and to the entrance of the hall. So many were gathering that a crowd spilled out onto the steps. His men began cheering as they noticed him, and the crowd parted to allow them through. Sebastien took her hand to guide her to the front of the hall.

Catriona broke away from her own maid and ran to Lara's side. At but six years, the girl had no idea of what was occurring, and she clung to Lara, wrapping her small fingers in her sister's. Cat tended to slip back to the nervous child she'd become with the arrival of so many strangers in their home.

With the death of her stepmother in childbirth, as her own had as well, Lara was the only person close to acting as a mother to Catriona, although lately Margaret served such a role as well. While the innocence of her age allowed her a smoother passage through the events of these last weeks, the changes and upheavals here unnerved the girl, and she usually remained in her chambers or in the solar when Lara was there.

Sebastien left her and called Malcolm to him. Philippe followed and Sebastien leaned over to speak with both of them. She'd never seen three more serious faces as the conversation went on for several minutes. Then Malcolm smiled widely at something Sebastien said to him, and he nodded. Without another word, Malcolm came to stand next to her. As Sebastien began his address to the crowd, she felt her brother's hand slide into hers and squeeze it.

He stretched up so he could whisper in her ear. "Sebastien says that we are his now and that he will care for us." She nodded to him without answering. He tugged her hand and she leaned down once more.

"He said we have nothing to fear from him."

She imagined that those words were the very ones spoken by the devil to Eve as he enticed her to sin. Lara glanced across the small distance that separated them and met his clear, green gaze. There he stood, the devil incarnate, tempting her to forget who she was and who he was.

The very worst of it was that she was very tempted to do exactly what he wanted.

Chapter Ten

Dunstaffnage transformed before her eyes over the next weeks—from home of the MacDougalls to prison to the home of the newly elevated Lord Sebastien. No longer restricted to the north tower, Lara was free to roam, and found no guards at her heels as she moved around the keep and the castle grounds.

Malcolm adored Sebastien and spent most of his time dogging his every movement. Catriona had taken a liking to him as well and had been drawn in by the small gifts he always seemed to bring her at supper. Margaret fancied herself in love with Sir Hugh and, although Lara suspected the knight had a nefarious purpose in mind, no words or warnings could convince the maid of it.

The new laird ordered barracks to be built a short distance from the castle, and the men still living in the hall moved there as soon as they were completed. His men seemed to find stationary living very different than their normal situation, but they all adapted to it. Sebastien organized a daily routine of patrols and training that suited those now stationed at the castle. Lara noticed that he stopped wearing his mail and armor while going about his duties—a sure sign of his confidence in their occupation of Dunstaffnage.

True to Sebastien's word and promise, all remaining soldiers and servants were given the choice of swearing loyalty to him and his king or exile. Although a few chose to leave, most stayed behind and merged into the fighting groups under his command or were assigned new duties by Etienne or Callum.

She overheard Sebastien tell Hugh that this was how Robert would govern once all of Scotland was in his control—in addition to his loyal vassals holding their own keeps, a system of castles under royal governance scattered across the land. Dunstaffnage was simply the first demonstrating this change in the way Robert the Bruce ruled his country. From ragtag groups of warriors, moving in stealth under night's cover, to well-provisioned and armed castles, the Bruce's force was stretching.

She continued to gather scraps of information and pass them on to her cousin, although she never heard much back. One day Lara discovered the list of planned supply movements and told Eachann about it. She even described Sebastien's method of having a heavily armed escort come to Dunstaffnage to travel back to where the provisions were needed. Over the next few weeks, his men were attacked by raiding parties and there were some injuries, but nothing serious enough to bring about retaliation from Sebastien.

Sebastien split the job of steward, assigning Callum to oversee those duties that pertained to the running of the castle itself, and assigning Etienne to oversee the task of moving supplies, men and weapons to and from Dunstaffnage as required. Now, with Callum taking care of things again, it almost felt like home to Lara.

Almost.

Nearly every task she'd done in the past—being in charge of the keep, its supplies and foodstocks, its servants and villeins, everything that did not involve her father's own duties—was now handled by others. Etienne never consulted her on matters pertaining to the villages or farmlands. Callum listened to her words or requests, but never sought out her opinions or suggestions or followed any orders she tried to give.

Everyone there seemed to know their place, and thrived under the care and control of the new Laird of Dunstaffnage. All but her. The worst part was that she could feel and see the ones she loved the most slipping away from her. And with discouraging news that arrived with each visit of her cousin or his man, Lara felt more and more lost and unneeded. It appeared that other than gathering facts and details for Eachann, she seemed to have no purpose here.

Mayhap, if Sebastien pressured her or forced her to the marriage bed, against her will, she would feel better about her spying. If she could hate him for the way he behaved toward her or her siblings, the passing of information and the subsequent attacks would feel more rewarding.

Instead, he treated her with infinite civility and politeness. After her rebuke of his request on the battlements, he'd not approached her about anything personal again. Strangely, they continued to share a bed. Each morning she awoke clinging to the edge on her side, as though afraid of reaching out to him while asleep. And if she tried to sleep in her chair, she always found herself in the bed and Sebastien gone when she woke.

If she were honest with herself, it was getting very difficult to ignore him. He dealt with everyone in his jurisdiction fairly and protected her family as he'd promised to. He'd created a home in Dunstaffnage where even her sister now moved freely and comfortably on her own.

Although his attempts to physically seduce Lara stopped, he did try to entice her with promises of a return to her previous duties, but she understood the cost of such a thing and could not accept the bribe. She managed to escape from such encounters, though it was growing more difficult each time.

The thing she could not escape from were the memories. Of his kisses. His touch. The way he made her body ache and then satisfied it. Memories invaded her sleep and she found herself watching the way he walked, the way he touched Catriona's small hand, the way he grasped his sword when training in the yard. Lara longed to reach out and touch the scar on his cheek and to feel the heat in his chest, but pride and fear kept her from doing so.

Eachann had called her a whore and she did not want that to be true. She could not lie with the enemy and keep her self-worth intact. She must continue to thwart his and his king's plans, and part of that was Sebastien's plan for her.

As was her custom, Lara was working on her embroidery in the solar when Malcolm sought her out. The morning had dawned clear and sunny and warmer than usual for a mid-September day.

"Come, Lara. Lord Sebastien asks that you join us on the firth," Malcolm said, grabbing and tugging on her hand.

"I am busy here, Malcolm. Please give Lord Sebastien my regrets." She shook free of his grasp. Errant thoughts of him now invaded her waking hours as alluring daydreams, and so the less she was in his company the better.

Margaret sighed loudly and Lara knew the meaning of the censuring sound immediately. The maid continued moving her hands deftly over the fabric and never missed a stitch. "Milady, you have made much progress on that. A bit of time outside might refresh your spirits."

"And give you time with Sir Hugh, Margaret?"

The woman's freckled complexion blushed at the comment. "I would accompany you, if you wish it. Sir Hugh is about his duties now."

"I cannot believe your boldness, Margaret. He is the enemy. And yet you…"

Margaret tucked her own needle into the tapestry and stepped to her side. Leaning down so that their comments were more private, she whispered, "We each have our own path, milady. Please do not begrudge me some small measure of happiness."

Lara felt small and mean-spirited at her irritation. Was it Margaret's fault or due to some weakness in her character that she could adjust to this new way while her mistress could not? In truth, Margaret had been at her side every moment that she was needed. And, in spite of the occasional kiss stolen by the man in question, Margaret spent every night in a bed in the children's chambers, Lara knew.

Leaning back and sighing, she looked at her brother, who stood tapping his foot and twisting his hands while waiting for her attention. Her throat had grown tight at Margaret's plea.

The maid sat back down on her stool and smiled at her.

"Please come, Lara. You can sew anytime. Please come," Malcolm repeated, ignoring the other topic being discussed in hushed tones.

"What is so important that I must come?" She slipped the needle into the corner of the tapestry so she would not lose it. "Another battle between you and Philippe? Another race on the shore?"

"'Tis a secret we have to show you."

Stretching her arms over her head, Lara tried to loosen the tightness in her neck. Mayhap Margaret was correct? A walk, a brief walk, would help her to rid herself of it? "Fine. Where is Lord Sebastien waiting for us?"

"He said he would meet us at the new dock. In a quarter hour." Malcolm's obvious joy made it difficult to stay aloof.

She smiled. "I will be at the dock then to see the secret that you and Lord Sebastien keep."

Malcolm jumped and yelled, startling the other women in the solar. "I must find Philippe!" he said as he ran out of the room and down the stairs.

She'd never liked surprises, so Lara walked to the

window that overlooked the firth and glanced out to see if Sebastien waited there already. Although not at the dock, he was there. As she watched, he walked out of the water, where he'd been swimming. And with each step, his naked form was revealed to her. Lara could not turn away from the display of his manly figure. Strong arms and shoulders led down to a narrow waist and hips. And…

She swallowed and tried to look away before all of him appeared, but her traitorous eyes would not obey. Another step and his muscular thighs and legs were exposed. Her mouth went dry and she shivered as she remembered the strength in those muscles and the pleasure of being covered by that body now revealed in the light of day.

Lara did not think she'd made a noise, but he turned his head and met her gaze. He pushed the hair out of his eyes and stared back at her. 'Twas then that she noticed the change. That part that he had filled her with, that had just now been at rest, grew hard and larger. Unable to look away, she nearly stopped breathing as he lifted one of his hands and touched…*it,* stroking it to an even greater size.

"Should I accompany you, then?" Margaret asked, but Lara was unable to respond. Heat pooled between her legs and her breasts tingled as she watched him smile knowingly at her. Then Malcolm's boyish voice called to him from farther down the shore and, without hesitating, he turned back to the water and dived under it.

"My lady? You look peaked," Margaret said, reaching her side—thankfully, after Sebastien had submerged. "It could be a fever. Let me feel your cheek." Her maid reached out and touched the back of her hand to Lara's indeed hot cheek.

"'Tis no fever, Margaret. Let me be." It was a kind of fever, but not one she wished to discuss with her maid and the others present behind her. Especially after her comments about such attraction. She waved off the attention. "I just need some air."

How could she ever face him now? She'd watched him and he knew it. But how could she not go as promised?

"Lara!" The shout came from outside. She dared not look.

Margaret glanced out and then waved. "My lady. 'Tis your brother and Lord Sebastien. They're calling for you."

Tucking her hair back inside the snood that covered it, Lara took a breath and walked to the door. She made her way down the stairs, through the hall and out through the yard. The guards nodded as she walked through the gate and across the drawbridge. Malcolm ran up to her and tugged on her hand, hurrying her along. In a few moments, they reached the new dock and Sebastien.

He wore trews now, but no tunic, and his hair hung down to his shoulders, still dripping water onto his chest and the ground around him. She knew her face was flame-red, but she answered his greeting in kind and looked everywhere except at his face.

"My lady! I am gladdened that you could join us."

Hearing the smile in his voice, she was tempted to glance at him. She fought the urge, one more in a line of provocative urges brought on by the sight or sound or nearness of him.

"Malcolm tells me you have a secret to share with me," she murmured.

Her brother was now back on the shore, calling out to Philippe to hurry. Lara watched his boyish glee and smiled.

"There are many secrets I could share with you, Lara," Sebastien said, in a voice so deep and warm it transformed her insides to liquid. Just as she began to turn to him, Malcolm raced by her, out onto the dock and then into the water.

The water?

Sweet Jesus! Malcolm could not swim.

To her horror, his running start projected his small body far out over the surface of the firth before he went under. There was no sign of him for what felt like hours, and without waiting, she ran to the edge and threw herself in after him.

The cold water shocked her and she felt it claw at her gown and tunic. She turned around and around, looking for some sign of her brother. Stretching down, Lara searched the bottom beneath her feet.

She touched nothing. Then the weight of her saturated clothing began to drag her down. Gasping and flailing her arms, she screamed as she remembered that she could not swim, either. All she could think of as she sank into the murky waters was one name.

"Sebastien!" she cried out, and then there was nothing but black.

Watching in disbelief, Sebastien could only wonder how people living so close to the sea did not know how to swim in it. He'd spent days teaching Malcolm to float and hold his breath and then how to take strokes to move himself through the water. Lara could climb, she could ride, she could fish, so how was it that she could not swim?

Malcolm's head came out of the water just as Lara sank into it, so Sebastien dived back into the firth to get to her. Luckily, 'twas in between the tides, so the water was calm. Deep but calm. Waving the boy off, Sebastien took a breath and aimed at the spot where Lara had sunk from view. He could only see a few feet in front of him, so he reached out, trying to grab her gown as it fluttered down to the bottom.

Pulling the heavy garment, he finally got hold of her and encircled her waist with his arm. With powerful kicks, he brought them both to the surface, then dragged her back to the shore. Margaret's screaming brought soldiers running to his aid. In a very short time, with Malcolm at his side, he carried Lara from the water and laid her on the edge of the beach.

Silence held all in its grip as they waited for her to take a breath. And waited. Just when he reached out to shake her, she convulsed, taking in a huge amount of air and forcing out a similar amount of water. Sebastien rolled her to her side and watched as her coughing turned to sputtering, and then she breathed clearly. Before she became aware of those around her, he waved them off, even the maid, Margaret, who had to be dragged away by Hugh.

Sebastien knelt by her side and waited until she opened her eyes. "I suppose you will never appreciate secrets now," he whispered to her.

"Malcolm," she gasped, trying to right herself and find her brother.

"Shh," Sebastien said, taking her in his arms and

rocking her. "Malcolm is well, as you shall be shortly."

The subject of her worry ran by, calling for Philippe to follow him. With a wave to her, Malcolm threw himself back into the water.

"Philippe! Have a care…" Sebastien pointed in Malcolm's direction and the squire nodded, acknowledging the order.

"He took to it as though born there." he explained to her, all the while holding her close. "I did not know you could not swim or I would have warned you."

"I thought he would die. I saw him go under and thought he…" Her words drifted off and she shook in his arms. He held her in silence, allowing her to cry out her fear. "I have only ever wanted to keep him safe. That is why I sent him from the castle the day of the battle. I thought you would kill him if you found him."

Confused at first by this shift in her words, Sebastien realized that the shock of thinking Malcolm in danger had released much more, from deep within her.

"Everything we'd heard about the Bruce and what he would do to us… I tried to get him away…even though my father said to stay inside. I tried… I tried…"

"Lara, he is safe. Malcolm is safe," Sebastien repeated, over and over until she quieted. "*You* are safe. Never fear, I will always protect you."

She leaned back and looked at him, as though seeing him for the first time. "You are so very different than I expected an enemy to be."

He laughed for a moment and then met her serious gaze. "As are you." Her teeth chattered and he noticed her lips were blue. "Come, you must get out of these wet clothes."

He stood up and helped her to her feet. After tripping over the sopping gown, he leaned down and lifted her into his arms. Instead of objecting or struggling as he thought she might, she collapsed against his chest. When they reached the drawbridge, he called out orders, and by the time he climbed the tower to their chambers, Hugh was on his way to retrieve the boys from the firth and Margaret stood ready with drying linens and hot water.

Sebastien released her into her maid's care, but did not leave the room. Turning his back, he tugged off his own wet clothes and found a dry pair of trews in his trunk. By the time he'd changed, Lara was sitting in the chair wrapped in a thick blanket. With a glance, he dismissed Margaret, who looked for a moment as though she would disobey his order to go.

He threw another piece of wood into the hearth and stoked the fire until it burned hotter. Then he crouched before Lara and waited for her to look at him. When she did, he reached up and touched her cheek. She did not pull away.

"It would have been better if you had forced your way in," she whispered.

Her words surprised him. "Forced my way in?"

"Into the castle. Into my bed."

Sebastien shook his head. "That is not my way." It had never been his way. When others preferred force, he went out of his way to avoid it. Force was the stupid man's method of getting what he wanted—and he had not gotten this far by being stupid.

"No, it is not," she said, gazing into his eyes. "You prefer guile and manipulation. By not forcing me, you have won everyone in Dunstaffnage to your side."

"Save one." He outlined her mouth with the tip of his finger. "For that one, I would give up all the rest."

Her lips parted then and she searched his face. "I cannot give in to you. I cannot be the wife you want without betraying everything I am."

Her voice shook as she told him the heart of her problem. He'd known it; she had told him in so many ways without the words being spoken. She had more honor in her soul than most of the warriors he'd faced in battle. This woman fought for her conscience when others sold theirs.

"Then you give me no choice but to force you," he said, standing and pulling her to her feet. Her hands clutched at the blanket, but she did not fight him.

"Men…people of honor can serve on each side of a battle," he began. He lifted her chin and brought her mouth closer to his so that his breath spilled onto her as he spoke. "This battle is not between the clans, is it," he whispered as he touched his lips to hers and then drew back. "It is between Scotland and England."

Sebastien kissed a path down her neck to the edge of the blanket, which she now held so tightly that her knuckles were white. "Robert stands for Scotland in the same way you have been standing for your clan." He kissed the slope of her breast. "In good conscience." He nipped back up to her chin. "With integrity." He touched her mouth with his and then looked into her eyes. "With honor."

His body surged just as it had earlier when she

watched him from the window. Everything in him was screaming for him to take her now, but he knew it would be a mistake. It must be her decision. It must be.

"Have I not kept my word to you?" he asked. She frowned at his words. "Have I not kept any promise made to you since I came here on the orders of my king?" He gave her a moment to remember all the steps along their path and how he had been true to his word.

"I cannot think when you touch me like this," she complained.

He let his hands wander over her, sliding over the blanket, knowing by the shivers and shudders that she could feel him. "Nay, Lara, the problem is that all you have been doing is thinking. It is time to trust."

He took her face in his hands. "Can you trust me?" He hoped he was correct in his knowledge of her. He prayed that his gut instinct was right, or he would lose everything…. He would lose her.

She did not give an answer quickly, but then nodded slightly.

"I swear to you on my honor that Robert should be king of Scotland. I swear he is the rightful and legitimate king and that I follow him willingly and without reservation. Other men of honor who have fought against him now come to his side. Men and women of good conscience support his claim. Can you trust me in this and come to *my* side?"

He kissed her then, openmouthed with all the passion he'd felt for these last weeks and weeks. He tasted her and his tongue touched hers, in and out, in and out, until she gasped for breath.

"Do not make me choose, Sebastien," she begged him. "Do not." She clutched at his hands now.

"You would not respect or trust me if I force you in this. It must be your choice." He dropped his hands from her and moved back. In his soul he prayed that she knew he would not betray her. That he would keep her safe. That they could live together.

"So, look now into your heart and tell me. For the good of clan and country, indeed even for your own good and mine, do you continue the battle or come to my side and accept all that I offer you?"

Sebastien held his breath, knowing that the decision about his life and theirs would be made in the next moments.

Chapter Eleven

It was only a small movement. Not what he thought would be needed to signify such a momentous decision. Not even an obvious one except that he was watching her for any sign.

Her hand slipped on the blanket and the woolen cover shifted off her shoulder. When he expected her to adjust it, she did not. Instead, she held her hand out to him in much the same gesture that he'd made on the battlements those weeks ago. The nervous expression in her eyes told him that she was not yet convinced, but she trusted him enough to try.

Sebastien reached out, took her hand and brought it to his lips. "I thank you for your trust, Lara. I will not betray it."

A fleeting look of pain passed over her face and then was gone. Had he imagined it? Then she nodded and stepped toward him, dropping the blanket on the floor.

"You do not need to do this, Lara. It can wait."

Dear God! Had he uttered those words? He was as hard as the first time he'd seen one of the kitchen maids in his mother's inn frolicking naked with a stable boy. The need to bury himself within Lara had made him boldly show her his desire in the light of day. He had thought endlessly of the moan she'd gifted him with when he'd touched that most private of places on her body. At this point, he thought he might have imagined it, but he wanted more than anything to find out...to make her soften at his touch, at his entrance.

His control stretched to its breaking point, and he wanted it to break. As though he'd spoken the words out loud, she smiled and let her hand rest over his hardness. Barely a touch, certainly not a caress. He felt the shudder ripple through him and he fisted his hands to avoid throwing her on the bed and burying himself. When she reached out for the laces of his trews, he gave a growl in warning that she did not heed.

Lara slipped her hand inside the loosened ties and touched him. He surged against her hand as he wrapped his arms around her. Flesh to flesh, her skin was hot and he only wanted to taste and smell her...and mark her as his own. Taking her by the shoulders, he dragged her with him until his legs hit the bed. Falling back, he lifted her on top of him until she straddled his hips.

Sebastien reached up and took her hands, entwining their fingers and pulling her down to kiss him. Her mouth was warm and welcoming and he could feel the heat of her, open above him. He lifted his hips and slid his hard male flesh against her until she began to move on her own. Unable to enter her without adjusting her position, and unwilling to let go of her hands, he simply enjoyed the sensations created by the friction of her wet flesh against his.

When her movements became frantic, he realized she did not know what to do. She'd been a virgin the first time they'd joined and had no experience to guide her. He freed her hands and slid his under her hips, tilting her upward, and then with one thrust he filled her.

The sound she made was the one in his dreams—from deep in her throat and so full of need that he nearly spilled his seed at the sound of it. Instead he rolled them over and plunged into her until he could go no farther. She moaned again and he hardened more at her response.

"Wrap your legs around me, Lara," he whispered gruffly. She did and he found himself deeper, at her very core. Pulling back until he was almost out and then driving back into her, she rewarded him with another moan, then another and another. He continued to wring them from her until he knew his release was upon him.

Taking her mouth, he filled her completely and felt the rush of his seed as it exploded from him. He moved within her, in and out, again and again, until every drop was spent inside of her. Sebastien was experiencing the last of his release when he felt the contractions around him, not as overpowering as his own had been. She came in a series of tightening waves until she shuddered and clutched at him. He held her close until her body relaxed beneath his.

It took some minutes for them to recover, and he waited before withdrawing from her. As he slid from her, sated for the first time in so long, he turned on his side and pulled her into his arms.

"Enemies no more, Lara," he whispered into her ear. "Enemies no more."

She tensed at his words.

If he noticed, he gave no sign of it, but settled his arm tighter around her and then fell asleep. Lara lay in his embrace and tried to pull her shattered control back into place. Convinced that he was indeed an honorable man, she decided to take this step and accept his offer. After saving her from almost certain death, he offered her another chance of life—a life of promise, a life of her choice.

Lara shifted on the bed, trying to ignore the pull to sleep. Her heart still raced from his possession of her body, and she could not let go of all the sensations moving through her. He lay against her back and shared his body's heat with her. He had not remained in bed with her the first time, so feeling him so close was new.

She shifted and he moved with her, sliding his leg over hers, tickling her with the hair on his thigh. How did men so easily accept changes like this? One moment they were strangers, living separate lives in the same place and time, and the next, they were…what? Husband and wife? Nay, they had been that for all the time they'd been together. Lovers? They were not in love, so that description did not work either. Bedmates?

Lara turned in his embrace and watched Sebastien sleep. His face was unmarred by the frown he usually wore. His hair, still damp from his time in the water, fell around his head. And the scar on his cheek still caught her attention and her curiosity.

Without warning, his hand followed her movements, gliding over her hip. The touch of it, even though unintentional, sent a shock through her. Would she ever grow used to being naked with him? Would she ever be able to lie next to him and not feel a strangeness?

A chill passed through her and Lara realized that they were lying naked on top of the bedcovers, and although he was still in his trews, she wore nothing. With no blanket in reach, she would either have to get out from under him to get one or wait until he woke. She glanced up at his face and noticed he was watching her.

"My—my lord," she stuttered as she pulled away from him, the heat of embarrassment filling her cheeks.

"Second thoughts, then?" He leaned up on one elbow and put his hand under his head, never taking his eyes from hers. "If you cannot call me by name, you must think you have made a mistake."

He rolled off the bed, reached down to the floor and grabbed the blanket that had fallen from around her. Holding it out to her, he sat on the edge of the bed and watched her with an intense gaze. The frown was back in place and her fingers ached to reach out and soothe the deep furrows that crossed his forehead.

Fighting the wayward urge, Lara clutched the blanket across her lap and scooted back in the bed until she reached the headboard. Tucking the cover more tightly over her legs, she pushed her own hair out of her face.

"So, Lara, did I take advantage of your condition, your confusion, after you nearly drowned? Or," he said, moving closer and touching her hand, "have we truly taken a step today?"

She did not want to lie to him, but Lara was simply not certain how she felt…other than warm in places she never thought about unless with him. There was such a hopeful look in his eyes and he rubbed the back of her hand with his thumb as he waited for her answer.

"I am not certain."

A momentary flash of regret or sadness passed over his face and then Sebastien turned his head away. Staring off for a minute, he nodded and stood up. He walked across the chamber and searched through the trunk that held his clothing. He tossed a chain of some kind over his head and then donned a tunic and belt. He faced her before he left.

She wanted to stop him, to give him some explanation, but she was so confused in her own thoughts and heart that she could not find the words at first. Lara shook her head and called his name.

"Sebastien, please wait."

Trapped by her nakedness, she did not want to leave the bed. He understood her discomfort and reached into his trunk once more, pulling from it the robe he'd worn on their wedding night. She'd not seen it since then. He held it out to her and she slid from the bed and pulled it on. Wrapping it around her, she stood near him.

"I still have such doubts in my heart, Sebastien. By giving in to you, I feel like such a traitor to my family and to my heritage. I know you are an honorable man, but I do not know if this can work. I wish, I truly wish that I could simply say my old life is behind me and we can start anew as though I was never the Maid of Lorne and you were not the man who defeated my people. But, I cannot."

"I understand, Lara. Can you at least give yourself

time to think on this and to consider it? I think that we could fare well in our marriage, but I know it will take time for you to accept your place with me."

He took her by the shoulders and kissed her on the forehead. "I have duties I must see to. Rest awhile here."

Lara knew she did not want to leave her chambers now; she did not know if she could face anyone yet. She nodded and sat back on the bed.

"Promise you will join me for supper in the hall."

She wanted to refuse, needing for some reason to deny him in some way. But the inviting smile he gave her, one that erased the frown on his forehead, would not let her decline.

"I will join you there," she agreed.

The hall was abuzz with the story of her mishap in the firth by the time she made her way downstairs a few hours later. After a brief and fitful nap, Lara decided to make an appearance. Delaying would simply make it more difficult, so she had Margaret help her dress and fix her hair under a respectable covering.

Once she left the tower and entered the hall, everyone she walked past inquired about her health. Even the irritating Sir Hugh asked if she'd recovered from her experience yet. The smirk on his face made her believe that he spoke more of the time in her chambers than what drove her there. However, she would not lower herself to confirm his insulting innuendos. Margaret took him to task in a whirlwind of furious whispering once Lara had turned away. At least their involvement was for some good purpose.

Sebastien had not yet taken his seat; indeed, he stood in the middle of the hall, speaking with a tall, broad-shouldered man she did not recognize. 'Twas not so unusual, since many new people lived here in the castle and in the small villages surrounding it. Some were his own soldiers and some carried out the Bruce's direct orders. Sebastien waved at her and broke off his conversation to meet her. Before he could say a word, Malcolm came running in from the yard, with Philippe following closely behind him. Skidding to a stop in front of them, Malcolm clutched her hand and whispered loudly to her.

"Have you heard, Lara? Have you heard the news?"

Sebastien cut off his words quickly. "Malcolm! Your sister is not yet recovered from her mishap of this morn. Give her some peace and quiet. See to your duties."

Malcolm's mutinous frown was the only sign that he might argue, but when Philippe grabbed him and tugged at him, he nodded to Sebastien and followed the squire. This week, Philippe was instructing Malcolm in the ways to serve his lord at table. Although Sebastien's methods of training the boy were more Lowlander than Highlander, Malcolm reveled in the duties assigned to him and the new tasks he was learning under Philippe's, Sebastien's and even Sir Hugh's tutelage.

"He did not argue with you," Lara said, surprised that Malcolm did as he was told to do. He usually bristled at any order given by her.

"Malcolm is learning quickly. His temper rules him at times because he is so young. Come," Sebastien said, offering his arm to her, "meet my friend."

"Your friend? You have never told me of friends."

"I have not told you much about me at all, Lara. But, as things continue to quiet and to settle, there will be time."

She walked at his side and began to worry at his friend's reaction to a MacDougall wife. His men could be ordered to show respect, but how would this knight treat her? Sebastien turned to her. "Something troubles you?" he whispered.

"Your friend…does he know of me?" Lara watched as the stranger continued in lively conversation with Sir Hugh and a few other knights.

Sebastien pulled her to a stop and turned her to face him. "Is this the same woman who challenged me and refused me entrance when she controlled Dunstaffnage? Is this the same woman who, only this morn, plunged headlong into the firth to save her brother when she could not swim? Tell me where this fear comes from?"

Lara struggled to understand it herself. Then she realized that no matter how she might want to make her life go back to what it had been, it would not. This morning, when she'd offered Sebastien, *her husband,* her hand, she had taken a step and there was no turning back from the decision. She had changed. Her life had changed.

"His opinion matters to you?" she asked.

"Aye. He has been a true friend for years."

"Then it matters to me as well," she explained, trying to put her fear into words. "I would not have him think less of you because you married an enemy's daughter."

He laughed at her words and then lowered his voice before continuing. "Lara, fear not about James. If I were a man who gambled, I would say that James is most likely the one who gave the king the idea of our marriage. He is the king's closest friend and counselor."

She began to argue, but he put his finger to her lips. "I believe him to be a fair man. Meet him and then tell me what you think of him."

A twinkling in his eyes warned her of something afoot, but he gave her no chance to object again. Sebastien guided her to the man he'd been talking to, and pulled her close. "James, let me present my wife to you."

Lara took a step forward and held out her hand to him. Sebastien's friend kissed it lightly and bowed. It was a graceful bow, one worthy of a nobleman in the royal court. He brushed his black hair out of his eyes and greeted her with a smile and a soft voice.

"My lady, 'tis a pleasure to finally meet the woman who held Sebastien of Cleish outside her gates." His hand was warm as he grasped hers for a moment more. "Not many have refused him entrance and lived to tell." He glanced over at Sebastien, who suddenly looked like a very nervous man.

Although she was certain that his words held another meaning, she smiled back. The knight's impeccable manners and pleasing personality put her at ease. "Have you eaten yet, Sir James?"

"It is simply James, my lady, for I have not attained knighthood yet. My thanks for your gracious invitation, but there are arrangements I must discuss with your husband before I can take my ease. Will you excuse us for a very short time?"

"Lara?"

Sebastien squeezed her hand, most likely because she was staring at his friend. A strange and puzzling twist at the bottom of her stomach tightened as a niggling suspicion bothered her mind. James? Friend and confidant to the Bruce? Lara pulled her hand from Sebastien's grasp.

"James," she repeated as she looked more closely at him. "James *Douglas?*"

A wide grin broke out on his face and he nodded. "At your service, my lady."

Others were beginning to watch their exchange, some of the servants and some of Sebastien's men as well. She could not keep her voice from growing louder, partly due to the shaking that seized her at the realization of the true identity of the man standing before her. She clenched her fists.

The very devil was in their midst.

"The Black Douglas?" She glanced over at Sebastien, who seemed interested now in the way the ceiling joints were arranged. "Sweet Mother of God, you've let the devil himself into Dunstaffnage!" Lara raised her hand to bless herself when Sebastien reached over and took hold of her arm, preventing her from completing the sign of the cross.

Silence filled the room as those who knew already and those who were just discovering that the scourge of southern Scotland, the man who Scottish mothers warned their children about, stood before them, focused their attention on the center of the room.

"He does not particularly like it when people cross themselves in his presence," her husband whispered as he held her hand firmly in his own. "He says he finds it to be insulting."

The man in question watched the scene unfolding and could hear every word Sebastien whispered. Lara was, however, about to tell the Black Douglas exactly what she thought of him when he leaned over to her, mimicking her husband's position, and whispered his own words in a gruff voice.

"And ye dinna want to anger the devil himself, do ye now, lass?"

She jumped back, for his voice took on a whole different tone and a menacing one at that.

"James, have a care here! You are terrorizing my wife and in front of me. Have you no shame?" Sebastien reached out and punched James on the arm, and Lara was tempted to run.

"Here now, there is no call for violence," Sir Hugh stated as he approached. "A messenger from the king is waiting to speak to you both."

The three men turned their gazes on Lara at the same moment. Feeling very much the outsider, she knew she must leave. But, here was an opportunity to learn important information from the Bruce's own men, his closest counselors and fighters. This was exactly what Eachann had pressed her about, what he wanted to know. A pang of regret and confusion filled her now. If she had taken a step toward being Sebastien's wife, could she continue reporting his plans to her clan?

The entire hall grew quiet once more and Lara became aware from the stares toward her that the men were waiting for her to leave. She made her decision in that moment of rejection—she would find out from the Black Douglas what Eachann needed.

"My lord," she said, curtsying to Sebastien and simply narrowing her gaze when she looked at James and Sir Hugh. "I would speak to the cook about the evening meal. If you would excuse my absence?"

Sebastien appeared to want to say something to her, but he gave her permission with a nod and she walked past them toward the kitchens' stairs.

And to the steward's chamber, where she could hear everything they said when they were not guarding their words.

Chapter Twelve

"**I** am longing for a good meal, Sebastien. Do you think she will poison it?" James asked with serious intents. "Should someone follow her?"

Sebastien turned and punched his friend once more on the arm. "You have brought it on yourself this time. What was in your mind to taunt her that way?"

James crossed his arms over his chest and frowned. "Taunt her? I was the model of decorum and courtly behavior. Did you not see how impressed she was with me?"

"Impressed, you say? Until she realized who you were, and then she seemed more afraid than accepting." Sebastien laughed now.

The reputation that James carried was well-earned by his actions; they both knew that. But, the rumors and stories and truths took on a life of their own as they spread from friend to foe. If it had not worked to their advantage many times, they would all, even the Bruce himself, squash the hearsay and correct the misapprehensions. Sebastien had witnessed one garrison of English soldiers surrender as one when they heard James shout out his battle cry. True, it was a small garrison, but they did lay down their arms, avoiding bloodshed on either side.

"So you think then that I should have someone taste my food while I am here?"

Hugh thought his jest was a good one, for it was his turn now to laugh. "From the expression on Lady Mac-Dougall's face, I would say you are each in danger. I for one will sit somewhere far away from both of you this evening and not share in your plates for fear of my life."

"Enough jesting. There is much we should discuss."

Sebastien walked to the long table in the south end of the hall and invited the two to sit. Once a serving maid brought tankards and ale and their thirsts were satisfied, Sebastien switched from the local Gaelic to French and reviewed with James the latest reports about the increase in attacks and ambushes to his men and those of the Bruce when transporting supplies over the western Highlands.

Each raid was not significant in itself, but there was an alarming pattern developing, and it seemed to spread out from Dunstaffnage itself. When he noticed the sameness in the timing, execution and details of each one, he knew that these were not simply random acts. Someone was directing them, and the attacks were too similar to be a coincidence and to not be related to the taking of Dunstaffnage.

"What do your spies tell you? Have the rest of the MacDougalls scattered or are they still lurking and plying mischief all around us?" James asked. Leaning in and looking from one to the other, he lowered his voice and asked, "And does your lady wife know about this?"

"That Eachann MacDougall is somewhere nearby? Nay, I have not told her that. She has been somewhat limited in her freedoms since I arrived here."

James laughed again and smacked him soundly on the shoulder. "Sebastien, must you chain your women to keep them in hand?"

"Your obnoxious jesting aside, James, with all the disarray and change, I thought it best to keep her secluded and safe. She has been little out of the castle grounds and then only to the chapel. And always with an escort."

"I suspect that Eachann and his men are behind the attacks."

"I, too, share that suspicion and have assigned Munro to the task. Munro can run any man to ground."

"In the meantime, we will target several places where the Comyns still have friends and uproot them from their keeps." James took out a small parchment from inside his tunic and spread it on the table before them. Pointing to three locations, James named them. "Invercreran. Here in Glen Gour on Ardgour. And here, to the south of Loch Awe."

Sebastien considered the locations, each one not far from MacDougall lands. Two could be reached by water, the other was in a valley to the northeast and would involve another journey much like the one through the Brander Pass. Once these places were cleared of enemies, the whole of southwestern Scotland would belong to the Bruce.

"In which order will we take them?" Hugh asked. "Or do we split our forces and attack at the same time?"

"Robert wants us to each take one of these—" James pointed to the last two "—and together take Invercreran."

"When?" Sebastien asked. He still had much to do here to get Dunstaffnage to the way it should be. And, now that things appeared to be more promising with Lara, he did not wish to be away for long.

"By the first week in October, for Robert plans to pursue the Earl of Ross then."

"No more truces?" Sebastien knew that the Bruce had signed a truce with both Lorne in the west and Ross in the north. One had been broken and the other had expired, and Robert was now anxious to gather them all under his control. Even worse, the Earl of Ross had captured Robert's wife, daughter, sister and one of his most ardent supporters, the Countess of Buchan, all of whom he'd turned over to the English.

James's smile was one of grim determination. "No truces. He submits or dies."

Sebastien noticed the servants waiting near and realized they were ready to prepare the table for supper. Standing, he invited James and Hugh to join him in the yard to meet with Etienne for a brief discussion of the supplies and men needed for these actions.

"I should tell Lara that we are done here," Sebastien said.

The other two looked at him and then each other, and James wiggled his eyebrows. "Ah, the life of a married man! For a warrior who was so dedicated to life on a horse, I am stunned that you are settling in so well here."

"We practically ordered her away. It is simple courtesy to let her know that our discussion has ceased."

"So it is," James acknowledged, as he folded the map and tucked it safely away. "Hugh and I can speak with your steward, if you'd like?"

"Enough! I will tell Lara and meet you near the barracks. Go now, before I demonstrate to everyone watching that the Black Douglas has no special powers."

James leaned his head back and laughed at the threat. "Very well, my lord. Seek you your wife and we will await your counsel in the yard." He bowed and turned and, with Hugh at his side, walked out through the hall to the yard.

Actually, if he were telling the truth, James did have special powers. Otherwise, he could not have accomplished as much as he had at such a young age. Just over a score of years had he, and yet the whole of Scotland and a good part of England knew of him. Thankful that he had never faced James on the field, Sebastien did understand how the man upset most people upon first meeting.

The king's business awaited him, so Sebastien headed to the corridor and stairs that led to the kitchens below to find Lara. He wasn't certain if giving her more time before supper was a good thing, but knew it was necessary. As he stepped through the doorway, Lara came running up the stairs. He moved back to make room on the landing.

"Lara, we are not done with our discussions and will return for the meal in a short time."

"As you wish," she replied. She tilted her head down

and Sebastien could not see her eyes. Then he noticed that she was breathing heavily and sweat beaded on her lip.

"Are you well?" He reached out his hand to lift her chin. Her face was a bit pale and her gaze wary.

"I must still be overwhelmed from this morn. The heat of the kitchens bothered me and I fear that running up the steps has left me breathless."

The lie did not quite reach her eyes. Sebastien was not certain why she was lying or about what, but he read the lie as easily as he read a battle formation.

"Have a care, lady. Come into the hall where it is cooler and mayhap guide the servants in preparing for the meal."

She accepted his hand without hesitation and Sebastien escorted her back into the hall. Once in the cooler room, she took a deep breath and released it. Granted, the heat from the kitchens, when the meals for dozens of people were being cooked, could be significant. The blush in her cheeks returned and he released her. James and Hugh were waiting for him.

He would think on this puzzle later.

She leaned forward once more and tried to peek around Sebastien at James Douglas. Her husband had suggested that he sit between them so that James's presence did not terrorize her. And rightly so! The Black Douglas was the scourge of those who opposed Robert the Bruce. A strange turn of events since the Bruce had, when fighting on the English side, captured Castle Douglas and turned him and his mother and sisters over to Edward Longshanks.

Lara peeked again. She could not believe that this young man was one of the Bruce's elite fighters. He was, she thought, at least five years younger than Sebastien. Lara glanced at her husband and found him watching her.

"Is he really the Black Douglas?" she whispered so the man in question would not hear her. "He looks so young."

"I assure you, my lady, that I have indeed attained the age of twenty and two years," he said in a voice that was both soft and cultured.

Lara gasped. He'd heard her. She sat back in the chair so he could not see past Sebastien. Then, damn him, Sebastien leaned back and exposed her to James's gleeful gaze.

"I do prefer just my name over the one that the English use."

The men all laughed at this. Sebastien joined them and then turned to her. "He is truly the Black Douglas, called that for many reasons." Sebastien lifted his goblet in a salute to the man on his left and called out, "A Douglas! A Douglas!"

James's men all stood at once, lifting their tankards high and answering back the same chant in thunderous voices. The hall shook with the intensity. Lara glanced around the table and saw that every person stared at James, including Malcolm, who watched from his place behind the table with Philippe. Instead of fear, excitement and awe filled his face.

Stunned by it, she looked around at the other Mac-Dougall servants and villagers who'd stayed on at Dunstaffnage. All joined in the revelry. Was she now the only one carrying on the fight? Then she felt Sebastien's hand on hers under the cover of the table and she met his gaze.

"All will be well, Lara. Truly," he said, trying to reassure her with his words and a gentle squeeze of her fingers.

She could say nothing, so she sipped from her goblet and watched as the hall quieted and the people went back to their meal. Exhaustion began to claim her and all she wanted to do was sleep.

"May I retire, my lord?" she asked in a low voice.

"Of course," he answered, waving to Sir Hugh at the other table where he sat with Margaret, to bring the maid to her lady. "I will join you soon."

He stood when she did, as did everyone in the hall. Startled by the sign of respect, she left the table and sought the comfort of her chambers. So many things were changing in her life and she did not know how to deal with all of them. Unfortunately, her room held not the comfort she sought, for it presented her with more choices to make.

Lara stopped at the entryway and looked about. Her father's chair stood on one side and the bed on the other. Where should she go? It seemed a farce for her to take her usual place in the chair, fully dressed, as she had each night since Sebastien's arrival. She turned and looked at Margaret, who seemed as confused about what to do as she was.

"Help me wash and take down my hair, Margaret. We'll figure out the rest later."

"Aye, my lady," the maid said as she crossed the room and gathered the things needed for her tasks.

With another glance at the bed, Lara sat on a bench placed near the hearth and accepted the linen cloth and soft soap from her maid. Once Lara had washed her face and hands in the basin held out to her, Margaret took the water away and returned with a brush. Lara allowed her thoughts to drift as first the snood was removed and then the intricate braids were loosened.

The maid's long, sure brush strokes through her hair calmed her. The tension in her shoulders and in her back from meeting a dreaded enemy melted away. It was as her head drifted forward and her chin fell onto her chest that Margaret spoke.

"He is a good man," she whispered. Lara was not certain if she defended Sebastien or Hugh until she continued. "I have watched how he treats the others of our clan who have remained behind. I think you are fortunate that he is your husband and lord now."

"But my father was—"

"Pah! Your father would have sold you to the highest bidder. We both know who he had in mind for your bridegroom, my lady. And we both know how things would have gone for you married to such a rogue."

Lara had not thought about the man her father had intended her to marry since the day Sebastien had arrived. Actually, her father had declared several men to be candidates for her husband, "to take the Maid of Lorne in hand and in control" were his words. Now, thinking on it, she realized the kind of life she might have had with another in Sebastien's place. A shudder raced through her at such thoughts.

"My thanks, Margaret," Lara whispered as she tried

to shake herself from the images of what might have been. She allowed the relaxed state brought on by her maid's sure hands and calming strokes to take over once more. After a few more minutes of silence, Margaret shook her gently.

"My lady, he is here."

Lara discovered that Sebastien was indeed there. He stood in the doorway, staring at her with an intensity that nearly frightened her. Her mouth went dry and she swallowed several times, trying to moisten it.

"Here now, my lord," Margaret said, walking to him. "Allow me to take that for you."

Lara blinked and then noticed the tray in his hands. He carried some kind of broth, a small loaf of bread and a wedge of cheese there. He'd brought food here?

"I noticed that you did not eat much at table. 'Twas probably due to the company." The corners of his mouth curved into a smile—an attractive smile that warmed her. Before continuing, he nodded to the maid, who took the tray and placed it on the table. "Hugh waits below stairs for you."

"Margaret…"

Lara thought to stop her maid from making the same mistake she had, but from the expression of joy on Margaret's face, it truly was too late. Sebastien closed the door behind her and leaned against it.

"They are in love."

"Hugh is a mercenary who will travel all over the land, fighting wherever and whenever and for whomever can pay his fee. He will not marry her." Her conviction was such that she shook with the words she spoke.

"They have a place here and wish to marry, but have feared asking your permission."

His announcement, almost whispered, struck her like a blow. Margaret had said not a word of this to her. Lara had spoken to her maid on the subject many times and, in a strange way, she'd hoped that it was simple lust. Lust would be easier to recover from when the worst happened. She drew back from the hurt that Margaret had not confided in her, and looked at him.

"But, as this shows, you are lord here and they need not my permission for anything."

Sebastien approached and took her hands in his, holding them firmly as if he suspected she would withdraw them from his grasp. "You are lady here and in charge of the women. She is your maid, Lara. I would never give her permission when it is your place to do so."

"My place?" He confused her constantly with his attitude. "But you are lord here now," she repeated, trying to convince herself more than him.

"Aye, and you are Lady of Dunstaffnage. All you have to do is take your place at my side to make it so."

"Your words make it sound as though it is easily done."

"'Tis not easy, Lara. But it is your place and I would have you there."

Standing with him, as he offered her everything she had truly wanted in her life, she could not find the strength to refuse. Her throat tightened and she could not get the words out. He opened his arms to her and she stood and walked into his embrace.

She felt his strength surround her, and for the first time, allowed herself to feel some bit of hope that this could all work out between them. Lara felt his hands tangle in her hair, and slid hers around his waist, holding him as he held her. Laying her head on his chest, she listened, or rather felt, his heart beating strongly there. His body was all hard muscle beneath her hands, and she allowed some of his strength to seep into her, into her heart and soul.

After a few minutes, he freed her hair and leaned away. Her body reacted on its own, following his direction to keep him close. He chuckled under his breath and untangled himself from her hold. "Come. It has been an arduous day for you. 'Tis time to rest."

He took her hand and led her to the bench where she'd been sitting until Margaret left. Grasping her shoulders, he turned her away and she felt his fingers move to the laces tied at her neck. With swift, nimble movements, he loosened them all the way down the back of her tunic. When she thought he would lift it over her head, he instead whispered in her ear from his place behind her.

"Do you know what the Church calls this style of tunic you wear?" She shook her head. "The gates that lead men to hell."

Lara looked down at the garment. "Truly?"

"Truly. One bishop in England has declared it a sin for women to wear it for it tempts men to lust and fornication."

Lara felt ill-informed and unable to figure out how a tunic and gown that covered every inch of her skin and her form could be a temptation to anyone. "You jest, my lord."

"Allow me to show you. Since we are married, it will not be too great a sin for me." There was teasing in his voice, but heat, too.

She gave him the permission he sought, and felt his hands begin at her shoulders and slide down her arms until he reached her elbows. She could still see no sin in this touch. Then he slipped his hands inside the tunic, where it hung open under her arms. With his palms, he stroked her belly and nearly touched her breasts, but did not. Then his hands moved softly over the tops of her thighs and nearly touched the juncture of them, but did not.

Heat grew within her, spreading from his hands into her belly and breasts and that place between her legs. Over and over he teased her until she writhed under his touch. Pressed against his body, she could feel the proof of his lust and hear it in his breathing. Still he did not touch her as she wanted him to. Lara was about to beg him when he released her. Even that was a teasing, for he slid his hands slowly away from the places that tingled and ached for more, until the tips of his fingers barely glided over her.

"And that is why the Church decries this kind of tunic. Even you can see the danger to men's souls if they are subjected to this kind of—" he did touch her then, reaching under the edge of the fabric and cupping her breasts in his hands "—temptation every waking moment of the day."

"I had no idea of it, my lord," she said in a voice that exposed her own sin of lust. "No idea at all."

All he had to do was take her. She would not resist him if he wanted to finish it now. Indeed, her body, heated by his sinful caresses, was ready—hot and wet and willing.

And, as was his custom, he did not.

Sebastien moved his hands down her legs now, grasped the bottom of the tunic and lifted it over her head. Flinging it over the bench, he began working on the laces at her shoulders to loosen her sleeves. She waited for him to do something, attempt some provocative touch, but none came. A few minutes later, after removing the sleeves, he slid the gown from her shoulders and let it fall to the floor.

When she was dressed in only the sheer chemise she wore under her gowns, he turned her to face him. His desire for her, plainly written on his face, encouraged her own. But she was not as naive as he thought her to be.

"I know your methods now, my lord. You have some experience in the ways of the flesh and are teaching my body *your* ways while hoping I do not notice."

He laughed and nodding, admitted it. "Am I succeeding in my attempts, my lady?"

Then, when she would have liked to deny him his victory, he untied his own tunic and pulled it over his head. His shirt was next, revealing the wide expanse of his muscular chest to her sight, and then his fingers reached for the laces on his trews.

"You triumphed weeks ago, Sebastien. I just did not know it." She admitted the truth to him now. "You have pushed me to the edge of my own control and have won the battle. I hope it pleases you."

He stopped and looked at her. His wicked smile spoke of his satisfaction in this battle of wills and wants. "Oh, lady, I am most pleased." But instead of reaching for her as she expected, he walked to the bed and pulled the blankets loose. "Come, the room cools and the bed will be much warmer for us."

Lara took the hand he offered, climbed onto the bed and slid over to the side where she usually found herself upon awakening. Sebastien turned away to tug off his trews, and then put out the candles that still burned and banked the fire in the hearth. She stared in fascination at the way his thighs and back flexed as he walked and how the color of his skin changed at his waist. Above was tanned from being in the sun; below was paler from not.

She noticed his reaction when he faced her; that part of him she'd felt against her back now stood straight up. He would fill the empty place in her that she had never even realized existed. In more ways than simply the physical way, he would satisfy her needs. "It is hard," were the only words she could think to say.

"It is that, lady. As it has been almost from the moment that I saw you on the battlements and you refused me entrance to your castle."

"You desired me then?"

He climbed on the bed and knelt before her. "Aye, there was desire, although more than once I could not discern if the desire to kill you was stronger than the desire to kiss you."

"And now?" she asked, needing no answer, for the proof was before her eyes.

Sebastien leaned forward and crawled over her legs. Grabbing her thighs, he pulled her down until she lay under him and then, grasping the edge of her chemise, he tore it until she was exposed to his gaze. He bent down and kissed her mouth. "I want…" he whispered as he moved his mouth to her neck. "I want to kiss you." His mouth was hot and wet against her skin. "And taste you."

Now he moved, kissing a path down her throat onto the slopes of her breasts. He suckled there, stronger and stronger, and he used his teeth against that skin until she thought she would scream. She did scream when his mouth covered the sensitive tips of her breasts, and instead of startling him, it seemed to urge him on. Moisture poured from that place between her legs and it began to throb and ache.

And still he used only his mouth. He pressed his face against her belly and then held her hips as he rubbed his chin against the place between her legs. Surprised by his actions, she discovered that the pressure created by his chin and the roughness of a day's length of beard aroused her.

"And taste you," he repeated as he moved between her legs and spread her open to his view and his touch. When he leaned down and suckled there, she could not control the spasms of pleasure that shot through her.

Lara tried to grab his hair to pull him away, even as she lost all desire to make him cease. He batted at her hands and, with a deep laugh, kissed and touched and tasted her in that most private place. Then, instead of stopping when her peak was upon her and filling her as he had before, he urged her over that precipice, making her body do as he wanted with a more insistent touch of his mouth and more ardent attention with his tongue.

When her body finally stopped spasming beneath his touch, she could not move. He still knelt over her and she waited for him to lie next to her. But, that part of him was still hard, and it looked larger than before. The expression in his eyes told her he was not done with her.

"I had no idea that a man could do such a thing to a woman."

He smiled gently at her. "There are many things a man can do to a woman." He kissed her belly and her body shuddered.

"Are there such things a woman can do to a man?" she asked, suspecting she already knew the answer...or some of it.

"Aye, Lara. Many things can be done."

He kissed her on the mouth now and she could taste the musky flavor of her own release there. "Can you show me another?"

And with very little urging, Sebastien taught her many more things that could be done between men and women before they slept that night.

Chapter Thirteen

The first time he awoke, he found Lara draped over him, asleep. After offering up a short prayer of thanks, he fell back to sleep, for how long he did not know.

The second time he woke, it was to Margaret's startled gasp at finding him and Lara still naked and entwined in their bed. With a shushing and a wave, he ordered her from the room. Although Lara mumbled a few words and shifted in his arms, she did not wake.

The third time he woke it was to the loud and not subtle presence of both Hugh and James in the next chamber. The subject of their discussion was not clear, but their intent to rouse him from sleep was. Sebastien eased Lara from his side and slipped from the bed. Striding to the door, he opened it and quietly cursed them both, warning them of a challenge later that day. He realized his mistake when Philippe, Malcolm and Margaret all met his gaze with incredulous stares. His body's condition was apparent even to the youngest of them. He slammed the door just as the laughter began.

"What is going on out there?" Lara asked, rolling

over and gifting him with the most wonderful view of her bare bottom and legs. His body responded to her voice and to the sight before him, but he knew he must leave her bed.

"Two men are asking for death," he said, smiling at her.

"Do you leave with James this day?"

"Leave with him? Nay. Although I must leave on the king's business soon, 'tis not now."

She yawned loudly and stretched her arms out before pushing the hair from her face. The movement was so stimulating Sebastien decided his friends would simply have to wait until he was ready to leave her. When he lifted the blankets and climbed back in next to her, she moved immediately into his arms. And wonder of wonders, when she felt his hardness pressed against her hip, she rolled onto her back, opened her legs to him and pulled him on top of her.

Then, she startled him as he moved to accept her invitation and to fill her just once more. He felt the walls of her core begin to convulse and shudder within moments. Lara arched against him and it took barely a minute before his own release. Nothing had ever felt so right to him before. No woman had ever felt like this. Sebastien could only describe it in his mind as finding a home.

Not wanting to rush, but mindful of those waiting, he lifted himself from her and kissed her softly. The wince that passed over her face told him that he may have been too aggressive with her in their love play.

"I apologize if I've hurt you, Lara. I have wanted you for so long, waiting for you to give yourself to me, that I fear I could not be gentle. Mayhap now that the commitment has been made, we can go a bit more slowly in our pursuit of all things between men and women."

She blushed, probably thinking about some of the actions and positions that he had shown her. "Commitment? What do you mean?" Lara slid up to the headboard and dragged the blankets with her.

"You made your first commitment to me when we exchanged vows. The second time was yesterday, when you agreed to try to be my wife and Lady of Dunstaffnage. The most important one so far was when you trusted me enough last night with your body. And trusted me to teach you what could be between us."

"So far? Is there more then?"

"You've given me your word and your actions and your body. Only your heart is left."

"My heart? You would want my heart?"

"Oh aye." He sat up and climbed from the bed, searching for and finding a new pair of trews to put on. Standing before her, he decided to tell her the truth of his life. "I grew up with nothing—a bastard whose mother married and had another family and five more children with her husband. My stepfather believed I would train with him to be a blacksmith, but I had no skill with the fire and iron."

"And your natural father? Do you know who he is?"

"Aye. My mother served in the public room of her father's inn. One of their guests, a nobleman traveling on King Edward's business, availed himself of her favors."

"Oh, Sebastien! Was she forced to it? Was there no one to protect her?"

He laughed and shook his head. "Forced? Nay, she gave herself freely to him, hoping to serve as his mistress and gain some measure of security that can come from that." She frowned again. "Come, Lara. You know how that works. She caught and bore a bastard, one in a long line for my noble father. It happens wherever the noble class and those below are involved."

"Like Margaret and Sir Hugh?"

"Just so, but he has made an honorable offer to her."

"So, then, who is your father?" She had held the question within for an admirable length of time. Longer than most would. She looked at him with such an air of expectancy that he felt tempted to break his vow to never reveal his name.

"I swore a vow not to speak of him."

Her lips thinned to a line much as Malcolm's did when the lad was faced with something he did not like. Sebastien reached out to run his finger over them, hoping they would soften beneath his touch as her body had. When they did, his own body hardened once more. He must leave now or he would never escape the chamber this morn.

"I did not begin this tale of woe to gain your sympathy," he said, pulling a shirt and then a shorter tunic over his head. "I did it to explain that I want it all." He wrapped the thick leather belt around his waist and buckled it. Sebastien reached under the bed to retrieve his sword and slid it into the scabbard on his belt.

"For so long, I denied that anything about this kind of life—" he waved his hand around the room to show her what he meant "—was appealing. I had the life I wanted—I was a warrior on the good side of the battle, giving my talent with the sword to a man I believe in. I owned my horse, my armor and anything I could carry with me. All I needed."

She nodded, but he could read her expression and knew she did not understand. She was trying, though, and that touched his heart.

"You have lived all your life with family around you, in one place—a home—with everything you need provided to you. With Robert's orders to wed you—"

"Or kill me. Forget not that part of your orders," she added, wagging her finger at him.

"When we wed and he made me warden here with his plans for Dunstaffnage, I discovered that I do indeed want everything I missed. A home. Marriage. Even, God willing, children someday." His boots were in the next room, so he stood before her, dressed and barefoot. "As I have come to know you, I discovered the woman I want as my wife."

"But that is a given here, Sebastien. We are wed. You have a wife."

"I want more," he said with a sigh. "There is so much within you, but for some reason or for many, you have not shared it with me." Turning to the door, he shook his head. "You will know, as will I, when that moment happens. When you give your heart to me, I will have everything I have ever wanted."

His words stunned her into silence for a moment. He walked to the door and lifted the latch.

"And *you?* Are you willing to give *me* all? Will you give me your heart?"

There was no reason to lie now, or to avoid the question.

"My heart has been yours from the moment I spoke my vows to you. I may not have known it then, but I do now."

Whatever he'd imagined would happen when he shared the knowledge of his love with her, the bewilderment and disbelief in her gaze was not it. "But I have been hostile and hateful and rebellious and dishonest with you from the beginning. How could you love me?"

Sebastien released the latch, walked back to the bed and held out his hand to her. She took it and he entwined their fingers together.

"I have seen a woman who is brave in spite of the dangers around her, trusting in spite of her fears, loving to those she calls family and stubborn in her resistance to a man who was her enemy. All traits I admire, lady."

A knock came on the door, reminding him of those waiting in the yard. "Now I must go and teach both Hugh and James a very important lesson in manners."

He leaned over for a quick kiss and then left the room. Lara still sat in the same position with the same stunned expression as he strode past Malcolm and Philippe and ordered them to follow. As he made his way down the steps, through the hall and out into the yard, with the boys at his heels, he realized that she'd admitted to dishonesty. It did not surprise him, for he would do the same to protect those in his care and would excuse it on those grounds.

But, when would it stop? When would she trust him

enough to come to him with whatever still haunted her and kept her from being completely his? He answered the question with the same words he'd spoken to her— *when she gave him her heart.*

Lara drifted through the day in a kind of haze. Sebastien had revealed so much to her, a glimpse of his childhood and of his heart. Astonished by his revelations, she struggled to think on it the rest of the day.

Had he truly said he loved her? Well, not in so many words, but he said he'd given her his heart, and what else could that mean? Lara sat in the solar, working on the tapestry again, and not having much success in figuring out her husband or in completing the section on which she toiled.

But, something was different this day. By the time she rose and dressed, Callum had asked to see her in the hall about the meals and about some household arrangements, Etienne had sent word about the newly completed storage rooms and Margaret approached her over the matter of marriage to Sir Hugh. The morning turned into a glimpse of what could be.

And the afternoon was beginning to follow that pattern as well—Lara was drawn into many activities she'd not done since her father had been in charge here. Callum sent her some trunks of clothing that Sebastien's soldiers found in the storage rooms, as well as one containing her mother's precious books, and along with Margaret's and Catriona's help, she sorted through them.

Lara was in the solar when she heard shouting outside. She looked out the window and was stunned by

the scene unfolding before her. Both James and Sir
Hugh faced Sebastien in the middle of the yard, bare-
chested, with swords drawn. Many onlookers circled
them and cheered them on. She could tell where
James's men stood, as well as her husband's from their
battle cries. Even Sir Hugh had a small group of noisy
supporters.

The warriors offered a few taunts to each other and
then the fight began. With sword and shield, they attacked and were fended off in turn. Although it appeared to be a friendly clash, soon the intensity grew
until blood was flowing. Margaret joined Lara at the
window and they both held their breath at the blows
given and taken. Lara tried with all her will to keep
from screaming aloud.

They were daft! Men were daft. Most likely, they
were risking head and hand to settle some wager. James
first disarmed, then knocked Sir Hugh to the ground and
held him there with the point of his sword at his neck.

"Do you yield, Sir Hugh?" he called out, while fend-
ing Sebastien off with his shield.

"Aye," Sir Hugh replied. And before Lara could say
anything to her maid, Margaret was running from the
room, her destination never in doubt.

Lara stood frozen in place there, watching as Sebastien went on the attack now, barely waiting for Sir
Hugh to gain his feet and leave the fight. She held her
breath and then gasped as each blow was struck. James
Douglas was an incredible swordsman and there was
never a moment's hesitation in his attack. Sebastien
seemed to be pacing himself and not allowing James
to goad him into any rash movements.

A long while passed as the men, matched in strength and endurance, continued to swing and hit, duck and bend, twist and turn. Then Sebastien's shield went flying out of his hand. Definitely at a disadvantage now, he maneuvered to James's shield side. Charging and then feinting, he managed to get close enough to slide his sword under James's and send it flying into the air.

Both men went running for it and Lara could hear herself murmuring Sebastien's name, hoping that he reached it first. And she let out a little cry as he did. Now with both swords and his opponent with only a shield, he attacked and beat the other man back and to the ground.

"I yield," the Black Douglas called out loudly.

"You what?" Sebastien demanded, holding his sword to the man's throat.

"I yield to the Lord of Dunstaffnage!" James answered.

As though absorbing the support that poured forth from the men he commanded, Sebastien stood over the prone figure of Scotland's most feared fighter with outstretched arms. Tears filled Lara's eyes at the sight of it. She knew it was simply a challenge between friends, but watching it had been overwhelming to her—forcing her to see just a bit of what a real battle was like.

And the dangers of it.

James rolled to his feet and held out the now battered shield to his squire. Sebastien relinquished James's sword to him and then the men bowed to each other and, turning, to the crowd that watched. The warrior leaned into Sebastien and spoke some words that only they could hear. Then, Sebastien handed his weapon to Philippe. Malcolm ran to his side and seemed to be asking many questions. Sebastien spent some time answering him and then waved both the lads off.

He had such patience with Malcolm's boyish curiosity, and interest in all things connected to his training. He had patience with her own behavior and her delay in accepting their marriage or even his presence here as lord. She sighed. He had such patience when another man would have retaliated harshly.

That was probably why, despite her best efforts to the contrary, she was falling in love with him now.

Sebastien chose the moment of her realization to look up to the window where she stood. He met her gaze directly and she feared he could read her thoughts. More than once he seemed to have that ability, but she was not ready to show this to him yet. She nodded and stepped back from the window until she knew he could see her no longer.

Lara took a deep breath and waited to see how this new awareness would feel. It could not be a good thing, for there were so many problems involved.

"My lady?" Philippe broke into her daydreaming. "My lord asks you to join him in the yard." The boy bowed very respectfully and waited for her answer.

"What is this about, Philippe?"

"I am not privy to my lord's thinking, my lady. He simply bade me to carry this message to you. Oh, your pardon, lady. He bade me tell you to bring your cloak."

He stood with such a serious look about him, as if delivering this message was a vitally important mission, that she did not have the heart to refuse this summons.

"Very well, Philippe. I will follow you in a moment."

He appeared inordinately pleased and he bowed to her and left. Lara took her cloak from the peg near the door and went to see what Sebastien wanted of her. She discovered him waiting close to the place where he'd fought with James. His hair was wet and he tugged a tunic back over his head as she approached him.

"My lord," she said, curtsying in greeting. "Felicitations on your victory over the Black Douglas."

"He is standing right behind you, Lara. I would not want to celebrate or gloat until he leaves."

She turned slowly and jumped when she discovered the man was truly a few feet from where she stood. Once more she lifted her hand to her brow to bless herself, until she recognized what she was doing.

"My lady, I know the news will not engender any sense of loss to you, but I fear that my men and I must be about the king's business," the Douglas announced.

"Now, James?" She tried to keep the joy from her voice. If she spoke the truth, she would be much more comfortable once the Black Douglas was gone from here. And gone far away.

"Now, my lady." He stepped closer and lifted her hand to his lips. "May I give your regards to the king when I see him next?" She noticed he did not release her hand.

"I have no doubt that you shall regale him with the story of our meeting, sir."

"Just so, my lady. For now, until we meet again, *enchanté*." He kissed her hand and then let it go.

"Merci, monsieur," she answered…in the same courtly French. The same language the men had spoken in the hall when discussing their plans for taking the last remaining keeps holding out against the Bruce. Was this a trap?

"You see, Sebastien. Your lady is infinitely talented. She speaks the language of the court, in addition to Gaelic and," he paused and looked at her directly when asking in that tongue, "English as well?"

"Yes, I speak all three and a smattering of Latin, although I do read it better than I speak or write it."

Sebastien stepped closer to her. "It comes as no surprise to me, James. I have known for some time of her talents."

Now she looked at him, for this seemed to be turning into a battle of words between the two men.

"Even before I met her, I knew of her vast education. She was, after all, the Maid of Lorne." He smiled at her. "As the one who carries such a title, languages, writing and reading, and even the duties of chatelaine, were expected of her."

"Well, Sebastien, now that we have established that your wife is a gifted woman, I must take my leave. The king and his business await."

She answered his bow with a curtsy and waited while Sebastien escorted him to the gates. A few minutes later, her husband was back. She shivered from the uneasiness James caused in her.

"Is that a chill? The weather is exceptional today, but here now, let me help you with your cloak if you are cold."

"I do not like that man," she stated, shaking off his attempt to do so.

"I confess I have never heard him baiting someone as he did you. He's used to having people simper around him." Sebastien held out his arm and she laid hers on it, allowing him to guide her steps. "James is a simple man, truly. Only those who are a threat to Robert need fear him. Since he pledged himself to the Bruce, that is the overriding law of his life."

Saying nothing would be better than attempting anything meaningful, so she nodded and followed his path.

"Are you not going to ask where we go?" Sebastien spoke in that deep and tempting tone that made her breathless.

"And would you tell me if I asked?" she asked.

"Nay, 'tis a surprise I've planned for us."

"Then, my lord, lead on."

The surprise was an afternoon away from the castle. Sebastien had two horses ready and they rode around the shoreline of the firth, exploring the beaches and even the caves where she'd played as a child and where Malcolm played more recently.

It was the first time since Sebastien's arrival that she'd been permitted to ride, and she enjoyed every moment of it. They returned to the castle in time for the evening meal and it was one of the most pleasant she'd had in such a long time. With James gone, the tension was much diminished for her and, it would seem, for everyone in Dunstaffnage. Even Catriona was permitted to join them, and for a short time, Lara could forget her cares and worries.

Sebastien made love to her gently and silently that night and then simply held her within his embrace until they slept. It was at that moment when sleep came to claim her that she realized what was wrong with this perfect day.

It was the fifth day since her last visit with Eachann, and she had not gone to the church to meet him. She'd overheard the most significant information to give him since the day of Brander Pass, and she simply could not bring herself to do it.

How did you willingly betray someone you were falling in love with?

Chapter Fourteen

⤜⤚⤜⤚⤜⤚⤜⤚

The next three days were just as exceptional, and everyone in Dunstaffnage scurried about trying to ready the castle, the keep and the outbuildings for the onslaught of the coming winter. Lara could also feel the growing tension within the soldiers, for they knew, as she did, that any battles would need to be fought before winter closed in. She simply was waiting for Sebastien to tell her that he was leaving soon to know that the plans were under way.

She'd missed the beginning of the man's conversation, for it had taken her several minutes to make her way to the room without being seen by anyone. Once in place in the steward's chamber, she'd heard the discussion about the king's orders. There were three more battles to be fought in this area and they would happen within the next three weeks. The Black Douglas would lead one strike, her husband another, then they would combine their forces for the last one.

Later on, from her vantage point on the battlements, she watched as the new storage rooms over the kitchens were being completed. Dunstaffnage's continued place in the Bruce's plan for Scotland was assured by the work that Sebastien had ordered and overseen. On a grander scale, he wanted to build a new wall and extend the protection of the castle to include the barracks and the new stables. Due to the rock foundation, this addition would take several months, possibly years, and the work of hundreds of men to complete. So for now, while the Bruce's focus must remain on fighting, only the necessary renovations were carried out.

After her daily walk around the high perimeter, Lara made her way to the kitchens, where the main tasks of the cook and his workers were butchering, salting and preserving the beef, mutton and pork they would need for the winter. Just as she reached the path to the doorway and stairs, someone bumped her from behind. Nearly falling, she was only stopped from doing so by the same person grabbing her shoulders and pulling her roughly to her feet. Lara spun around to see who it was and gasped.

Eachann MacDougall.

"Here now, my lady," he said as he released her. Then he continued in a muted voice that only she could hear. "Hush now, Lara. I have but a moment here. I amno' happy that you are avoiding me." He had a cloak on and, with the hood pulled down low, his face was hidden.

Lara looked around to see if their exchange was noticed by anyone. No one seemed to be watching them. "I have nothing to tell you, Eachann," she whispered. "So I will not be meeting you anymore."

"Think ye no'? High and mighty, are ye now? Well,

I have word from your father for you." He closed the distance between them and took her arm. "Be there as I've told ye to be, and bring something personal of his."

Lara shook, hearing her cousin's angry and threatening tone of voice. He was unpredictable and dangerous. "What do you mean? Whose?"

"Dinna be playing the fool for me, Lara. Yer husband is who. Bring some personal tidbit or trinket of his." He released her with a push.

"Lara!"

She turned and saw Malcolm running to her. He must not see Eachann. Facing her cousin, she whispered, "You must go now. Sebastien will hear of this."

"Oh, I see how it is now. *Sebastien,* eh? If ye dinna bring me what I ask, I will be back. I can slip in and out of here with no one the wiser."

"Go now, Eachann. Please," she implored him. She did not want Malcolm to be in danger.

"I will be going. Do not disappoint me, lass. The next one I visit will be the boy," he threatened as he nodded in her brother's direction. "Be there."

"Lara!" Malcolm called out again, and Lara turned her body to try to block Eachann from the boy's view. She looked back over her shoulder and saw her cousin melting into the crowd in the yard.

"Malcolm! What is it?" She reached out and brushed his hair from his face.

Malcolm leaned over and looked behind her. "That looked like Cousin—"

"I did not see anyone, Malcolm. Here now, tell me what you are so excited about."

Malcolm shook his head but did not ask again. In a

few minutes he was so involved with his story about going fishing with Sebastien's men that he forgot about who might or might not have been there. Lara walked with her brother to the gate and released him to Sebastien's men after being reassured of their supervision. Then, she went to her chambers to try to figure out what to do about Eachann.

Once there, she glanced at Sebastien's trunk. He never wore jewelry or any kind of decorative belt or badge. For what possible reason could her cousin need something of Sebastien's? She might not understand his need for it, but she understood the clear threat if she did not provide it.

Malcolm.

She shuddered at the thought of Eachann gaining control of her brother. Her sister was not safe, either.

Mayhap if Lara gave some trinket to Eachann he would leave and not come back. She could convince him that this area, indeed Scotland itself, would be completely in the Bruce's control soon, and then Robert would turn his sights on the English.

Lara walked to the corner and carefully opened Sebastien's trunk. Looking through it would not be amiss, since she was the one who usually placed his cleaned garments there. After a minute of just thinking on it, she convinced herself that there would be no harm in seeing what lay at the bottom. Sliding her hands under the layers of cloth, she lifted them up to check beneath them.

She did not notice the pouch at first, for it was tucked into a small pocket in the lining of the trunk. She moved the clothes aside and slid the leather pouch free, untying the laces and tugging it open. It felt empty, but when she turned it over, two objects fell into her palm—a gold cross and a bejeweled ring.

She examined both items closely. The cross was plain, with no markings, and it was tied onto a leather strip that served in the absence of a matching chain. The ring had a large blue gem on the front and an inscription on the back that she could not read in the shadows of the chamber. When she would have moved nearer to the window for a better view of it, she heard someone climbing the steps toward the chamber.

Hurriedly she placed the items back in the pouch and the pouch back in its hiding place. Putting the clothing over it and smoothing it into position, she closed the lid of the trunk and stood just as Sebastien reached the doorway.

"I saw you in the yard," he said, before crossing the threshold of the room. "You looked upset."

Dear God! Had he seen Eachann as well? "Upset?"

"I told him he could not go without your permission. I feared you would throw yourself in the firth after him if you had no knowledge of the plan." His smile warmed her.

Relief flooded through her as she realized he spoke of Malcolm's fishing trip rather than her cousin. "I am not upset by it. Your man explained the safeguards and the supervision and I think it a fine plan," she said.

When she took a moment to think on it, Sebastien had surprised her yet again. Believing her upset by the thought of Malcolm on the water, he'd sought her out to comfort and reassure her. Even as she had been plotting against him, he was caring for her. Her sin was glaringly clear and she almost decided then not to go the chapel as Eachann had ordered.

Almost.

Her father had sent word to her. She'd heard nothing about him from anyone since the day he'd been exiled. If he was sending word to her, she should at least go and find out what that message was. She noticed Sebastien was staring at her then.

"I have hesitated to offer it, but I could teach you to swim as well so you would not fear the water."

She must have shaken her head without realizing it.

"Mayhap when the water grows warmer again?"

"I will have to think on your offer, my lord. It simply does not have any appeal to me."

He stepped closer and she smelled the scent of him—an enticing mix of leather and male. Taking her hand in his, he pulled her to him and kissed her. She relaxed into him and slid her hands to his back as he plundered her mouth. The kiss went on and became something more as he moved his hand up to the back of her head. Tugging off the netting over her hair, he loosened her braid and entangled his fingers in her locks.

Sebastien moved his lips down to her neck and loosened the neckline of her tunic as much as he could without untying the laces. She knew he would use his mouth to drive her wild. Then just when her body tensed, waiting for it, he stopped and drew back instead, touching a spot on the slope of her breast with the tip of his finger.

"I did that?" he asked, drawing her attention to the purplish bruise on the skin there.

"And who else could have?" she countered.

"I did not know. Why did you not tell me that I was hurting you?"

"It did not hurt, my lord. My mind, I fear, was somewhat distracted by other things you were doing to notice this…" Lara paused, not knowing what to call the mark left behind by the intense action of his mouth and teeth.

"Love bite." He provided the answer, but frowned as he said it. "Although the sight of your skin marred in such a way makes me regret my actions, I confess that the thought of kissing you like that makes me want you now even more."

The proof of his words could be felt even through the layers of her chemise, gown and tunic. Although her body began to warm to his words, she could not forget about Eachann and his threat. Before she needed to make any objection, voices carried into the chamber from the stairway.

"Hugh! Hugh, stop!" Margaret's whispered warning was not subtle or quiet.

"He has been in there long enough, Margaret." Hugh sounded exasperated. "He is needed in the yard. Now."

More movements on the stairs accompanied hushing sounds.

"They might be… He might be… I will not go any farther!" Her maid sounded embarrassed and Sebastien began laughing.

"Then move aside, lass, for I will." Some grunts were followed by more sounds of movement, then footsteps on the stairs.

Sebastien took Lara by the hand and led her out into

the other chamber. They stood waiting for Sir Hugh to make it up the stairs in spite of Margaret's best efforts not to allow him to. He reached the landing first, followed by the more hesitant maid.

"See? As I said, they are not naked again."

Margaret covered her mouth at Sir Hugh's rude words, but Sebastien only laughed. "A few more moments of privacy and who knows what could have happened," he said, causing Margaret's blush to deepen and spread over her cheeks.

"Your pardon, my lady," Sir Hugh began, without acknowledging Sebastien's words at all. "We have need of your husband in the yard."

"Well, my love," he said, lifting her hand to his mouth and kissing it, "I must see to this need below. I will find you at supper?"

"Yes." She clutched at his hand. "May I walk to the chapel before then?"

He waved Sir Hugh and Margaret away and leaned in closer to her. "If it is necessary."

"Necessary?" she asked, as part of her hoped against hope that he would refuse her permission. If he ordered her to stay within the walls, she had a reason, albeit an excuse, to not answer Eachann's call. Lara waited and prayed silently that Sebastien would stop her from doing something that might hurt him, and herself.

"You always seem more agitated upon your return from your prayers. I cannot see what peace you gain from such visits."

Please. Please. Please stop me.

"But, if it pleases you in some manner, if it fulfills some need in you, then go, with my blessing."

All she could do was nod, for words of any kind might reveal more than she should.

"I will have an escort for you when you need."

"Guards?" she asked.

"An escort, for your safety, lady. I have hesitated to tell you this for I do not know your feelings on it, but…" He paused, lowering his voice. "Your cousin Eachann has been sighted close to Dunstaffnage. He murders without care, his victims innocent or not, and leaves a trail of dead bodies as he moves through the countryside."

She gasped. She'd known he was about, but hadn't realized Sebastien was aware of it as well. He misinterpreted her surprise and continued.

"I know he is kin, but you must have recognized the kind of man he is and the danger he presents to any who oppose him. That is why I want you to have an escort anytime you leave the castle walls."

"Murder?" she asked. "He murders?" She knew her cousin was capable of much cruelty, but had never any inkling of this.

"Three crofters in the next valley were murdered as they slept. Two more near the loch."

"But it could have been anyone, Sebastien."

"Except that he cuts his name into their flesh…." He stopped and looked at her. "I did not want you to hear this."

"My lord!" Sir Hugh's booming voice filled the stairway and the room, startling her in its loudness.

"I must go, but you must promise to have a care."

She could only nod her head in agreement. He kissed her and released her hand, trotting down the steps to answer Sir Hugh's demanding call. Lara's body shook as she went back into the chamber, closed the door and leaned against it.

Did this change anything? Was she truly ignorant of Eachann's ways or had she simply not admitted to herself that she knew? Would he harm her when she refused him? Lara shivered as she realized he would if she did not hold some worth to him.

She remained in her room until most of the afternoon had passed, sending Margaret off on various errands and assigning her tasks to keep her away. Finally, when she knew she must leave, Lara knelt in front of Sebastien's trunk and lifted the lid. Sliding her hand down the side, she retrieved the pouch and took out the pieces of jewelry again.

After studying at both, she decided that the cross was the best one. It did not look costly and it might not cause a stir if he discovered it was missing. Turning the ring over and over in her hand, she thought something was familiar about the insignia inside of it. Finally, unable to solve that puzzle, she placed it back in the pouch and hid it back in its pocket.

The walk to the chapel was a blur to her. The guards who escorted her were pleasant and shared with her the gossip of the castle and nearby villages. 'Twas clear from their talk that they considered this their home and not a stop along the way to another battle.

How would things change if Robert was defeated? Would her father return here to claim everything that had once been his? Where would she go and what would happen to Sebastien?

The guards stopped at the door and allowed her to enter alone. She made her way to the front of the church slowly and waited for some sign of Eachann's arrival. Despite the daylight outside, the stone walls and small windows did not allow much light inside.

"Ye made the right decision, cousin," he whispered from the shadow near the altar. "I feared ye would no' take me seriously."

"I think I know what you are capable of, Eachann. I take everything you say seriously." She hoped her voice did not tremble.

He walked over to her and reached out his hand to touch her cheek. She tried to stay still and not pull away, but it was difficult.

"Ye have the look of a well-ridden whore, Lara. If I were to smell your skin, I would wager I could smell his seed on ye. They say he takes ye to his bed for hours and hours."

She stepped away then, from his touch and his disgusting words. "Stop this, Eachann. I do not have much time here."

He started at her words and she waited for his reaction. "And, 'twould appear that ye have grown a backbone. I will enjoy watching ye be tamed once more when yer father returns. Oh, aye, it will be a sight to see." He slid his hand down now and rubbed himself as he spoke. "Spare the rod and spoil the child, the book does say. Yer father will no' spare the rod on ye when he finds out the filthy things ye have been doing with the enemy."

This was becoming dangerous, and she feared she wouldn't be able to escape if he attacked her. Lara walked away and put the altar between them. Then she realized what he'd said. "What do you mean, *when* my father returns?"

He gazed at her as though lost in thought, and then shook his head. Reaching inside his tunic, he removed a folded parchment and held it out to her. "This is from yer father. He said to read it and then I'm to burn it so that none know about it."

Lara took the parchment, broke the seal and opened it. Holding it close to the candle that burned on the altar, she read her father's greetings, news of his triumphant entry into England and into Edward's favor and his appointment as Admiral of the Western Seas.

"He be an admiral now. His fleet is growing and will give the Bruce's allies here in the isles much to worry about." Eachann nodded at her.

After Eachann's frightening words, the tone and wording of the letter came as a surprise to her. First her father apologized for the humiliating scene the day of his capture; he explained that it was necessary in order to make her husband believe she'd been repudiated. Her father praised her for keeping the children safe and for the unfortunate burden she'd had to bear over these last few months as wife to the enemy. He promised a warm welcome and his favor once that same enemy was routed from their home and the MacDougalls reclaimed Dunstaffnage, as was their right.

His closing words entreated her to continue to pass information on to Eachann for their use, to undermine her husband in any way she could, and to stay faithful to the clan. He promised he would make arrangements for her safe return when the time came. She felt the tears gather in her eyes as her doubts about what she did lessened. She had not been abandoned at all.

Something within her sent off a warning. This was too favorable to her. Too ingratiating. Too confusing. Who could she believe in this? Her father, who now stood on the brink of a return, or her husband, who treated her with respect and honor and...love? Eachann was watching her as she considered the letter.

"When did he write this, Eachann?"

"He gave it to me just three days ago. The day ye should have been here to receive it, but ye were in that bastard's bed." His expression changed and his words and tone softened. "But, he says he understands that ye must do such things as ye must do."

She feared this instability in him and wanted to leave as quickly as possible. She tore the parchment in pieces and gave it back to him. Without a word about the cross she carried or what she'd overheard, Lara turned to leave.

"Here now, Lara. Ye have something for me?" he asked as he held out his hand to her.

"Why do you need something of his?"

He was around the altar before she could finish her question. With a punishing grip he pulled her to him. "Ye should no' question my methods, lass. I do what needs doing, too." He shook her and then pulled her to him again, holding her so close she could feel his breath on her cheek. "Did ye bring something for me?"

She nodded and reached into a pocket in her cloak for the cross. He tore it from her hand and held it up to look at. She thought he might let her go now, but, after placing the cross in his pocket, he smiled at her in a way that made her skin feel as though it were on fire.

"Ye have been entertaining some important people there. Surely ye heard something when the Black Douglas was sitting at yer table?"

How could he have known that? Did he come and go freely, with no one noticing? She knew he'd done it at least once, when he approached her in the yard in the full light of day, so 'twas possible he'd done it before or since. Or…?

"You have other contacts within the household?" she asked.

"Aye. A few well-chosen, well-placed, faithful Mac-Dougalls are there with ye. But ye are the best placed by far, with the most *intimate* access, shall we say?"

Now that she thought on it, it made sense to her. Lara suspected that she knew at least one of those who still reported to Eachann. And who probably gave an accounting of her behavior as well.

"The sun is going down and I must be on my way, so tell me what you know. What did the Douglas say?" Eachann twisted her arm tighter, until she gasped, and then asked again, "What did he say?"

She did not answer fast enough, for he backhanded her across the face and she fell to the floor. "He is not worth it, Lara. You are trying to protect the Bruce's spy and it's no' something ye need worry about." He yanked her to her feet and spoke quietly now. "What are they planning?"

"Spy? He is not a spy," she said, so dazed from the blow she could not focus her thoughts. "He is a warrior."

"Ye are sleeping with the man who controls all the spies used by the Bruce. Sebastien of Cleish and I are old acquaintances and have faced each other many, many times, Lara. 'Tis like a game now between us. I leave him signs and he answers them in kind. 'Tis fitting somehow that ye should be his downfall."

"Signs?" She covered her cheek with her hand. It burned from his blow. "Like those people you killed?"

"Just so. Yer husband does the same when he gets close to my trail. 'Tis just sport among those of us in the game. But ye're wrong in this one—he left them for me, no' the other way round. They died at his hand and bear his mark."

"You think this is some kind of game?"

"Oh, aye, 'tis that. Tit for tat. He makes a move, I counter it. He found out about the ambush at Brander Pass. I found out about the gathering at Kilcrenan, but the bastard changed the location and we missed our opportunity to capture the Bruce himself."

"So, he did not go to Kilcrenan?"

"Nay. The bastard used St. Modan's instead. He defiled our own priory. But dinna worry, for he will pay dearly for that sacrilege." He turned his gaze back to her. "Dearly."

Eachann leaned her back against the altar and faced her, his hands free and menacing before her. "This is the last time I will ask ye. If ye do not give me what I want, I will fetch sweet Catriona and we can finish this with her to spur on yer words."

"No!" she cried.

"Good. Then speak yer piece and ye can go."

"The Douglas said that they need to take but three

more keeps to control this area. Invercreran is to be last, Glen Gour and the southern tip of Loch Awe first." She could see him thinking on her words.

"When do they make their move?"

"By early next month. Then the Bruce will seek out the Earl of Ross." She related to him the details of the attacks and the specifics about how many would be involved in the plan.

"Verra good, lass. Next time do no' make me waste time waiting for ye to come or to tell me what I need to know. I will tell yer father that ye are glad to hear of his return."

He stepped back and disappeared into an opening in the wall before she could agree or not. Before she could tell him that she would not do this again.

Lara gathered her cloak around her and wondered how she would ever conceal this from Sebastien. From the pain in her face, she knew it would be obvious that she'd been struck. What could she say? How could she explain it?

She stumbled to the door and pulled it open, for the need to breathe fresh air was overwhelming to her. The two guards stood a few yards from the entrance and they turned as she left the church. Positioning the hood of her cloak over her head, she tried to keep her face hidden in its folds. When they arrived at the path that went up the embankment to the drawbridge, she stopped.

"I am not ready to go in just yet. I would like to walk on the shore there for a few minutes." They glanced at each other and looked as though they would argue, until she pointed out the guards on the battlements and at each corner of the castle, on the beach. "I will be observed every moment and will be quite safe. I need only a short time."

With a nod, they allowed her to go on, and she walked to the water's edge. Crouching down and dipping her hand into the water, she knew its chill would soothe the growing pain in her face. Taking the end of her cloak, Lara wet it and held the cold cloth on her cheek. When it warmed, she dunked it again and repeated the action until the pain lessened.

The sun dropped behind the trees and she knew she could not remain much longer. She shivered, both with cold and with trepidation over the coming scene with Sebastien. Now that she knew his true role in the Bruce's campaign, how could she face him? If he and Eachann were involved in some personal war, did he know *her* role?

Her legs were tired from being in this position for too long, so she immersed the edge of the cloak one more time and then stood with it against her cheek.

"Tell me what brings you to the water's edge? Surely you cannot mean to swim now?"

Sebastien's voice was light, even playful, but his face when he saw hers was nothing like that. He wore a deadly expression and she watched him change into the forbidding warrior he was. "Give me his name," he ordered. "Give me his name!"

Chapter Fifteen

Sebastien strode to her side and took her by the arms. When Lara winced, he released her but did not move away. She was shaking and the dark, spreading bruise on her face told of her being struck. But she would not meet his eyes, so he summoned the two guards assigned to her.

"Explain this," he ordered as he pointed at her. The two men paled at the sight and said nothing. "You were guarding her. How did this happen?"

"Sebastien," she called out in a weak voice, "it was not their fault."

"I will speak to you both later, but now summon Hugh and go back and search that chapel for anyone, anything suspicious." They seemed frozen in place, so he raised his voice. "Now!"

They turned and ran at his orders. Lara watched his every move as though she would bolt. The terror, fresh in her eyes, overpowered her and her body shuddered. He approached her slowly now and spoke softly. Suspecting he knew the culprit, he needed her confirmation of it.

"Lara, who did this to you?"

"He said that you two know each other. Is that true, Sebastien?"

"Aye, Lara. 'Tis true." He did not bother to question her or to deny the identity of the person they both knew was responsible for this.

"He said that you are in charge of the Bruce's spies."

Before he could respond—and he was candidly not sure of how to answer her—Hugh and a small contingent of men ran down the shore from the castle with swords and axes drawn. They needed to move quickly if they were to find or follow him.

"Jamie, escort the lady back to our chambers. Do not leave her side until I am there," he said. The young soldier moved forward and took Lara by the arm. To another soldier, Sebastien said, "Search the north tower before the lady enters it and take the children there as well. Let no one join them but her maid."

He watched as Lara moved with Jamie, not resisting his orders. When they were far enough away that she could not hear him, he turned to Hugh. "Search every inch of that church. Eachann MacDougall was in there."

Hugh nodded and turned to do as ordered, but Sebastien stopped him for a moment. "I suspect there is another entrance there. Find it, Hugh."

He needed to secure the castle and make certain that Eachann was gone. If he knew the man, Lara's cousin would not be found here. Munro had been having no luck in tracing Eachann's movements over these last weeks. How long had he been this close? Shaking his head, Sebastien recognized that Lara was at the center of this.

It took nearly an hour to accomplish, but the keep and the castle, as well as the surrounding grounds and chapel, were searched completely. Once satisfied of this, Sebastien made his way to the north tower to face Lara and the questions that hung between them.

He stopped in the solar and checked on Malcolm and Catriona before climbing the stairs to their chambers. A guard stood at the top of the steps and another inside the doorway. Jamie took his orders seriously, for he was in the same room as Lara. She sat in the chair and stared at the flames in the hearth. Sebastien did not say a word, but the guard and Margaret left.

He walked to the window and looked out at the deserted yard. No one he did not know personally was inside the walls now, and the same restriction would continue until he was certain Lara and the children were not in danger.

He did not wait for her to ask. Without knowing what Eachann had revealed, he would tell her the truth. Then, he knew, she would lie to him.

"'Tis true, Lara. I do spy for the king. I have since the beginning of my service to him nigh unto three years ago. Although I have some talent for fighting, Robert discovered that I could gather information. I have men all over Scotland, in cities, villages and in the countryside, who provide Robert with the most accurate information about his enemies, their troops, their plans."

Lara sat unmoving in the chair. From his place by the window, he could see that her whole cheek was bruised.

"So you kill as he does? He said those villagers were murdered by you."

"I do not kill innocents. I do not turn away from doing what must be done in carrying out the king's orders, but those not involved in the fight need not fear me."

He thought she glanced at him then, but she lowered her gaze quickly if she had. What was her part in this?

"Was Eachann there when you arrived?"

"Aye."

"How did he come to be there?"

"Sebastien, he was here in the castle this morn. He told me to meet him there or he would come back to harm Malcolm."

"He was here and you did not tell me?" he asked, already knowing the answer.

"I could not," she said.

He faced her now and asked again. "Could not or would not?"

Lara met his gaze and repeated, "I could not. He threatened the children if I did not meet him in the chapel."

"He only has the power you give him, Lara. If you could have trusted me and told me, he would never have gotten close enough to do that—" he pointed to her cheek "—to you. And he would not get to the children, either."

"I do trust you, Sebastien. But he is family…." She stopped and looked away when she realized what she'd said.

"And I am still the enemy." His heart hurt as though stabbed. She was holding on to the past with both hands, and there was no way to move forward in their lives, in their marriage, when she did so.

"For each step we take ahead, we seem to stumble two back. I thought you were becoming accustomed to our marriage. I thought you might even be accepting it. Was it Eachann's visit that make you doubt again? What did he tell you that is making you look at me with such fear?"

"Eachann said that you killed those villagers as a warning to him."

"Look at me, Lara. Who is lying in this? You know my ways. You have witnessed how I run this castle and how I carry out my duties to Robert. Have you ever known me to kill without reason? I could have slain every man and woman the day I came here. 'No quarter asked and none given' is the battle cry. I could have, but I chose another way to get in the castle."

"Yes, you lied to me to get in."

"Lied, yes, and bluffed, and humiliated you as well, but you and those you care about the most are alive, when most who refuse the king's orders are not."

Lara stood now and walked to the other side of the room, as far as she could go. "And if you've lied to me all along, why should I believe you in this? It will be easier if you can convince me to accept your words over my cousin's."

His anger flared, so much he wanted to scream it out at her. But, he realized that she was doing the same thing she had in the past when afraid of her own feelings or of something she faced—striking out so that she could be driven away. Did she even know she did it?

"What is behind this, Lara? What else did Eachann say that has made you doubt me?"

She did not answer quickly, indeed she crossed her

arms over her chest and for a few minutes appeared to be thinking over her answer. She still kept her secrets, the ones he knew about and the ones he prayed he was wrong about.

"Tell me of my father," she whispered.

Ah, so Eachann had told her of her father's return to the fight. "Your father is now serving as an admiral in Edward's forces. Although he has returned to Scotland, his activities so far have not been in this area. Mayhap he does think to protect the ones he left behind as hostages?"

"So you did know?" she asked.

"Of course I knew. I was the one who informed Robert of it. Eachann was right about one thing—I am the king's spy."

She flinched at his words. "What else do you know about him?"

"Lara, he fights for England, hoping to recover all he has lost. He wants to use you as a wedge—causing enough trouble to distract me from my duties to Robert and using you as a figurehead to draw his allies into the fight."

"Me? How is he using me?"

Apparently Eachann had not revealed the whole plan to her. "His aim is to, in his own words, free the Maid of Lorne from her captor and return her and this castle to their rightful place."

"His own words?"

"I have one of the letters he sent to several of his former allies, all of whom have sworn allegiance to Robert now. He is using you as a rallying cry and nothing more. This is not about him caring for you, 'tis about his own goals."

She looked confused. But she did appear to be considering his words. That was a good sign, but not enough to remedy this situation, which put all of them and especially him and his men and their mission for the king in danger. He could not and would not do that, not even for the woman he loved.

"Every good spy has a contingency plan. Situations change, allies become enemies and enemies become friends," he explained. "'Twould appear that we have need of one now." Her eyes widened at his admission. "Sit and let us discuss mine."

Lara moved back to the chair and sat. He noticed her favoring her arm. "He hurt you there, too?" At her nod, he went to the door and called for wine to be brought. "Has Gara seen to you yet?"

"Nay. You ordered that no one could enter and Jamie took your instruments very seriously."

"Good. I do not like to have my orders disobeyed or ignored."

He stood at the door and took the pitcher and goblets from Margaret when she returned with them. After telling the maid to summon the healer, Sebastien filled the cups and handed one to Lara. She accepted and drank most of it in one swallow.

"Go slowly or you will be asleep before I finish telling you of my plan."

He'd thought on this for many weeks. The future, one with her as his wife, was just ahead of them if he could only make her see the rightness of it. If only she could trust him or if she wanted to trust him, it could work out well. But, without her full support, it would not work at all.

"As Robert's commander here, I perform many duties for him. His decision to leave this castle standing when his tried-and-true method is to destroy such keeps is based on my ability to carry out my orders. My first responsibility is to hold this castle and area in his name. My second is to organize and maintain supply lines from here on the coast to many locations. My third task is to continue to gather information and use it against his enemies."

He paused and drank some of his wine. "Your *inclination* to favor your family over me is causing problems and preventing me from successfully carrying out those duties."

"Me? I do not understand. How do I interfere here? I have no power, nothing with which to stop you."

He smiled at her. "If I have to worry that you are being dishonest with me, or giving aid to your cousin, who is my bitterest enemy, or that you are in danger here, I cannot be effective." He drank down the rest of his wine. "And I must be effective or it will cost lives."

"Am I to be a prisoner again? As in those first days and weeks?" She shivered and he knew she was at the end of her endurance.

"Nay, not a prisoner. You have a choice to make and not much time to make it."

"I made my choice—I have been trying to be a good wife to you. I have begun taking over the duties that should be those of the lady and chatelaine. What more do you want?"

"I want your unconditional surrender."

She was about to take a sip of her wine but stopped and stared at him. "What do you mean?"

"In battle, when one side is overwhelmed by the enemy, an unconditional surrender is the only way out. I told you that I want everything I never had, Lara. I want it with you. But, you must give yourself to me, in mind and body and soul and, most especially, in heart. I must be the family who claims your loyalty, your trust and your support."

"You ask much of me, Sebastien. Do you know the cost of this to me?"

"Aye, love, I do. But the rewards will be great."

"And if I cannot give you what you ask?" She frowned and he was pleased that she wanted to know all the conditions before accepting or rejecting his offer. She was thinking, which was better than acting in haste.

"You have two options. If you want to remain my wife, but cannot stay here in the thick of things, I can send you to a cousin who lives in the east. You and Malcolm and Catriona can live with them until this is over, and be safe there." He paused and then explained the next part. "If you do not wish to remain my wife, if you wish to return to your clan, I will send you back to them."

"You will put me aside?"

"Aye. Robert has enough bishops on his side that I am certain one or more could be convinced to annul the marriage. You can go on as before and your father can choose your husband."

"Malcolm and Catriona?"

"They must stay in my control, but I will send them to my cousin for safety."

"You will not allow them to return with me?"

"Nay, they are in the king's custody and not mine to release. Your father will have no compunction about attacking here if they are returned to him." Sebastien stood and walked to the door. "Since I leave on a mission for the king in four days, you must decide by then which you choose."

"Four days?" she asked, shifting on the seat. It was such an uncomfortable chair, he wondered why she'd chosen it for their chambers.

"Aye, four days and then I must handle some matters for the king."

He watched for any reaction to his words, for he suspected that she did know the details of the upcoming battles. Other than looking paler than a few minutes ago, she revealed nothing. They would hold to the plan; however, there were additional precautions he would put in place to prevent Eachann from benefiting from anything he'd forced from Lara. Sebastien opened the door and nodded to Gara, who stood waiting there.

"Come and give assistance to your lady," he said.

When Gara and Margaret entered, he stepped aside to let them tend to her. It was obvious that he was not needed, so he left to find Hugh and Etienne. There was much to do and little time in which to accomplish it.

Chapter Sixteen

~~~~~~

She awoke in the middle of the night, the pain in her face pounding. Lara sat up in the bed and realized she slept alone. The draft that Gara prepared had made her sleep, but obviously not long enough. Shifting under the covers, she turned to the other side so that her cheek would not press against the pillow. That was when she saw him.

He slept in her father's chair, hunched over. A snore broke the silence in the room, then he twisted around and leaned back once more. Lara pushed the covers away and walked softly to his side.

"Sebastien. Sebastien, wake up," she said, shaking his shoulder gently. He came awake with a start and reached for the sword that usually hung from his belt.

"What is it? Are you well?" He sat up and looked around the room. "Why are you out of bed?" Stretching his arms and rolling his shoulders, he stood and frowned at her.

"You cannot sleep in that chair. Come to bed."

"I was asleep, Lara. I can usually sleep anywhere—in a bed, a chair, even on the ground."

"Well, if there is a bed here, why not avail yourself of it?"

"I did not want to disturb you when I came in. I thought it best to rest here," he explained.

"Please come to bed. There is no reason for you to avoid it."

He looked as though he might object, but then he glanced at the chair again and accepted. He waited as she climbed back in, then followed. She leaned against the pillow and watched as he slipped under the blankets. Lying quietly, she waited for sleep to claim her…which it did not. Lara turned her head to look over at him and found him watching her.

"Are you in much pain? I can summon Gara if you need her," he said. He reached out his hand to touch her cheek and stopped himself.

"There is no need. I just cannot sleep."

They lay there, not touching, not sleeping, for a few more minutes until she could not bear the silence. Leaning up on one hand, she asked him a question that had bothered her since he'd mentioned it the first time.

"You have told me all that you did not have as a child. Pray thee, what did you have? What was Cleish like?"

He glanced at her and for a moment she thought he would not speak of it. Then he turned and lay in the same manner as she, so that he faced her.

"Cleish is a wee village not far from Stirling. 'Tis truly small but, being just off the main roads, many travelers pass through it. My mother's da had an inn there and she took to running it when he died."

"And you were how old when she married?"

"I had five years." She could almost see him at that age, not much younger than Catriona was now, with light hair and his green eyes sparkling as he ran and played.

"How many brothers and sisters do you have?" She found herself curious about details of which they'd never spoken.

He paused and the strangest expression lit his face. "I have two brothers and three sisters, the youngest now ten-and-three. I had thought to have her come here to live, but that discussion is for another time."

If she were still here, Lara thought. "When did you find out who your real father was?"

"When my mother died. Her husband gave me a few things she wanted me to have. I discovered who he was and where he lived."

"Did you go to him? Did he know of you?"

He laughed. "Nay. I decided I would wait and make my own way in the world and not be beholden to a name. My stepfather gifted me with my first sword and he arranged for me to train with one of his cousins."

"And once you made a name for yourself, did you tell him?"

A sad smile crossed his face. "Nay, Lara, for he died years ago without knowing that I was his son."

Saddened by this news of his solitary life, she felt tears gathering in her eyes. Lara reached up to wipe them away.

"Here now, I did not mean to upset you with this."

"I think I am overwrought from the day's events."

"And you need to rest. Close your eyes and let sleep come."

She did as he said, shutting her eyes and rolling onto her back. As she did every night, she moved over until she could feel his warmth. If he thought it strange with all that was between them, he did not hesitate to wrap himself around her, draping his arm over her waist and resting his chin on her head.

With his heat seeping into her and his strong arm around her, Lara felt the call to sleep. She heard and felt his breathing become even and slow, and knew he was on the brink of sleep as well. The words escaped as she drifted off.

"If I did not love you, none of this would be a problem."

A few miles away, off the coast on a boat hidden among the small islands in the Firth of Lorne, Eachann spoke with his uncle of their success.

"You have a trinket then?"

"Aye, Uncle. Lara brought it as she was told to." He held out the small cross to him.

"What was her reaction to my letter?" John of Lorne asked, taking it from him and slipping it into his tunic.

"She was much pleased by it. She was about to bolt until I told her about you and gave it to her."

"Was she? Is she enamored of this bastard who married her?" he asked, shaking his head. "She is a weak woman, like her mother was. She just needs some guidance."

Eachann laughed and felt his cock harden at the thought of being the man who tamed his beautiful cousin's willfulness.

"I dinna care how much he has used her, Uncle. I

want her when this is over." If last night was any indication of her resistance and strength, it would take much to break her. He shuddered with pleasure at the thoughts of all he could do before finally killing her. She would scream… He reached for his cock, enraptured by the very thought of what would be.

"Not yet, Eachann. Control yourself until we have what we want. Then she will be yours, since she will never be welcomed back."

"Yer pardon, Uncle," Eachann said. He could wait. One thing he'd learned in his years as a spy was how to wait. And she would pay with her flesh for every day he waited. He pulled his thoughts back to their plan. "So, we will warn Invercreran, Glen Gour and Awe of the coming attacks?"

His uncle's mouth curved into a smile that made him nervous. "Nay. The bastard knows she told you something. She is not smart enough to have carried this spying off without having slipped up during this time. Knowing him, he already suspects her. So, we sacrifice the first two and let him doubt whether or not she gave you anything we could use. We will gather our forces and make him pay at Invercreran."

"Sacrifice them? But there are hundreds in those keeps."

"They will further our goals of reclaiming Dunstaffnage and defeating the Bruce's forces. And no one will be the wiser for it."

"And Sebastien of Cleish? When do we remove him?"

His uncle laughed. "Patience, Eachann. You will make certain to place this—" he patted the place where

the cross was stored "—on one of our men, who will
live just long enough to claim that Sebastien of Cleish
told us the battle plans. Once James Douglas or the
Campbells hear of it, it will take him out of the game."

"But Douglas is his friend."

"Ah, but he is first the Bruce's man. If he suspects
Sebastien of anything, he will take it to the Bruce. If
the Campbells find this proof, they will proceed with
it, for they hunger for Dunstaffnage almost as much as
we do. Either way, he will find himself charged with
treason and most likely executed before he ever real-
izes we were behind it."

Eachann thought on the plan and smiled. "And then
I get her."

"Aye, Eachann, the stupid bitch is yours."

She ached from head to toe when she opened her
eyes in the morning. Well, her eye, since the other one
was swollen shut from the blow to her face. Groping
across the bed, she discovered that Sebastien was already gone.

Lara lay back down and thought on his words last
evening as he'd spoken of his childhood. When she
considered what he'd told her, she decided mayhap
making his own way was better than being claimed by
one family. He was not bound by anything but his conscience and his honor. He answered to no one but to
those whom he chose. There was a certain attractive-
ness to such a life when she thought of her own dilemma.

Tied to her family no matter the cause or the
argument.

She wished she had someone to share her thoughts with and to discuss matters such as these. The only one close enough to her was her mother's sister, but she had not seen her in over three years. Sitting up now, she slid to the side of the bed and climbed out. Margaret responded as always at her first movements and opened the door.

And dropped the tray she carried onto the floor with a loud crash.

"Oh, my lady!" she cried out as she knelt down to pick up the broken jug and bowls. "Your face…your face!"

Surmising that she looked worse than she felt, and she felt poorly, Lara knew she would be staying in her chambers for the day. Going to help Margaret clean up the steaming porridge from the floor, she gasped as three heavily armed guards rushed up the stairs and into her chambers. Before she could give an explanation, they drew their weapons.

Sir Hugh followed a moment behind them, sword drawn and ax in hand, and then Sebastien only a few steps behind him. Margaret looked up at the fierce warriors before her and fainted to the floor. When Lara tried to catch her, they all moaned as they caught sight of her face.

"Here now," Sebastien said as he hurried to help her. "What has happened?" He, too, paused and glanced at her injured cheek before lifting the maid into his arms and passing her off to Sir Hugh, who stood behind him.

"You should have warned me or them about my face."

"Truly, it did not look this bad before. 'Tis only full daylight that brings out all the colors."

She thought he might be trying to jest, but his horrified expression matched those of the other men, and she shrugged. "I would have thought that this bruise would be nothing to battle-hardened warriors like yourselves. There is not even a trace of blood." She touched her swollen cheek and they hissed as though in pain.

"Blood is no' a problem, my lady," Jamie said. "Or even severed limbs…."

"Do ye remember the time that Old Hamish lost his eye?" another chimed in. "Even seeing it hanging by a thread down his cheek didna bother me."

The third began to regale her with another injury incident when Sebastien—thank the Lord!—interrupted them. "I think," he said, and then louder, "I think it is seeing it on a woman that makes it more grievous than in battle."

"Aye, my lord. Ye have the right of it," Jamie said. "If the skin did not break—" he pointed to her face "—ye probably willna even have a scar."

The other men just stared at her and then nodded at the apparent wisdom of their comrade. She looked to Sebastien and cleared her throat. He got the message.

"The lady is safe, so go back to your posts," he ordered.

The soldiers put their swords back into their scabbards and bowed to her. She heard their footsteps as they trod back down to where they were assigned, apparently not too far away. Lara peeked into the outer chamber and noticed that Margaret had regained consciousness…in Sir Hugh's arms. The woman would be worthless for the rest of the day, so Lara waved her off as Sir Hugh helped her down the stairs.

"Are they truly necessary, my lord?" she asked, gathering the remnants of her meal and placing them on the table.

"Until I am certain that Eachann is no longer a threat to you, aye, they are." He picked up the cloth that had covered the tray and began to wipe up the porridge from the floor with it.

"He is probably long gone, back to my father."

"Mayhap or not, I will not take any chances with him," he said. His lips moved into a slight smile. "Not as long as you are my concern, that is."

She nodded, understanding that one of her choices was to leave him and go back to her family.

"I would say one thing on the matter of the choices before you, if I may?" He looked to her for permission. Lara nodded. "If your decision is to leave our marriage behind and seek an annulment, I would urge you to consider going to someone other than your father."

"Why?" He did not know of the conciliatory letter and the tender greetings and promises made to her by her parent.

"In my dealings with your cousin, I've learned that he is a man who enjoys giving pain to others."

"And in your dealings with other spies, have you never caused pain?"

"Aye, I have. But, when I forced someone to spill their secrets by heavy-handed methods, they were soldiers or spies, and even then, I had some measure of regret over their hard use. Eachann does not regret any methods he uses. Indeed, he relishes the giving of pain."

She remembered her cousin's shoving and hitting and how he seemed to get sexual pleasure from it. Lara's mouth went dry.

"You do understand, then?" Sebastien asked. "So, consider seeking another refuge if you decide on the annulment."

She turned away, not willing to let him see the tears in her eyes. "I will think on your words, my lord."

"Good. I will send someone up with another tray for you and I will warn them of what to expect so we have no more fainting."

"My thanks," she said, finally able to look at him.

"Oh, the children have asked to see you. I did tell them of your injury, but I did not reveal the cause of it. So, if you want to tell them that you fell…?"

"That might be an easier explanation for them, and it is not far from the truth."

He stood for another minute as though he had something more to say and could not get the words out. He offered her a bow and then left her alone.

Part of her longed to stop him and to throw herself into his arms. She wanted to accept his strength; she needed it when she felt this weak. Another girl knocked on her door with a tray of fresh porridge and bread, and it was her expression that sent Lara searching for her looking glass. When she saw what the others had, it put her off her food for the rest of the morning.

With the maid's help, she contrived a hair covering that included a loose veil she could draw down to hide most of the swelling. By the afternoon she was ready to see the children, or at least as prepared as she could be.

Malcolm, as most boys his age, did not seem affected by it at all. He entered her chambers and proceeded to ask all kinds of questions about Sebastien and the axes the soldiers carried and the new boats. Catriona broke into tears and climbed into Lara's lap. Every few minutes she would lean back, stare at Lara's face and utter her new favorite word—*horrendous*.

"Lara, it looks horrendous," she would say, drawing out the word to make it last more than the count of ten. After the sixth time, Lara asked who had taught her such a word.

"Sir Hugh said it first. He told Margaret that your face looked *horrrendousss*."

Lara reminded herself to have a talk with Sir Hugh about what he said in front of her sister. Catriona would use this new word endlessly for days until she discovered another she liked better. "Catriona, a lady does not point out someone's misfortunes."

"But it looks h—"

Lara grabbed her hand and put it back in her lap. "Aye, love, it does." Guiding the girl to her feet, she stood. "Come, let us go down to the solar. Mayhap we can coax Margaret to join us."

She walked down the steps and discovered the soldiers standing guard on the landing. In spite of her veil, they all shook their heads and scrunched up their own faces at the sight of her. Waving off their attention, she entered the bright chamber and decided to work on the tapestry that still taunted her.

Malcolm whined about being shut up and not permitted outside. Once Philippe arrived with some rope and a new knowledge of knots to share with him, both boys were occupied for a time. Margaret did join them and she spent her time brushing and arranging Catriona's hair into elaborate braids.

After losing stitches and needles, Lara realized that her sight was impaired by the swelling, and gave up again on trying to embroider. So she contented herself by watching the boys practice their skills, and even learned one or two herself under Philippe's tutelage. Gara came and applied a paste to her cheek, which she assured Lara would help with the swelling. In the late afternoon, when Philippe was called back to his duties and Catriona and Margaret were napping in Catriona's bed, Lara realized that one source of information sat right before her.

"Malcolm, tell me what you think of Lord Sebastien."

Her brother began by outlining all of Sebastien's accomplishments and abilities and manly skills in fighting.

"Nay, Malcolm. I know all of those things. I would hear what your thoughts are on his character."

The boy stared off into the distance for a few minutes, then met her gaze. "He is a good man, Lara. You could not find a better man if you had sought one of your own choice."

Stunned by the wisdom in one so young, she repeated in her mind his words. *Could not find a better man...*

"I think you are correct in this, Malcolm."

"He does not rule through anger and fear as Father did, Lara. His men serve him of their own will. They know he would give up his life to protect any one of them, and it makes them pledge to him without hesitation."

Where did this come from? How could one so innocent recognize the leadership in Sebastien? Surprised by his words, Lara thought on them.

"Philippe's father is an earl, but Philippe will pledge to Sebastien when he finishes his training. As will I," he said proudly. "We will be knights together in the service of the Bruce."

Reeling from this declaration, she shook her head. Misunderstanding the gesture, Malcolm stated, "Sebastien said it will be my choice to make when the time comes."

"So he is not forcing you to this way of thinking? Or is Philippe persuading you somehow?"

"Nay," he said, shaking his head now. "Sebastien said that men of honor follow their consciences and honor their pledges. I want to be a man of honor."

Sitting back in her chair, Lara was overwhelmed by the lessons taught and learned in just these last few months under Sebastien's guidance. Her husband had treated them all with infinite patience and care and honor. Oh, she knew he manipulated her at times, but he never did it to hurt or harm her, and she recognized when he did it. Mayhap that was part of his plan?

She sought her bed earlier than usual that day, exhaustion driving her to it just after eating with the children. She was no less confused when she woke up in Sebastien's embrace in the middle of the night. Once more he warmed and protected her, with no expectation of a return on his actions.

In the morning, when her face was less swollen and

she could see more clearly, she sought out one of the books in her mother's collection, an illuminated history of the MacDougalls. One of the pictures portrayed her great-great-grandfather pledging himself to the king who had granted their original charter of lands and titles.

Looking at both the men involved, Lara noticed first that there was nothing subservient about her ancestor's stance or gaze as his hands were held by those of his liege lord. And there was nothing prideful or gloating in the appearance of the king as he accepted the words spoken by his vassal.

As she translated the pledge from Latin, she let the meaning flow over her. Everything became clear to her as she contemplated what Sebastien offered and promised her.

She took to her chambers, chasing all away with a tale of tiredness, and spent the day thinking on the words that could express her decision to Sebastien. Finally, when Margaret brought news that he and his commanders would meet in the hall before their supper, Lara knew it was time.

Time to make her choice.

Chapter Seventeen

◦━━━⟡━━━◦

Lara could not wait for supper to do this, for her stomach rebelled due to nerves. It had to be now. She made her way from her room to the hall where Sebastien met with his own commanders. His troops were divided into six companies, each with a different skill or superiority in some aspect of warfare. One contingent was skilled with bows, another with sword and lance and another with ax and pike. As Malcolm had explained to her in the last day, some had trained with the Black Douglas before coming to Sebastien, and some of his men had fought with Sebastien for the last three years.

She walked with a boldness she did not feel to the front of the room where they had maps spread out and were deep in discussion over their upcoming mission. One of the men noticed her and called out to Sebastien to bring her to his attention. Soon the room had quieted and, after each man stood and bowed to her, they waited to discover her purpose here.

Standing before Sebastien, she wondered why she had ever thought to betray him. How could she do anything but love this man who had given her so much and saved her from so much else? Lara saw the puzzlement on his face and smiled at him. Then she knelt before him, with her hands extended out to him and her head bowed.

The words that she had practiced all morning and most of the afternoon swirled around in her thoughts, and she began to repeat them out loud for all to hear.

"By the Lord before whom I, Lara MacDougall of Dunstaffnage, swear this oath, and in the name of all that is holy, I will pledge to Sebastien of Cleish, Laird of Dunstaffnage, to be true and faithful, and to love all that he loves and to shun all that he shuns, according to the laws of God and the order of the world. I swear that I will not ever, with will or action, through word or deed or omission, do anything unpleasing to him, on condition that he will hold to me as I shall deserve it, and that he will perform everything as it was in our agreement when I first submitted myself to him and his mercy and chose his will over mine. I offer this unconditionally, with no expectations other than his faith and favor as my lord and husband."

She finished the oath and waited, with head low and hands outstretched, for his reaction. No one spoke a word. There were no whispers or noises in the hall in spite of the large number of people who were watching her submission to her lord and husband. He stepped closer and she felt his hands cover hers. She noticed, in that moment, that his were shaking as badly as hers. Then his voice poured over her as he spoke in response.

"I, Sebastien of Cleish, Laird of Dunstaffnage, do accept this oath of fealty as sworn here before these witnesses, and do promise as lord and husband to protect and defend the person and properties of Lara MacDougall of Dunstaffnage who here pledges on her honor that she will be ruled by my will and by my word. I agree to the promises contained herein this oath unconditionally, with no expectations other than her love and faith and favor as my lady and my wife."

The cheering and clapping that filled the hall in the next moment was deafening, but she heard the word that he had added in his pledge—her love. She raised her head and met his gaze then and read, there on his face and in his eyes, all that he had promised and more.

Sebastien drew her to her feet and pulled her into his arms, wrapping them around her and lifting her to him. And he kissed her in a manner that had little to do with the formal kiss of peace usually shared in this ceremony, opening himself to her even as he claimed her in front of his men and any MacDougalls still present.

"I think they are pleased for us," he said, leaning close enough to her ear that his breath tickled her there.

"And you, my lord? Are you pleased?" He'd said that this was what he wanted, but how did he feel now that she had made this choice?

"I am well pleased by this, Lara." He kissed her again.

"My lord? We could finish this later," one of the commanders said.

Sebastien laughed. "We are that obvious, are we?" He turned back to her. "I would ask your leave, my lady. There are things that must be finished now." He did not look happy about it, but she knew the truth of it.

"As you wish, my lord. I will await you in our chambers," she answered as she sank into a deep curtsy.

He said nothing in reply, although the wanting that showed on his face told her so much. Her body reacted to it, warming in preparation for his claiming. Lara walked through the hall to the tower steps.

Callum stepped out of the corridor and stopped before her. "My lady," he said with a bow of his head.

"What is it that you need, Callum?" She suspected she knew the topic, since Callum was one of Eachann's men here in the keep. She'd known since the day she listened to Sebastien and James Douglas through the wall. He'd warned her of Sebastien's approach.

"That was quite a show, my lady. He is already fascinated by you—this should keep your duties to Eachann a secret still."

"Callum, I am done with that. My cousin has no place here any longer." She felt stronger now knowing that she had her husband's protection.

"You may think that, but Eachann will have something to say, something you might not like." He stared at the bruise on her face and nodded. "That is nothing compared to what he can do, will do, if you betray him."

"Callum, I will not tell my lord of your mixed loyalties yet, but I would suggest that you consider joining my father's household wherever he is. And do so with haste."

The old man started at her words. It was not what he expected to hear, since Lara had always been an obedient child and woman. Until now. Until Sebastien's love showed her that there was a life without fear to be had as his wife.

Callum seemed to collect himself. "And I willna inform your cousin of this change of heart, my lady. 'Tis you who should be thinking of your place and the results of this." He gestured to where she'd stood while making her oath to Sebastien. "It could be dangerous when Eachann hears of it."

Sir Hugh chose that moment to approach with a question, and she dismissed the old man with a wave of her hand.

"My lady," the knight began, and then lowered his voice. "My lord says that your presence is a distraction to him."

Lara found it difficult not to smile. She turned around and noticed Sebastien, indeed all of his men, staring at her. Her smile broke out then and she curtsied again and climbed the stairs to wait for him.

Stunned by her public commitment and surprised by the manner in which she did it, Sebastien found it difficult to concentrate on the important matters under discussion. All he could hear in his mind were her words: *to be true and faithful, and to love all that he loves and to shun all that he shuns.*

He recognized some of the words she spoke from the ceremonies he'd witnessed when Robert was crowned at Scone two years earlier and the nobles present there submitted to him as king.

The giving of his own oath to the king had been much simpler, since no lands or titles were exchanged. Sebastien held the lands only as royal warden and guardian of Malcolm and not in his own right. When that time came, he would use words very similar to what Lara had spoken to him.

The silence caught his attention and he realized that he'd stopped speaking in the middle of his explanation of the attack plan. His men, he could see, knew exactly what was pulling his focus from them. Sebastien tried to gather his thoughts, but he could not remember what he'd been saying when the most wonderful images flashed before him. From earthy to ethereal, they all involved Lara.

He stared at the doorway across the hall that would lead to her. She had given her body and soul and her heart to him, and everyone in Dunstaffnage had heard it. Without hesitation, she'd pledged to him of her own free will. The things that he'd always wanted, the things that mattered in life, were about to be his now that Lara had made her choice.

Someone was coughing quite loudly and he shook his head to clear his thoughts, and turned to the men again. "Yes, Hugh. Are you having some problem?"

"Aye, my lord. I am having some difficulty absorbing the news."

"The news? Has there been news?" What had he missed while thinking about the woman who waited for him above stairs?

"I find myself quite moved by the sight of Lady MacDougall pledging herself to you. Quite moved," he said, not even trying to be serious. "What do you think, men? Were you not affected by the emotional scene before us?" Hugh held his hand out, gesturing to the others to add their comments.

"Quite moved," called out Connor.

"I, as well, my lord," said another.

"So moving it was, my lord, that I would beg a short respite to reorganize my thoughts."

"A respite, my lord!" It was Connor again.

"A short time, my lord. To regain our…attention to the matters at hand," Hugh explained.

Though tempted not to give in, and to fight the urge to go to her immediately, he caught the smiles and knowing glances of his men and the others in the hall. Giving up the battle, he nodded, threw down the parchment he was holding, and strode through the hall toward the north tower…and her.

"'Twould seem that my lord has decided to take a respite," Hugh said loudly, and his men joined in the laughter.

Sebastien did not care. There would be time later to finish their plans. Hell, they were almost complete now. His feet moved without effort up the stairs, past the astonished gazes of the guards, whom he ordered away now. When he reached the outer room, he paused for only a moment before entering their chambers.

She stood much the same as the day of their wedding—before the window, with her hair loose and flowing down over her shoulders. Most of the time she wore it braided and covered, and he was pleased to see it thusly. Nothing encouraged his rampant desire as much as the thought of tangling his hands in it and stroking its silkiness.

Lara faced him and this time it was she who held out her arms and he who walked into her embrace. Sebastien lifted her off her feet and held her high enough off the floor that her toes could not touch. Without taking his gaze from hers, he kissed her on the mouth and then let her slide down his body.

"You are mine, now, my lady," he said as he took her lips again and again.

Lara leaned back and laughed at him. "As you are mine, my lord." Then she kissed him with her mouth open, mimicking the way he always kissed her.

"You make me wild, Lara. I fear I cannot hold back what I am feeling for you right at this moment."

"Then do not hold back," she said quietly.

His body tightened, and his cock, which had been hard from the moment she knelt before him, now rose even more. His heart pounded and he found it difficult to stop kissing her.

"But your poor face," he said.

"You will not hurt me, Sebastien. I do not fear your passion."

"And I do not fear yours. Let it go and let us revel in it."

"Aye, my lord. It is as you wish and command."

Her saucy tone excited him more and his body reacted by hardening as he slid his hands to the back of her neck and untied the laces there. He was not certain how all of their clothing was removed, but in a few minutes they stood naked next to the bed. There were so many things he wanted to do, so many places on her body that he wanted to touch and taste. There were so many ways he wanted to draw out that moan that she made when overwhelmed by pleasure.

"You appear to be confused, my lord."

He threw back his head and laughed. "There is so

much I want to share with you. So many thoughts and desires are racing through my thoughts and I do not know where to begin."

"Start by simply loving me. The rest will come as we go."

"That sounds good to me."

He started with a kiss. He touched his lips to hers gently and drew her closer. He felt her hands gliding over his skin, around his waist and even down onto his arse. He arched into her, unable to stop and wanting more. He was careful not to touch that side of her face where the bruising was. Sebastien led her to the bed and he sat on it…and smiled. The height of it and his own height put his mouth directly in front of her breasts. Spreading his legs, he pulled her between them and kissed her breasts.

As he watched, her head fell back and she began to make the enticing throaty sound that spoke of pleasure. Her nipples tightened and he moved from one to the other, licking and sucking on them until she did moan. Steadying her with his hands on her hips, he moved his mouth down to her belly and kissed almost to the place between her legs. He felt her clutch at his head, and laughed.

"Am I pleasing you, wife?"

He did not wait for her response in words, for her body answered him and, as he slid his hand between her legs and into the very core of her, wept a welcome for him. She shook and her legs trembled as he continued to draw that moisture out and spread it on the swollen bud there. She shuddered and shivered as he pressed his palm against it, and he felt her tightening around his fingers.

Lara was so close to her edge and he wanted to be inside of her, filling her, when she reached it. He slid backward on the bed and helped her climb up. Instead of laying her next to him, he guided her across his legs until she sat facing him. Taking a moment and hoping it prolonged what was to come, he moved her legs around his hips and bent his legs around her to keep her where he wanted her. With little effort, he pushed forward and entered her. Although doing so nearly killed him, he sat unmoving until she opened her eyes and looked at him.

"You stopped?" she said, in a husky, passion-filled voice.

"Aye, my lady." He held her steady with his arms wrapped around her. From chest to hips and more, they were touching each other without using their hands.

She squirmed, or tried to, but he was stronger and held her fast. "My lord, this is not fair. Do you not want to take me?"

"'Tis simply the consequences of disturbing my work. I saw the way you moved your hips as you walked out. You knew I would be thinking of doing this." He arched now, pushing more deeply into her and then drawing out. "And this," he said as he repeated it. She did not resist him, indeed when urged on by his hands and words, she lifted herself closer so that he could capture the tips of her breasts with his mouth.

"Sebastien!" she cried out. He could feel the tension in her body and knew she wanted release. He was simply not ready to give in.

"Are you aching for me, Lara?" He took the now tender nipples between his first two fingers and squeezed them gently, then rubbed his thumbs across them until she screamed. Then he released them and blew on the tight buds to soothe them. Another shudder shook her, but still no release.

His own body screamed for it, too. He knew it was close, but he drew in and let out a couple of deep breaths until he felt more in control. But that did not relieve the tightness of her sheath around his cock. Or the heat and wetness that so aroused him.

"Sebastien," she whispered. "Please? Please now? It aches like an itch that needs scratching, and I cannot reach it."

"Then let me help you, love. Give me your hand," he said as he took her fingers and guided them down between their bodies. He moved his fingers around hers and spread the wet folds until he—they—could touch the treasure within. "Can you reach it now? Move your fingers with mine." He waited for her to follow his instructions. She gasped once, and then again and again, as their fingers teased and touched the center of her ache.

"I cannot…" she began, and then the words trailed off as her peak came upon her. He felt it probably before she did, for it spread from inside her sheath out to the bud they teased togethered. Her body tightened and arched against his hands and around his cock. He thought he might come, but he was watching the expressions on her face and managed to hold it back.

She keened, emitting that sound, and he was ready. Lifting her from his lap, he slid down on the bed and settled her over his legs, on her knees this time so she could move. Lara knelt above him now, with her hair streaming over both of them. He took two handfuls and wrapped his fists in it, pulling her forward to his mouth.

Her expression was one of confusion when she gazed down at his hardness. "Will you not take me?"

"Nay, lady. 'Tis your turn to be doing the taking. I promise not to resist you too much."

"I can take you?"

"Oh, aye. I know your skills in riding. Ride me, Lara."

After considering it for a moment, she smiled, and he knew that, more likely than not, it was the same smile on another face that had tempted Adam to sin in the Garden of Eden. When she began to move and then found her gait, he knew it for certain.

He stroked the fistfuls of hair over her belly as she moved against him, and then up to her breasts. She gasped with every touch, and he knew she would come again. He arched his hips against her, aiding her movements and filling her more with every thrust. Then he felt his seed ready to burst forth and he did not to resist it. The muscles deep within her contracted again and again and pulled every drop from him.

He smiled, satisfied in more ways than just the physical joining. This felt so right. As if he belonged here, he was home. He waited for her to collapse, which she did a moment later. He held her tightly and rubbed his hands over her back.

"I do love you, Sebastien," she whispered to him. "In spite of the mistakes I've made, I truly do love you."

"Hush, now, Lara. We will both make mistakes along the way. The important thing is that we have found love and it will help us in times of doubt and trouble."

She did not answer him. He knew there were many secrets she still held, as did he, but together they would find their way. He rolled to his side and gathered her close.

"All will be well."

It was at that moment that he realized in his haste to bed her, he'd left the doors to their chambers open, as well as on the landing below. Most likely, everyone in the hall had heard every sound between them. Lara would be most grievously embarrassed.

As sorry as he was over that, and he was, it was best if they learned now what life would be like as they accepted their marriage. He would keep her in his arms and in his bed as much as possible once he returned home from the next two battles.

Home.

Aye, he was truly home.

Chapter Eighteen

"No, Philippe."

"But my lord… 'Tis my place to be at your side."

Sebastien let out a frustrated breath. "I would rather you be here to help my lady wife while I am away from Dunstaffnage."

"But, I was there at your side at the Brander Pass. I have trained. I am ready," Philippe said with all the bravado of one of ten-and-two years. But his mutinous feelings were demonstrated with a quivering lower lip. Malcolm's influence on the boy, no doubt.

Sebastien turned to Lara for help in this matter. He did not want Philippe at his side, especially if treachery was in the air. Not certain if she or anyone else had known the details of their plans, he would rather not take the chance and put the boy in danger. As commander of this raid, he and his men would be in enough peril without the added complication of a boy.

"Philippe, Malcolm will be devastated if anything happens to you, and he would welcome your company while your master is away," Lara said to the lad. "And I would be happy for your help while my lord is gone."

But even her soft tones and lovely smile did not wipe the displeasure off his squire's face. There was simply no other way to do this.

"Philippe, you are nearing the time when you will train as a knight. If you cannot obey my orders, I cannot accept you into training." Sebastien crossed his arms over his chest and glared at him. "So, what is your answer?"

Philippe looked at him, then Hugh, Etienne and Lara before replying. "As you command, my lord," he said, bowing to Sebastien. But his face wore a frown of disappointment that nothing would remove. Sebastien knew; he'd worn one himself enough times to recognize it.

"You are my responsibility, Philippe. I must answer to your father, to the king and to my conscience if I allow harm to befall you."

"I understand, my lord."

"Nay, you do not now, but one day, when a boy in your service stands before you with just such a look on his face, you will," Sebastien said, trying to soften the blow to the youth's honor. "Now, I must speak with Sir Hugh and my lady. See to your duties."

Philippe left as he was ordered and Sebastien turned to the truly difficult conversation of the day...or the week...or his life. He had never left behind a wife, a woman he loved, before. He had never tried to prepare anyone for a death that might come at any time. Hell, he never thought on it at all, but now there was so much to worry about.

"Etienne, did you bring the box?" he asked.

"Aye, my lord," the steward replied, holding out the wooden chest that Sebastien used for all of his private papers. "Would you like me to leave?"

"Nay. I want you and Hugh to know what I have done so there is no question of my wishes." He took in a deep breath and let it out, not yet meeting Lara's eyes. "In here is my will," he began.

"No!" she cried out. "Do not talk of such things, Sebastien. There is no need." Her eyes filled with tears and his own throat tightened as he continued his explanation.

"Lady, I would know that you are cared for if something should happen to me. Not just this day, but for all days forward from now."

"I do not like this, my lord," she insisted. "I do not!" She clasped her hands together and laid them in her lap. He could see that they were shaking.

"Your expression looks remarkably like the one Philippe was just wearing. Mayhap he learned it from you?" He watched her face for a sign that his attempt at levity was working. If anything, her visage became grimmer.

"Upon my death, the lands given to me as your dowry will be returned to you to use or sell as you wish. Malcolm's guardianship, with the king's approval, will be granted to you and Hugh together, as will that of Catriona. Hugh will serve as royal warden of Dunstaffnage until the time when Malcolm can pledge himself, or not, to Robert. There are a few other personal bequests—" he smiled at Lara "—but those are the clauses you need to know about in the presence of each other."

"If you are through, I would like to be excused," she said without meeting his gaze.

He knew this was a thorny matter, but he had never before had lands, and a wife, to worry about. She was scared. Part of him, that part within his heart that loved her, was thrilled that she cared so much. Part of him, again the part that loved her, was terrified that he might not return to her. His emotions, since the day she'd pledged herself to him, were a jumbled mess.

"I will finish with Hugh and Etienne in a short time." He held out his hand to her and she took it. He kissed her fingers as she stood, then released her.

They waited for her to leave the hall, then he invited Hugh and Etienne to sit. There were other things that needed to be spoken of before he left. Lara thought he would depart in the morning, but he preferred the cover of night to aid their movements north.

"I would have you both follow her orders as if they were mine."

"What do you mean, Sebastien? You leave *her* in charge?" Hugh asked.

"Aye, I do. She has the knowledge and the experience to protect the place. Even more importantly, as my wife, she has the right."

"She is a MacDougall. How can you trust her?"

"We cannot choose the blood that runs in our veins, Hugh, but we can choose those whom we trust. I trust her in this."

"'Tis not your arse in danger if she changes sides again," Hugh said, swearing under his breath.

"If any other man had uttered those words, he would

be dead. 'Ware your words about the lady," Sebastien whispered.

Hugh realized how close he'd come to trouble then, and he nodded his acceptance of the rebuke.

"The only time this castle has been taken, it was done by deceit and trickery. With you at her side, there will be no way for that to happen again. Keep her and the children inside the walls during the day and within the keep at night. Let no one in if neither you nor Etienne know them personally. I will handle any problems when I return."

"Does the lady know of these instructions?"

"Not yet. But I will speak to her about them and about your power to overrule her if you think she makes a dangerous or foolhardy decision."

"And if she does not accept my ruling?" Hugh seemed to be thinking of all the potential rough spots in the road ahead.

"Lock her and the children in the north tower. Tie her up if need be, just do not allow her on the battlements or out to the chapel." They had yet to discover the secret entrance there that he knew must exist.

"I understand about the church, but the battlements?"

"She can, I suspect, climb as well as James Douglas. I do not think you need worry, but I thought you should know."

Hugh whistled. "Is there no end to the lady's skills?"

"Etienne, carry on only the resupplying that you can with the limitations I have placed on visitors inside the castle. If we must make someone wait a day or two at most for supplies, so be it. I will answer to the king.

"Now, if you have no questions, I am to bed for a short rest before we leave." He handed the box back to Etienne for safekeeping.

Neither man said anything, so he nodded to each of them and walked to the tower stairs. Everything was ready for his departure—the men, the boats, the weapons. Everything but himself. But that would be handled when he spoke to his wife.

Well, the sooner started, the sooner finished, he thought as he climbed the last few steps. Of all the duties he'd carried out in his life, he'd faced none to prepare him for what waited inside his chamber. He opened the door quietly and found the room dark, save for one candle by the bed.

Lara sat in the chair, wrapped in a blanket. At first he thought her asleep, but she whispered a greeting to him. He walked to where she sat, and asked her to stand. When she did, he sat down and pulled her onto his lap.

"I do not know how you can sit for so long in this chair. It is the most uncomfortable piece of furniture I have ever used."

"It was my father's chair," she said softly.

"Aye, it makes sense. A hard chair for a hard man." He shifted and then repositioned her so he could see her face as they spoke. "Now, if this were another foot or so wider, it would have its uses."

"As what? 'Tis a chair." She frowned and shrugged.

"You see, love. With more room on each side, your knees could slide in here and we could…you could…" He let his words drift off. At her beautiful blush, he knew she understood what he meant. "And you could use the back to steady yourself for the ride." He moved his hands there to give her some idea of it.

"It would be worth trying," she said, smiling this time.

"Now, before I carry you to that bed and wear you out with my affections, there are a few more things you must know."

"Sebastien, please do not say more." She placed her fingers over his lips. "I cannot bear to think on such things."

"Once I am assured that you know the essential information, I will not say another word about these arrangements." She nodded and he explained. "You are to hold the castle until I return."

"Hold the castle? But Sir Hugh…"

"Hugh will be at your side, but the decisions are yours. For your safety and the children's, you must stay within the castle walls—no chapel and no battlements."

"I have not gone to the chapel since…" She stopped abruptly and nodded her assent.

"And you will not until the secret entrance is found and sealed." He paused, for he had never asked her directly about her knowledge of Eachann's escape. "Do you know where it is or where it leads?"

"I only know that it is in the wall behind the altar. I did not detect how he opened it or closed it. He threw me to the ground and then left through it. I did not see."

"Eachann seems to have left the area, but I cannot be certain. So, stay within the castle."

"And the battlements? You know that I love to walk there."

"Mayhap with Hugh or Connor or Jamie at your

side, but not alone. An arrow shot from many different places could reach there."

"Very well, I will stay off the battlements," she agreed. "But now tell me what you hesitate to say. It must be bad for you to hold it in for so long."

He kissed her then and laughed at how close to the truth she came. "Hugh has the power to overrule any decision you make if he thinks it a danger to you or the children or my men or the castle." He waited for the explosion and the anger that did not come.

"A sound decision."

"What? I thought you would be opposed to it." He lifted her chin so he could see her eyes.

"I would not have Dunstaffnage fall again on my account."

"Lara, you are softhearted and I do not want to see anything happen because you could not make the decision needed. Hugh knows you are to be obeyed unless there is some extreme situation."

She nodded and then curled up against his chest. "How long will you be gone?"

"If all goes as planned, no more than three days."

"So, it is close, then?"

"We sail to Glen Gour on Ardgour, across the firth to the north."

"Have a care, Sebastien. My father sails those waters…"

"I will, and I will send word if we are delayed." He shifted in the chair and slid his arms under her legs. "If we are done talking, there are still some things I must say before I can sleep."

He stood and carried her to the bed. Laying her on

it, he stripped off his clothes and boots and knelt next to her. Peeling back the blanket and lifting the chemise over her head, he loved her with everything in him and made certain she knew it. As he entered her body with his, he let his love spill out to her.

"Lady of my heart," he whispered.

"Forever," she answered. And, when she gifted him with the passionate sound he would never tire of hearing, he knew he would remember it to his dying day.

Chapter Nineteen

It was a shameless act, performed before so many that it could not be denied later when she came to her senses. So blatant as to not be mistaken for anything else. Lara's face flamed now even thinking on it.

Three days had passed since he'd left in the night from her bed to go off on this mission of the king's. Three long days and three torturous nights when she'd lain awake and worried about what her father and cousin were arranging to thwart the Bruce's, and her husband's, plans.

She'd managed well enough in the light of day. After ordering one of the carpenters to work on her new piece of furniture, she set herself to work on the other things needed. Keeping her hands busy somehow made it bearable, and the thoughts of the terrible things that could happen to Sebastien did not take hold until the night.

Her dreams were filled with images of his broken and torn body being dropped at her feet by Eachann. Her father was there as well, calling her all the foul names that the Bruce's soldiers had used against her. When she ran from them, they were behind her or in front of her and to her side. The third time she woke up screaming loudly enough to draw Margaret's attention, she knew sleep would escape her grasp until Sebastien was home safely.

Malcolm and Philippe took to avoiding her—the lack of sleep and the constant worrying over Sebastien made her a miserable companion. Catriona was using her favorite word again, but now used it to refer to Lara's mood. Lara knew she should have more patience toward the child; however, at the tenth use of that word she lost any hope of decorum and ordered her out of the keep. She knew that Sir Hugh had quietly countermanded her orders, but she chose to ignore that.

She'd almost succeeded in regaining control over herself when that damned James Douglas arrived. Just his appearance was bad enough in her eyes, but when he sat at her table, in Sebastien's seat, and would say nothing to her about her husband's condition or whereabouts, she threatened to use one of Philippe's training swords on his "valuable bits." After crossing himself and then making a hasty retreat, he relocated himself and his men to the barracks outside the castle walls.

Then Sebastien was there, just off to the west in the firth, heading for the shore and the dock. He stood in the boat and waved—she was sure it was to her as she watched from the battlements—but she could not raise her arm in greeting. Instead, just as he stepped off the boat and was welcomed by Hugh and James and Etienne, she crumpled on the stone walkway and sobbed so hard that she lost her breath.

Lara heard his voice in the yard and tried to stand. One of the guards came running to her and helped her, crying out to Sebastien at the same time. She was on her feet when Sebastien reached the battlements and called out her name. Leaning against the wall and uncertain of what his true mission had been, she said what came to mind first.

"Did you kill my father this time?"

Horrified at the insult, she put up her hands to fend him off. Then, even worse, with everyone watching from the yard and from the battlements, she called out to him.

"And I do not love you!"

He continued his direct path to her and waved the guards off as he neared her. Putting his hands on his hips, he challenged her. "Oh, yes you do, lass. And I love you, too."

Overwhelmed and exhausted by worry and lack of sleep, she could not think of what to do or say next. She stood and waited for him to make some move. All he did was hold out his arms, and she ran to him. Jumping into his embrace, she wrapped herself around him and just breathed him in.

"Here now, love," he whispered to her. "I know it has been difficult for you since I've been gone."

She leaned into the curve of his shoulder and let his strength seep into her. "I have not slept since you left. I have offended most of your men and all of my family. And I chased James Douglas out of my keep."

"So I heard. James appealed to me on the docks and said he would not enter until I did something about you."

"He said that?" Now that Sebastien was holding her, none of it seemed important. "'Twas his fault, after all. Sitting in your place and not speaking a word about you." She shook her head. "Oh, Sebastien, it has been horrendous without you. *I* have been horrendous."

"So, Cat still uses that word? You have not been able to entice her from it with something new?" She shook her head again. "Come, then. Now that I am home we will have to try."

He walked down the stairs, through the hall and then back up to their chambers without ever letting her go. It was a shameful display, both her actions and her words, but most especially the way that she clung to him as though she were a clinging vine on his wall.

No one spoke as they passed by. Finally, they were in their chambers, and she knew he'd seen her gift as soon as he began to laugh. He released her legs and she tried to stand. It took her a few times before she was able to let him go. Then, the expression on his face was worth all her efforts.

It was one plank wider than her father's chair, and deeper in the seat area. She'd sewn pillows and a cover for both this new one and the old one, and they made for much more comfortable sitting. She could see the exact moment when he thought of the use for such a chair.

"An excellent welcoming gift, but I fear I would not put it to good use this day."

"Oh, Sebastien! I have not even given a thought to your needs." She would never survive this kind of life with him—watching him leave on the king's business and never knowing what he would face or if he would return to her.

"Etienne has set up food and drink for the men in the hall, love. Fret not over that."

She scanned his body, from head to toe and back again. "Have you been injured? Did you lose any men?" She shook her head. "What happened at Glen Gour?"

He lifted his hauberk over his head and fussed with the mail under it. "Not much. We approached in the hour at dawn. Some of my men climbed the walls and overpowered the guards and opened the gates. When the laird woke to our swords at his throat, he surrendered."

"You sound disappointed."

"Nay, not in taking a keep without losing a man. Just confused, for I expected more resistance. But," he said, finally lifting the mail over his head with her help, "there is simply no way of knowing what to expect."

"Do not your spies tell you those kinds of details?"

"Aye, most times. However, until a man is threatened with losing his life or those he loves, there is no knowing how he will act." Stretching his arms over his head, he moaned. "I did not realize how unaccustomed I was to wearing this lately. Three days and nights in mail is enough to suit anyone." He dropped it in the corner and walked her across the bedchamber.

"I do not want to soil the bed with this sweat and grime. There is a bath waiting for me in the kitchens and I shall return as soon as I am clean and have eaten something. Will you wait here for me? Warm my bed until I can warm you?"

Truth be told, now that he mentioned it, she realized she was exhausted, and the thought of crawling into the bed and waiting for him was quite appealing at this moment.

"Aye, I will wait for you here," she answered.

He helped her into bed and smoothed her hair away from her face. It felt so good and so comforting that she could sense the sleep that had eluded her these last days finally within her reach.

"Sebastien?" She called his name and he leaned down and kissed her mouth sweetly.

"Aye, love. I am still here."

"I know that I have been horrendous to everyone while you were gone. I do admit it to you, but I cannot apologize for worrying over you."

"It warms my heart to know that you love me, my lady."

"Aye, my lord, I do love you."

She remembered nothing after that, until a night and a day and another night hence.

"My lord, I beg of you! If you must leave, either take me with you or take the lady. I could not stand another three days as the last ones have been."

Sebastien laughed. "You are whining like a babe, Hugh. I thought you a better man than that."

"In God's name, Sebastien, she chased the Black Douglas, the scourge of Scotland, from your hall! That should say something about the events here since you left." Hugh rubbed his face and drank half of the ale in his tankard.

"Better yet, send her into your enemy's keep and I promise she will drive them out, screaming like madmen, within a few days," James added sarcastically. "She could be the Bruce's secret weapon."

"I thought that was you, James."

"I would gladly yield the honor to the lady. This could be the turning point in the war."

The men up and down the length of the table, some who had traveled with him or with the Douglas and some who had remained on duty here, laughed at the thought. Sebastien knew it was all in jest, but he needed to make it clear that no one could malign his wife.

"When she cares, she does it from deep within her heart. I am honored that she has chosen to feel this way about me."

"Just so," Hugh called out as he held his tankard high. "To the lady! Huzzah!"

"To my lady!" Sebastien added, and he drank deeply in her honor. Once the men went back to drinking and eating, he turned his attention to his friends. "James, tell me of your raid."

"'Twas the same as yours. They did not know we were coming and I had my men over the walls before they woke."

"Mayhap MacDougall resistance is broken? Eachann has not been seen or heard from in some time. The MacDougall is in the waters to the west and makes no secret of his appointment by Edward. My spies and yours have reported no large movement of troops in the area," Sebastien explained. James and Hugh nodded. "Or possibly taking Dunstaffnage has accomplished what Robert sought to do—a base with enough presence and enough men to awe those left behind when John went to England?"

"And the winter comes soon. Anything left unsettled then waits until spring," Hugh added.

"True," James said. "So, let us plan this final attack so that we can all settle in for a long Highland winter."

"Dear God in Heaven!" Hugh exclaimed under his breath. "Please say that I will go with you. Do not, I beg you in the name of all things holy, do not leave me with her again. Not this soon."

Sebastien smacked him on the back and laughed. "I would trust no other with her—she is that dear to me."

He permitted Hugh to grumble for a few more minutes, and then turned the talk to their plans. James had already sent half of his men on ahead to begin the approach to Invercreran. Now finished with Glen Gour and Awe, they would join forces and take for the Bruce the last holdout keep of any importance in the area.

They would prepare their attack and leave within a few days. No need to let word spread too widely that Robert's men were on the move. Of course, that meant telling Lara, and even worse, it meant leaving her again.

"I always knew that when some woman stole your heart, you would fall hard," James said quietly.

"Harder than I ever thought possible," Sebastien answered. "I want this over and done so I can enjoy the fruits of my labors."

"And the lady?" James added with a raised brow.

"And the lady," he answered.

Her reaction was much better than he or anyone in Dunstaffnage thought could happen. She heard him out and accepted his words. She asked many, many questions and pointed out flaws in their plans. She repeated her concerns about their safety. But, she did not lose control as she had when last he left.

They spent their time preparing for his departure, and it was not until the night he went that she demonstrated how far they'd come in their love.

Lara had looked at him with horror in her eyes when he revealed his plan to take Philippe along on this mission. Between their uncontested raids on Glen Gour and Awe, and the presence of James and his men, Sebastien believed this would be an acceptable mission for his squire and soon-to-be knight-in-training to accompany his lord.

"Please, Sebastien, I beg you, do not take the boy."

"Lara, 'tis his place and 'tis time for him to learn."

She knelt before him and took hold of his hand. "My lord, my father and my cousin are ruthless and will stop at nothing to kill you."

"How do you know this?" he asked. He suspected that Eachann was making bold claims and promises, but had no direct knowledge of it.

"He said it to me that night in the chapel. Your insult to the MacDougall honor by using our priory for the Bruce's gathering has made this a matter of personal vengeance for them. The loss at Brander Pass does not sting as much as that."

He'd known what he was doing, and had insulted their honor on purpose. Now he knew that they knew. He smiled.

She stood and shook her head. "You wanted him to know? It was part of your plan that they should know?"

"Aye, Lara, for I enjoyed the chance to run roughshod over their honor and squash their treasonous arses into

the ground. What good is an insult if they know not
of it?"

She screamed and he backed away. "So, this is a
game to you as well? You and Eachann prick at each
other to see the blood flow. When does it stop?"

"With one of our deaths. 'Tis the only way it can
end."

Her face paled and she shook her head once more.
"Have a care, my lord, and watch for the ambush.
Eachann is intent on your death and I would not have
him succeed." She began to turn away and then looked
at him once more with haunted eyes. "Keep Philippe
close, my lord. Protect the boy."

"I protect those who are mine, Lara. Nothing will
happen to him."

They spoke no more of it and he departed in the
night while she slept. It was easier than seeing her on
the battlements as he left.

Chapter Twenty

They'd been gone for seven days and, with the passing of each one, her fear and anxiety grew. If Sir Hugh noticed it or thought it unreasonable for the circumstances, he said nothing. Lara controlled her behavior better this time, but the knowledge that her family knew of this coming attack terrified her in a way she could reveal to no one.

The tension finally drove her from the hall to her chambers. Unable to pace away some of it in view of Sebastien's people, she sought the privacy of the tower. And pace she did. Minutes and hours passed as she stood at the window, walked to the cold, empty hearth and back again. Sometimes she sat in Sebastien's chair and tried to push away the guilt within her.

Lara knew she'd caused many deaths this day, some within her clan and some of her husband's warriors. Try as she might, she found it impossible to think of them as only the enemy now. She lived with them. She ate and drank with them. She knew their names. The acts she attempted to justify to herself as rightful resistance to an illegitimate ruler screamed out at her when the truth of her efforts sank in.

People would die because of the plans she'd forwarded to her father.

Mayhap even her husband.

The husband she loved.

Her stomach rolled at the thought of him dead. She could see in her mind his tall form lying slashed and bleeding on the cold, hard ground. His face twisted in the grimace of death. The expressive light in his eyes extinguished because of her words. The meager contents of her belly pushed their way up and she barely pulled the pot from under the bed before they escaped her control. Wave after wave of nausea pulsed through her. Then, empty and spent, she fell onto her side on the floor.

Was he dead? Had she killed Sebastien?

Lara pushed the hair out of her face and took in some slow breaths, trying to calm the tremors that shook her. Her stomach began to calm and she dared to sit up. With a huge amount of concentration, she did not collapse. When she felt stronger, she grasped the covers of the bed and used them as support to gain her feet.

This was why women did not involve themselves in war. Oh, aye, they were victims often enough of the violence of men's conflicts, but this was too hard to do. Living in oblivion while her father planned the death of his—their—enemies was much preferable to being a part of it. How did people live with knowing they killed both innocents and willing participants? How did they form friendships or care about anyone, when they might send them to their deaths with a word? 'Twas too much to bear.

Lara stumbled to the window and opened it to the cool night air. Letting it pass over and around her, she tried to understand the difference between men's souls and those of women. She had known, but never accepted, that the results of her actions would end this way. Now, the truth was so close, so strong, that the reality made it difficult to take a breath.

A sudden clamor in the yard drew her attention. The drawbridge slammed down and horses and men thundered over it. At first, she thought the keep was under attack, but she recognized one of her husband's men carrying his banner, and knew he was here. Tears poured down freely and she sobbed out before she could control it. He was alive.

He was alive.

Then she saw him ride through the inner gate toward the keep. He looked neither left nor right and sat stiffly on his mount. One of the stable boys rushed forward and grabbed the reins from him as he slipped from the saddle. Even from this distance, Lara could tell something was wrong.

But he was alive.

Surprised and confused once more by the strength of her relief, she stepped back from the window. Should she go and greet him? Should she stay here? His men spread throughout the yard and many others poured from the keep to assist them. She stood frozen by indecision until a noise in the hallway made her move. Rubbing the tears from her face with her sleeve, she ran to the far side of the bed and waited for him to enter.

The door of the chamber flew open and slammed into the wall. She jumped at the force of it. Watching from across the room, Lara saw several of Sebastien's retainers enter, carrying his targe, his sword and helmet. Usually Philippe carried those for his lord, but she did not see him among those crowding the chamber. Then Sebastien was there.

She drank in the sight of him filling the doorway, outlined by the torches held behind him. Servants followed him, carrying buckets of water and jugs and platters. Who had ordered this? Etienne had obviously carried out his duties as steward, even as she failed in hers as lady.

Staying in the shadows of the room, she watched as Sebastien walked over to the window and allowed others to take the last remnants of battle from him. After his armor was removed and the worst of the blood washed from his face and hands, he waved everyone out, and still she waited. The door closed quietly, almost reverently, and Lara wondered what to say to him or if he even knew she was there.

With obvious effort, he took the few steps to his chair and collapsed into it, landing hard on its wide, sturdy seat. He leaned his head back and closed his eyes, and she could feel his despair and sadness before he spoke of anything. What had happened?

"My lord?" The words were out before she could stop them. He did not move or acknowledge her, so she thought he must have known she was there. Lara edged closer to the light and closer to him. "Are you injured?"

His words were near to a whisper. "Aye, I am that."

She took another cautious step toward him. "Should I call for Philippe? He could summon Gara the healer."

"Philippe is dead, Lara."

Her breath hitched and the very air around her sparkled before her eyes, blurring her vision. Philippe was dead? How could this be? He was more child than man and not trained for battle.

"Dead?"

"His only sin was that he carried my banner. Your uncle and his allies cut him down rather than fighting me. They used that boy to draw me away and killed him without a moment's thought."

His words, cold and empty, filled her with horror. Philippe was full of life and humor. He'd always had a ready word of reassurance for her. He had made friends with her brother and kept him company when he was not at his duties.

Philippe was…dead. Nothing could stop the tears now, but as she was unable to speak, they fell into the anguished silence that surrounded them.

He pushed himself to his feet and began to peel off the layers he still wore. The steam from his body escaped into the chill air of the room, reminding her once more of her failures and her guilt. If he noticed that the hearth was empty, he did not mention it. Then, when she thought he would climb into the bed without saying more, he broke the silence. His voice was frightening in its bitterness.

"Someone will pay for this betrayal. I will find those responsible and I will see them hanged in my yard in punishment for the lives they took this day."

"My lord?" she asked, praying that her own guilt was not made clear by the shaking of her voice. Clenching her teeth and clasping her hands tightly to keep them still, she waited for him to say more.

"They knew my plans. They knew too much. I will discover the spies among us and they will pay in unimaginable ways before I allow death to release them for what they have done." His face hardened with the vehemence of his pledge, and she backed away, afraid of him as she had never been before. For the first time since his return, he faced her.

"I do not want to look on another MacDougall this night. Go now from here. Sleep elsewhere. I have not the strength left to pretend that I feel otherwise."

Lara stumbled back against the door as she lost her balance, terrified by the hatred that spilled out of him. Try as she might to keep the sobs within her, they erupted. Fueled by honest grief and dishonest guilt, she cried out as she ran from the room, down the hallway and stairs and out into the courtyard. Grabbing up her skirts, she staggered through the confusion of men and animals and raced out the gate and across the drawbridge. If anyone tried to stop her, she knew not. Blinded by tears and the dark, she ran to the only place that had ever held any refuge for her. As it was now the site of her worst betrayal, she wondered if peace could be found there.

Entering the chapel, she struggled toward the altar. Falling to her knees, she prayed for forgiveness for causing so many deaths with her betrayals. All she could see was Philippe's face before her, and her imaginings of his death tormented her. Unable to even kneel, she fell prostrate on the steps and cried out her grief and guilt and sorrow until she was spent. Exhausted, and with no other place that would welcome her, Lara fell asleep on the cold stone floor.

Before dawn came, she roused from her troubled sleep to the sound of the doors of the chapel opening. Sir Hugh stood outside. Struggling to her feet, she waited on his word, half expecting him to accuse her. Instead, he did something much more horrible. Stepping back, he allowed two soldiers to enter. They carried a plank between them and on the plank was a body.

"There is a priest on his way to say the Mass for him," Hugh said, his voice flat and devoid of any emotion. "Sebastien would not leave him behind."

Lara walked to meet them and lifted the bloody sheet that covered the boy's body. Philippe appeared to be sleeping, his face unmarred by whatever death blow had killed him. As she raised the sheet more, Hugh took her wrist to stop her.

"Do not, lady."

She stared at him for a moment, but it was enough to make him free her hand. The boy's face was apparently the only place not touch by the violence of the battle. A grievous wound split his shoulder and neck and another cleaved open his chest. Gasping and unable to control herself, she fell to her knees and wept openly.

She had caused this. Her need to feel important. Her need to regain a place in her clan had killed this boy as surely as if she'd held the ax in her own hand. Her refusal to accept her husband and his king—and now it was too late. Too late for the boy and the others who had perished this day.

Even Malcolm had warned her that no good would come of her resistance. He had urged her to grab hold of the life that Sebastien offered her, and she had ignored him, taking the route of deception and betrayal that had led her here—to this lad's death.

Sir Hugh's strong hands clutched her shoulders and lifted her to her feet, allowing the men to carry Philippe's body to the front of the church. She stumbled after them. A boy so young should not lie alone in the dark. She knelt next to him and reached under the sheet to take hold of his hand.

"Lady, you should come now," Hugh said softly.

"Nay, someone should be with him." Lara shook her head.

"Lady, please come away?" His touch on her shoulder followed his plea.

Shrugging his hand away, she screamed out at him. "Get away from me. He should not be alone in the dark. I will stay."

She did not turn to see if they obeyed or not. Dawn could not be far away and then the priest would arrive. Until that moment, she would stay to keep Philippe company. Rubbing his cold hand, she touched it to her cheek and bowed her head to murmur a prayer she knew would be for naught.

"Forgive me, Philippe. Forgive me."

Indecision and guilt tortured her the next weeks. The Mass and burial tore the heart out of everyone at Dunstaffnage. The sight of Malcolm's thin shoulders sobbing silently at his friend's death nearly destroyed her. Cat walked the halls carrying the pieces of rope that Philippe had used to teach knot-tying. Even worse than her choice of words, the child now retreated into the silence of grief. Callum disappeared from Dunstaffnage and, to many, his departure spoke of treachery.

But no one was more painful to watch than Sebastien. He dealt with the boy's death by ignoring it and carrying on each day as though nothing had changed. Once, when he seemed to forget, and called out Philippe's name for some task, Lara ran crying from the room at the pain of it. He spoke not of it, to her nor to anyone, as much as she could tell, and she carried her grief and guilt in her heart.

Lara was able to learn the details of the raid that turned into a battle through a series of people. Sebastien gave a report of it to Hugh, who in turn shared some of it with Margaret. Then, Margaret gave her an account that made Lara's blood run cold in her veins.

When Sebastien stood frozen over Philippe's body, frozen in shock and grief, her cousin and his men had surrounded him and taunted him over the death. They'd taunted him with the treachery that had led to it, and promised they would take back Dunstaffnage and all that was theirs. It was only the quick action of James Douglas that had saved Sebastien's life and turned the battle into a complete rout. Screaming for vengeance, he'd become the Black Douglas that everyone feared, and had led the king's forces to victory.

Margaret whispered that none were left alive when they were done. Only a handful had escaped into the mountains surrounding the keep on the River Creran. Lara suspected that Eachann had survived, even if he had had to sacrifice others to insure his own safety and escape.

Sebastien finally came back to their bed after nearly a week of not sleeping, or sleeping elsewhere, but he was changed. Only once had he turned to her in that bed and made love to her, with a desperation that frightened her. Other than that, he kept his grief completely within himself. Even when word came of the Earl of Ross's surrender to the king at the end of October, it did not seem to lighten his spirits or his grief.

Truthfully, Lara knew not what to say or what to do. There was so much guilt inside her that she thought of making a confession to him. Perchance she could explain why she had done what she had, and he could forgive her? One look at his expression that day told her of her folly.

But, when her courses did not come for the second month in a row, Lara knew that she must do something, she simply knew not what. The furtive delivery of a sealed parchment to her by a man she did not know took the decision out of her hands.

Chapter Twenty-One

Lara carried the letter for more than three hours before finding the courage and a safe place to read it. Huddled in one corner of the storage rooms, she broke the seal and opened it. Once past the greetings her father wrote, his message struck fear into the very core of her.

Her role had been discovered and the king's men were on their way to Dunstaffnage to arrest her for treason. The only way to avoid it was to follow her father's instructions and escape with the children before the men arrived.

Her hands shook so badly she could scarcely read the words. She tried to steady herself and comprehend the instructions in the letter, but the terror of being found out and turned over to the king's justice made it impossible.

For a moment she allowed herself to believe that she could go to Sebastien and tell him the truth and beg for his mercy and his protection. She laughed at her folly—he was faithful first to Robert the Bruce and he would never stand between the king and a traitor, especially not one who could have prevented Philippe's death with but a word of warning.

She read the letter again. A distraction would take Sebastien's attention just before sunset, and that would be her chance to get Malcolm and Catriona and take them to the chapel. Someone would meet them and bring them to her father and safety. She should not delay in leaving, and bring nothing with her but the clothes she wore.

Lara stood and collected her thoughts. This was the only way out for her now. Once Sebastien knew the truth of her actions, he would abandon her, anyway. Even if what she suspected was true and not a result of the constant emotional strain on her these last weeks, he would never want a child from her. Once away, and when the truth became obvious, she would figure out a way to raise the child herself. The irony that his child might grow up as he had, fatherless, struck her, but she forced that aside for now. If she did not leave, her life would be forfeit.

Knowing her path at last, she left the storage rooms and returned to the north tower. Seeking the children, she stayed close to them so that she could move quickly when the time came.

She did not let herself dwell on the pain of leaving Sebastien behind. Once with her father, she would write to him and try to explain everything. And she would never see him again.

"Fire! Fire!"
The screams began just as the sun sank low in the

west, and were joined by more calls and warnings. Lara ran to the window and was aghast to see that the storage rooms were on fire. As men ran to save what they could and others brought buckets of water, she grabbed her cloak and the children's from hooks by the door of the solar.

"Come, Malcolm. Cat. We must leave the castle now."

Malcolm would have fought it, but she told him of the fire and that they must leave before it spread. She took their hands and led them down the steps, through the hall and toward the gate. Everyone was so involved with fighting to keep the fire from spreading that no one noticed them. They were through the gate and past the barracks in a short time.

She hurried the children down the path and inside the chapel and pulled the door closed. They did not have much time before someone would be there to take them to their father. She'd followed the instructions, but the heaviness in her heart made it difficult to walk away from her home...and from Sebastien. There would be time for regrets and contemplation later. For now, Lara made certain the door was secure, and then turned.

Sebastien stood before her. Her heart leaped at the sight of him.

"Lara, you must not do this," he said.

"What do you mean? Do what, my lord?" She clasped her hands to slow their trembling as she stood before the man she was about to betray for the last, and worst, time.

"Wait," he ordered her. Then he crouched down before Malcolm and Catriona and spoke to them. "Malcolm, you must take your sister back to the keep and wait for me there. It is safe now, the fire is nearly out. Do you understand? Follow the path and none will stop you until you come to the gates and find Sir Hugh."

"Malcolm, you must stay with me," Lara argued.

"I have given my word to protect you and your sisters, Malcolm. Do you believe me?" Sebastien waited for her brother's answer. She held her breath.

"Aye, my lord," the boy whispered.

"Then go now and follow my instructions." Malcolm looked at her with sad but resolute eyes. "You have my word, Malcolm," Sebastien repeated, when the lad would have wavered.

"Malcolm…"

"Lara, they must remain here at Dunstaffnage," Sebastien explained, in such a calm, rational voice that it made her want to scream. "Malcolm, do you stand by your word?"

"Aye, my lord," he answered softly, all the while his sad eyes meeting hers. He reached out and took Catriona's little hand in his and tugged her along to the door. "Farewell, Lara."

She had to look away or else she feared changing her mind as well. Sebastien led them outside and directed them on their way. Then he came back in and closed the door once more. He stood before her and just stared at her.

"Why, Lara? Why?"

"My father offered me a chance to return to my clan," she said, but the words rang untrue even as they left her lips. Giving up any attempt to mislead him, she shook her head. "How long have you known?"

"That you are one of the spies in Dunstaffnage? I suspected a connection for several weeks, but I knew for a certain just before Glen Gour. I knew before the battle when Phillippe was killed."

Ah, the darkest time in her life. The death of a child, his blood on her hands and marked on her heart forever.

"I did not mean for him to die, Sebastien. You must believe me," she pleaded, but he interrupted before she could offer any excuses.

"Who did you think would die, then? How many of my men, who you sat at table with, have you sent to their deaths? How many of your own clan died because of Eachann's use of the information you passed to him?" He stepped toward her and grabbed her by the arms. "What did you think would happen?"

"I thought you would leave!" she cried out. "Eachann said that if he…we…made things difficult that the king would give up Dunstaffnage and move on. He always has before. The Bruce does not have a standing army."

Sebastien's eyes were filled with disappointment as he watched her. "And now? What do you do now? Where were you taking the children?"

"I must leave." She said the words with as much conviction as she could. "My father sent word that the king's men are on their way to arrest me. You are not the only one, it seems, who knows of my treachery. I know that you cannot stand for me to the king, so I must accept my father's offer of escape."

"And when did you come to me and ask for my help? When did you come to me and tell me the truth?"

"When I asked you who you were, do you remember what you told me? How you defined yourself?" He frowned at her. "'First, I am a faithful vassal to my king,' you said. I could not ask you to forsake your honor for me, not when the charges are true."

"Lara—" he began.

"Nay, Sebastien, there is no other way for me. My father is regaining—"

"Nothing," he said, interrupting her. "I swear to you, Lara, that your father will not possess Dunstaffnage again while Robert is king. With the taking of Dunstaffnage and Invercreran, the Comyns, the Mac-Dougalls and their allies have been crushed. Now, with the Earl of Ross pledged to him, the only enemies that remain are Edward's forces." Sebastien took her hand in his. "You must stay here, Lara. It will not be safe for you to go if Eachann is there."

"But you know what I am. You know that I have been spying on you as your enemy. Surely you cannot promise my life or even my safety once your king discovers the truth."

"I swore to protect you, Lara. That pledge still stands."

"You will never trust me again, Sebastien. We both know that. And any love you felt for me is surely gone now that you know the truth."

"I told you that I have known the truth for some time. I knew when you finally gave yourself to me that you were a spy."

Lara felt the heat in her cheeks. He'd told her that

they would both recognize the moment when she declared to him, and they had. Unfortunately, her sins were so great that they could not be forgiven. Not by him with his honor. Most likely not even by the Almighty.

"I do love you, Lara. Do not run this time. Give me your trust and let me find a way for both of us."

"Ah, but you see? That is the problem. There is no way out if I stay here. Your honor will demand that you turn the spy over to your king. You will have no choice." She stepped back from him. "This way, you can disavow me. Let me take the children, for Robert will seek vengeance on them for both my and my father's acts. Let us go now before it is too late."

"It is already too late if you love me." He faced her and asked her again. "Do you love me, Lara?" He held his hand out to her, as he had so many times before, and waited for her answer.

She spied the movement in the shadows too late to warn him. With one blow to his head, Eachann laid him low. Lara began to scream, but her cousin stopped her with his hand over her mouth.

"Yer pardon for interrupting such a touching scene, Lara. Yer father waits offshore for us and we dinna have much time to reach him before the alarm is raised."

Jerking herself free, she fell to her knees next to Sebastien and lifted his head from the floor. Blood streamed from the wound on the back of his skull and he did not move.

"Why did you have to kill him?" she cried.

"He is not dead, but we shall be if we stay," Eachann

said as he wrapped his hand around her arm and pulled her away. "We go now." He pushed her toward the altar and, after placing something inside Sebastien's tunic, he followed her.

When they reached the altar, he walked to the far corner and pressed a certain place on the stone wall. The door she'd never seen open swung back and, after lighting a torch, he stepped in first and waved for her to follow. The damp, fetid air in the low corridor made her nauseous. She covered her nose and mouth with the edge of her cloak and tried to stay with Eachann.

It took almost a quarter hour to traverse the tunnel. Once they reached the end, he lit a small, covered lantern there and extinguished the torch. Pushing on the wall, Eachann pulled her out the tunnel and along a rocky path. They were in one of the caves on the firth, to the southwest of the castle.

Eachann motioned for her to stay back as he stepped out cautiously and surveyed the beach. Was he looking for guards? Then he lifted the lantern, uncovered it, and waved it to and fro for nearly a minute before lowering it and stepping back inside the protection of the cave.

Numbed by what had happened between her and Sebastien and then Eachann's attack, Lara slid down on the floor and began to shake uncontrollably. Her cousin eyed her with amusement on his face. He stood watch at the edge of the cave until he whispered her name a short while later.

Eachann lifted her to her feet and wrapped his arm around her waist. It was then Lara noticed a small boat coming to shore. Her cousin tugged on her arm and they ran from the cave, down the beach to the water's edge. He handed her into the craft and pushed it back into the water, climbing in as it moved away.

The boat bobbed about in the waves, and Lara's stomach rebelled. Three times she was forced to hang over the side of the small vessel as nausea gripped her. The cold water terrified her, and she clung to the side, closing her eyes and offering a prayer for Sebastien's safety. She did not ask for herself, for she deserved whatever suffering she got.

The journey to her father's ship took a long time, and she was exhausted by the time she was handed up to him. Instead of a warm welcome, he simply nodded to her and directed her to a place on deck where she could sit. Puzzled, she watched as he and Eachann exchanged words and laughed together. The glances they threw her way made her nervous.

Finally, the ship moved into smoother waters and she fell asleep, huddled under a blanket on the deck. Some time later, as dawn broke over the water, she was awakened by harsh whispers.

"Does she know?" her father asked.

"Nay. She believes that she is the one they came for."

"Eachann, this is working better than I had hoped. She is here believing that we saved her. The bastard is left behind and the king's men have the proof that he is the spy. His honor and sworn oath will prevent him from ever admitting she is the guilty one."

"Aye, Uncle. The king will execute him and our path will be clear. And the children?"

"Another way to guarantee his silence—if the Bruce believes him to be the spy, he will not take action against either of them. And the letter left on him will implicate the bastard even more."

They laughed again and Lara tried not to open her eyes.

"When will she be mine?"

"In good time, Eachann. In good time."

"I would like just a sample of what will be mine, Uncle. Let me have her just once and let me tell her the truth. Ye can watch if ye like."

Though revolted by his words, Lara could do nothing, lest it give away the fact that she listened. Her father did not want her back. She was his means to destroy Sebastien and, ultimately, the Bruce. And the thought that he would give her over to Eachann, knowing the disgusting things he wanted to do to her, turned her stomach again. The sound of flesh striking flesh drew her attention. Daring a peek, she realized that her father had punched Eachann in the face.

"Nay, Eachann. She has her uses in my plans before she is yours, and I will not have her damaged before then. She is the key and the safeguard. Once the bastard is executed, she is yours for whatever uses you wish."

Eachann backed away from her father, and Lara pulled the blanket tighter around her. Knowing the truth—that her escape trapped Sebastien and that he would protect her because of his honor—Lara knew she must get away from them. But how? On the sea, she was at their mercy, and she knew not where they were talking her. She decided that she must wait and watch and come up with some plan. Sebastien told her that a spy always has a contingency plan. She offered up a prayer that she could come up with one now.

Chapter Twenty-Two

"Tell us, traitor, what did you gain from your treachery?"

The man questioning him backhanded him again, and Sebastien struggled to remain upright. With his arms bound behind him, it was difficult. When he did not answer, the man punched him in the stomach, and as he bent over from the force of it, punched him in the face again. That blow landed him on the floor, and as he fought to take a breath, a kick followed and then another until he lost consciousness.

He was still on the floor when he woke. Blood poured from his nose and from the wound on his head, and he could not feel his hands. He thought at least one rib was broken, possibly more, making it difficult to breathe.

He lifted his head and looked around. They'd thrown him in the cell that faced the firth. The large barred opening allowed both wind and rain in, and so he was bloodied and cold and wet. Sebastien could not tell how long he'd been there. The same rain that pelted him now had put out the fire in the storage rooms. He'd known the blaze was a distraction when he'd seen it. Leaving the tower, he'd rushed to the chapel because he knew it would be the only way she could get away.

Sebastien knew that Eachann must have crept up behind him and hit him. When he awoke there, she was gone and the doorway, the one he could never find, stood open, as if glaring at his stupidity. He did not bother to follow, for he knew it must lead to the shore, and that they were long gone.

The king's men were in the hall when he entered, and, led by Patrick Campbell, they arrested him for treason. Patrick had him searched and claimed to have proof of his guilt. It could not have been much, and so the beating commenced to try to get more from him.

Sebastien would never give them anything. He'd promised to protect Lara and the children and he would do that, for if Robert believed that she was a spy, he would think nothing of executing the children as punishment for her crime. After keeping them with him and putting them in danger, Sebastien would have to keep silent to protect them now.

He moved slightly, and pain shot through his arms and chest. He needed to get off the floor and out of the rain. Ignoring the pain, he brought his legs up and rolled onto his knees. It took a long time for the sharp biting ache to ease and for him to be able to breathe. As he did, he heard a guard call out. Soon, the cell was filled with Patrick and his men. They pulled him up by his arms and forced him to stand.

"You will suffer less if you tell us the truth. I promise a quick hanging if you tell us what you gave to the MacDougall and the names of your accomplices."

Sebastien steeled himself for the blow as he watched the man make a fist and draw his arm back. But it did not come.

"Campbell! Another blow and I will lay you out."

Sebastien chuckled at James's threat. There was no love lost between the Black Douglas and the Campbells, so this would give him the chance to take them on without fear of repercussions. Although Sebastien could hear the heated words between them, he could not see them now for the blood pouring into his eyes.

"The king said to hold him for questioning."

"Aye, I heard him. But the bastard tried to escape, so I had to prevent that."

It was a lie—they all knew it—but James would not call him on it. That was not his way. "Clean him up and bring him to the hall."

"Oh, aye," Patrick said in a bitter voice, one that spoke of being forced to obey.

Sebastien heard James stride away, and waited. Patrick would take at least one more strike at him before releasing him to the Douglas.

"Clean him up? He will be cleaned."

They dragged him to where the rain fell the hardest and held him there. Patrick left and returned, followed now by several men carrying large buckets of water. They lined the buckets up and forced him to his knees. Grabbing his hair, they pushed his face into the first one. He struggled against their hold, but they were too many and he was weak. Just as he started to pass out, they pulled his head out of the water and threw what was left in his face.

"Nay, lads, not yet. He is not clean yet."

He tried to take a breath before they grabbed him again, but his chest would not respond. His struggles were for naught and he was held in the next bucket and the next until everything began to fade to black.

At least she was safe. If he had to die to protect her, then it had to be.

"Damn it, untie his hands, I said!"

James again.

Sebastien forced his eyes open and discovered that he now lay in the middle of the hall, on the floor. He felt the slice of a dagger cut through the laces that bound him, and through his skin as well. He could not feel his hands or move his arms, but within a few seconds, they came screaming back to life.

No one said a word as he struggled to his feet. Without the blood in his eyes, he saw that he was surrounded, by his men, James's men, the Campbells, and none of them looked very happy.

James stood and walked over to stand in front of him. "There are some charges that you must answer to, Sebastien. I am here for the king, to find out the truth."

"We know the truth, Douglas! He's a traitor."

Sebastien did not know which of the Campbells called out, but his men yelled their own insults back at the accusation. A riot threatened. James instructed his men with a nod, and with swords drawn, they surrounded him and separated the others. Sebastien pushed his matted hair out of his face.

"We are here to seek the truth," James said, looking at him. "Will you answer my questions?"

Sebastien did not reply, but James continued anyway. Holding out a small object, he asked, "Is this yours?"

Startled at seeing his mother's cross in James's possession, he nodded. "'Tis my mother's." The last time he'd seen it, it had been stored safely away in his trunk…along with his father's ring.

"You see? The bastard gave us up to the Mac-Dougalls!"

As more yelling and pushing began, James called out to them. "Hold! In the king's name, hold!"

James walked to the table and brought back a document of some kind. He held it out to Sebastien. "Do you recognize this?"

Sebastien took it and peered at it. It was a letter to him from John of Lorne, and as he read it, he shook his head. "This is not mine."

"They found it inside your tunic when they searched you. You are saying it is not yours?"

"It is not mine," he repeated.

He could see that James was in a quandary—he wanted to believe him, but the evidence pointed to his guilt in this very serious matter of treason.

"We will hold him until the king arrives," the Douglas called out loudly.

The Campbells argued, but there was nothing they could do here in the hall, outnumbered by James's men.

"Sir Hugh, he is your prisoner until the king relieves you of him. Secure him and see to his needs."

Hugh approached with Connor and Jamie and took

him by the arms, helping him back to the south tower, but to the cell above where the Campbells had held him. While the two stood guard, Hugh left and brought back something dry for him to wear. After locking him in, Hugh stood at the door.

"Do not be a fool, Sebastien. We know you are not the traitor. Even James knows."

"Do you?" he asked, as he stripped off the wet tunic and gown.

"And we know the most likely suspect, as well. Your life is at stake here."

"My honor is at stake, Hugh. Nothing less than my honor."

Hugh mumbled under his breath and banged on the door. "Do not protect her, Sebastien. Tell the truth and save yourself."

He walked to the door and spoke quietly to his friend. "I am nothing without my honor, Hugh. We have fought together long enough for you to know that I keep my word."

"Aye, but you pledged to the king. What about that oath?" When he did not answer, Hugh asked, "Do you truly think that they will let her live?"

"Nay, not for long, once their purpose is attained."

"So you admit that you protect her?"

"To you? Aye," he answered. "But, if the king believes that Lara is in a plot with her father, he will have no choice but to kill the children as an example to those who would defy him and break their truces. Hostages are worthless if they are left alive after betrayal." With a great amount of pain and difficulty, Sebastien finished dressing in the dry clothes.

"What will you do?"

"Once I know that she is safe, nothing at all. The king will draw whatever conclusions he must from the evidence."

"Safe? How will you know that?"

"Surely, Hugh, you know that all spies have a contingency plan?"

"My lady? My lady? Please wake up," the quiet voice said in the darkness.

Lara opened her eyes and struggled to sit up on the small cot where she lay. Then she realized she was not alone and almost screamed. His hand over her mouth prevented her, and he whispered for her to be silent. She nodded her acceptance and he dropped his hand.

"Who are you? What do you want?" she whispered as she moved as far as she could from this stranger.

"My name is Munro, my lady. I am your husband's cousin."

"How did you find me?"

"I have been working for your father for weeks, keeping a watch on him for Sebastien."

"You are a spy?" she asked.

"Hush now, my lady. I would not want someone to hear you. I have come to get you out of here, but you must hurry and do as I say."

Sebastien had directed him to find her? "My husband sent you?"

"Nay, but I am under orders to do what I must, and this seemed the right thing to do." He handed her a sack. "There are clothes in there—change quickly and bring your own cloak as well."

It took her only a few minutes to dress in a man's garments. She handed him her clothes and he stuffed them under the blanket to appear as though someone slept there still.

"Are you ready? We must move quickly and not look back. Do not look back."

Catching sight of the bloodied dagger in his hand, she nodded, though not sure at all. But something in his gaze told her that her life depended on getting away from here, and that he was the way to do that. And with what she knew, she needed to return to Dunstaffnage before they executed Sebastien.

James Douglas leaned back and let his laughter roar out. Then he shook his head as he looked once more at the pair of scraggly men standing before him. Well, one man and one woman. Her displeasure at his mirth was clear.

"James, this is a serious matter. You know he is not a traitor."

"Aye, my lady. Just as I know that you are," he said with a nod of his head.

"Touché," Lara answered. He had to admit that her voice did wonderful things with French words. Her tongue curled in the just the correct manner to soften the sounds…and heat a man's blood. Even filthy and dressed as a man, she was appealing.

"I must see the king on Sebastien's behalf."

"I fear not, my lady. I do not trust you enough to allow you access to the king."

"So, then, you would allow the king to execute his own brother and not tell him so?"

"My lady, you try my patience!" Then he heard the last words she'd said. He searched her face for some indication of whether she spoke the truth or not.

"Aye, James Douglas, you heard me. Sebastien of Cleish is Robert's own brother."

"You have proof of such a claim?" He crossed his arms and waited for her reply. The defeated expression on her face told him the answer.

"But there *is* proof. If you let me into Dunstaffnage, I can get it and bring it to the king."

He laughed again, but she stopped him with a poke in his chest. "If you are his true friend, you will at least see the proof and do what you can to help him."

He stopped laughing then and accepted the inevitable. "Tell me what I must find, lady, and be quick about it."

The news reached even the most isolated place in the castle—the Bruce had arrived. Sebastien heard one of the servants tell the guard when they brought him food. He'd thought about his dilemma and still saw no way out of it that did not damn her or the children or his honor. He knew that Robert would most likely seek a private word with him before reviewing the matter in public, so he waited.

James had not been back to talk with him, nor Hugh, but Sebastien suspected that was to avoid any challenges to their authority. He wondered what his men must think of this. Well, there was not much to do now. He was not sure that Robert would understand the choices he'd made, but he would comprehend the need for his word to stand.

The guard came to the door and announced a visitor, and Sebastien stood and waited for Robert to enter. Instead, a much smaller man entered and stood before him. Surprise turned to shock as he gazed at his wife's face. Before he could respond, James Douglas pushed her forward and entered the cell behind her.

"'Twould seem all your good efforts are for naught, Sebastien. Look who returned to Dunstaffnage this morn."

He could not look at her or he would waver. She must get away or everything would be in danger. *She* would be in danger.

"James, if you are my friend, take her from here and let her go. For all the times I covered your arse, let her go."

"I tried that, but she will not be put out," James said. "I am having nightmares over her threats of bodily harm if I do not come to *your* aid." He laughed. "Between the two of you, I do not know which to fear most."

"Lara, you must go. James, please." He would beg if that's what it took.

"But Sebastien, she tells such an interesting tale. You should hear it before you send her away."

"Lara, do not say a word."

"It is too late, Sebastien. I have told him everything—about my family's plans, about the information I provided to them, about…you."

"What about me?" What did she mean?

"Everyone knows you are a man of honor. No one can believe that you would betray the Bruce, a man whom you pledged your word to, a man I know is your brother."

The light in the cell changed somehow, and he gazed at her across the small distance. She knew? How did she know? Words would not form in his mouth, but from the knowing smirk on James's face, this came as no surprise to him.

"How did you find out?" he asked. Only Hugh knew, and he would never have betrayed Sebastien's secret unless Sebastien gave him leave to do so.

"I should have realized it when I saw the two of you together, and I cannot believe that canny James Douglas has missed the resemblance for this long."

"Lady, you are trying my patience once more," James growled from his place near the door. "I would have you beaten if you were my wife."

"Your coloring is different, of course, but you share the same nose." She laughed then, a sound welcome to his heart, and one he did not think to ever hear again. "And, more importantly, the same father."

"It means nothing, Lara. If I had wanted the protection of his name I would have sought it out long ago. I have made my own way all of my life and will not hide now behind a name."

She continued as though she'd heard none of his words. "I found the ring when I took the cross from your trunk, Sebastien. I did not recognize the insignia as the Bruce's family mark until I saw the documents carried by Munro. I realized then that you were one of them."

"Munro saw you to safety then?"

She nodded.

Good. His man was in the right place at the time of most serious need, as he'd planned.

"And killed Eachann," she said, her voice trembling now, and Sebastien fought the urge to go to her side.

He nodded, pleased that Munro understood completely what had to be done and did it, although deep inside a part of him wished he had wielded the weapon causing his enemy's death. He hoped it was not too swift a death.

"Do not try to distract me, Sebastien. I saw the same seal on the documents he carried to ease his way through the Bruce's camps."

"Anyone can have a ring." He did not know why he fought to keep it a secret still. It truly did not speak to the issue of treason and the evidence against him.

"Aye, but I also read your will."

"My will? How did you get to these things?" If she'd read his words, then she knew for certain.

"James the Canny sought them out for me." She gestured to him with her head, and Sebastien held in his laugh. "He did not trust me in the same castle with the Bruce."

"You know he takes his reputation and his duties very seriously, lass. I would not be insulting him. He will be your safe passage out of here once you both understand what must happen next."

Lara walked to him and touched his cheek. "I would do anything for you, Sebastien. I will even save you when you will not save yourself."

"There is no need for you to say anything."

"I heard my father's plans. I heard how he—they—used the information I gave them, not just to attack the Bruce's forces, but to destroy you as well. Even they who have no honor recognized that you would damn yourself before you broke your word to me. And they willingly used me, just as you warned they would do."

"Lara, please, say no more. James will have no choice but to tell the Bruce, and I will have no way to save you." He shook his head and tried to step away from her, but she followed him.

"Sebastien, you need to know this. They attacked one of their own men and left him for dead, telling him that you were his assailant. They put that cross in his hand, and that is how you were linked to his death. Eachann put a letter inside your tunic when he struck you to provide them with 'proof' that you were plotting with my father to hold Dunstaffnage for yourself."

He leaned in close to her and said softly, "I know that their proof is false, Lara. It changes nothing. The only choice I have is to sacrifice you, and that is not an option."

"Mayhap the king will hear my words asking for his mercy. Mayhap he will understand the weakness of a woman trying to protect her own siblings and people, as he has had to do. Mayhap he will wait until the babe is born before deciding its mother's fate."

"Babe? Babe?" he stuttered. They were to have a bairn of their own?

"Mayhap he has, lady?"

The voice that came from behind Lara was not James's. She gasped as the king pulled open the cell door and entered.

"Sire," Sebastien said, bowing to his brother.

"You are wrong about one thing, Sebastien. Not just anyone can have this ring." Robert held out his father's—their father's—ring to him. "He told me he had them made for his sons, both legitimate and natural. He may have known only of your existence when he gave this to your mother, but he would have summoned you to him if he'd had an opportunity to do so. I have only recently lost brothers, and cannot so easily allow another to die in defense of his wife." Two of Robert's brothers, and his half brothers, had been executed by Edward in a hideous manner after their capture.

"Sire, she was forced to help them. She was beaten, anyone here can tell you—" he began to explain.

The king held up his hand to stop him. "And everyone has told me. You have the most opinionated group of men serving you, Sebastien. And the women are no better. One, called Margaret I think, has no fear." He looked at both of them and shook his head. "I knew that you would face challenges in your marriage to her, but this is more that I expected any of my vassals to face. I could intercede on your behalf if you wish for an end to it."

The king turned to face James and then turned back. "I am willing to forgo any judgments or punishments until we have had a chance to talk about all of these things and about why you have not brought news of our kinship to me before this." Robert walked to the door. "She has promised to be a good and obedient wife from now forward, Sebastien, and I will take her at her word. With your strong guidance and her remorse, I believe she can be controlled and not repeat her offenses."

James coughed as though choking, but stepped back to allow the king passage. Shaking his head, he followed Robert out of the cell. Sebastien could hear his words, for he was certain that James made no attempt to hide them. "She has not been yet, sire, why do you think she will be now?"

Sebastien suddenly realized they were alone, alive, and the door was open. He opened his arms to her and she stepped into them. "Obedient? You promised him you would be obedient?"

"Well," she said, smiling at him, "other than this, I have been obedient."

"Other than leaving against my orders, coming back against my orders and revealing what I told you not to reveal, when did your obedience begin?"

"You would have sacrificed your life for me," she said, putting her head on his shoulder.

"I promised you that I would protect you. If you could trust me, we might have avoided much of this."

"If I had trusted you, so much loss could have been prevented." She leaned back and looked at him, her eyes bleak with the same thought he had. "Philippe. The other lives shed because of my words. I will regret their deaths forever, Sebastien."

"Lara, the boy's death was my fault. I knew that Eachann had my plans by then. You were not the only one of his spies here. I should have protected him by leaving him behind. You did warn me. You begged me not to take him. Although I did not know why, I should have listened to you."

They were quiet then and he thought of the smiling boy whose life had been lost in his service. The king was no doubt handling matters of treachery and clearing their way above stairs, so they should follow.

"Come, Lara. We should see what the king wants of us. And you should change out of these clothes."

"I used to wear something like this when I learned to climb the walls of the castle."

He felt faint. Blinking, he shook his head. "Never tell me that you climbed the walls to get in here today."

"Oh, nay. I just threatened a pox on James's essential parts if he would not help me."

"I do not wonder why he fears you, lady. He needs those if he wants to start his own family."

"Come now, Sebastien," she said, as he took her hand and led her out of the cell. "He needs those parts to pleasure a certain kitchen maid named Peggy."

Sebastien laughed for a moment, knowing that Lara would give James no quarter in the future. "We have much to discuss and many things to do."

The Lord and Lady of Dunstaffnage were greeted by their people as they entered the hall. The Campbells were gone, and apparently the king's declaration that Sebastien was still in his esteem had smoothed the way quite nicely for them.

Sebastien was not happy when he discovered that Robert would stay for several more days…and use their chambers, as befitted his station as king. But he knew that the Bruce, having not visited there for some time, would not miss the strange, large chair from the bedroom.

Epilogue

"I baptize thee in the name of the Father, and of the Son, and of the Holy Ghost. Amen."

Father Connaughty poured the final amount of water over the bairn's head and smiled as his outraged howls filled the chapel. Handing him back to his godfather, the king, the priest stepped away and allowed them a moment of privacy.

"A handsome boy," Robert said, as he turned and held the babe out to her.

"Aye, sire. He has his father's eyes."

Lara dried Philippe's head and soothed him back to sleep. Sebastien offered to return him to his nurse, but Lara held him. They had spoken often of the first Philippe over these last months and it seemed fitting that they should name their son after him.

"Raise him well, Sebastien. I need good warriors on my side."

"We will, sire. If he has his mother's daring—"

"Dear God in Heaven, save us!" James finished the

sentiment, although Lara knew it was not what Sebastien had been planning to say.

"I did not know you could enter a church safely, James. There are rumours, you know." Lara relinquished the babe to Margaret's willing arms.

He held up his hands in surrender and walked away. "You will have to teach me that skill, lady. Even beating him to a pulp does not gain his surrender to me."

"'Tis simple, Sebastien. He has a secret that I know and he fears I will reveal, so he acquiesces to me."

"And that secret?"

"I cannot say, my lord. Mayhap one day he will tell you himself."

"Lara, as your lawful husband, I command you to tell me," he ordered.

She laughed. It was such an inconsequential thing, but always important to men. And she had such fun using it against James. To share it would lessen its power.

"Let us go back to our chambers and discuss this obedience you desire."

"Oh no, Lara. I know your ways. We will go there, you will seduce me and I will never find out."

She moved her gaze over his body until it reached the part of him that would react to her words. "And would you like to do that or not?" She licked her lips and he tensed. "The king will be using our chambers this night, but if we hurry…"

"Damn!" he said. "Very well, I will allow you to seduce me then."

She leaned up and kissed him. "And I will allow you to seduce me the next time."

The sparkle in his eyes spoke of his passion and told her he knew her game.

"I am always your obedient wife, my lord."

"Or you let me think you are."

"Oh, aye, my lord."

He kissed her then and swept her out of the church to their chambers, where their laughter filled the keep with love.

Author's Note

I based my story on a factual event, the battle of Brander Pass, which was fought on August 11, 1308, but I confess to taking "literary license" with some of the real history of the time. The Bruce did indeed defeat John of Lorne, who escaped to England and was appointed Admiral of the Western Seas by Edward I. As a hostage, John left behind his elderly father, not his children, as I used for my story. The eldest daughter of the Lord of Lorne, and head of the MacDougall clan, was given the honorary title of "Maid of Lorne."

I fear I did not give James Douglas enough credit, for it was his battle strategies that saved the Bruce that day. James, who was later called "Good Sir James," was Robert the Bruce's premier fighting machine and guerrilla warfare expert, and fought in more than sixty battles during his lifetime. Robert the Bruce so trusted him that he asked James to take his heart to the Holy Land to fulfill a promise to go there on a Crusade. James died in Spain on his way to the East, and Robert's heart was returned and buried in Melrose

Abbey, while the rest of his remains are in Dunfermline Abbey in Scotland.

I think I owe the MacDougall clan an apology—their actions were no better or worse than any other noble family in this struggle that was both a civil war and a war against England. Fathers and sons, brothers and sisters, even husbands and wives, often found themselves on opposite sides. Extremes in brutality and mercy were seen throughout this war. As I mention in the story, Robert the Bruce originally fought on Edward's side, but changed loyalties during the struggles after being inspired by the actions of William Wallace—and perhaps his own desire to be king? He was also known to forgive former enemies; Thomas Randolph and William, the Earl of Ross, are some dramatic examples of mercy he showed when it was politically correct.

Dunstaffnage Castle, home at one time to the legendary Stone of Scone, was seized after the Battle of Brander Pass, and a royal warden was appointed to hold it. It was one of very few castles that the Bruce's forces did not destroy during his campaign to take back Scotland. Eventually, after Robert's death, John of Lorne regained it, and later it passed into Campbell hands. As Sebastien predicted in the story, John of Lorne would never get the castle back while Robert lived—and he did not!

One final bit of history—although the first formal "parliaments" of Robert the Bruce were held in the spring of 1309, there are a few mentions of a gathering held at Ardchattan Priory, a monastery a few miles northeast of Dunstaffnage, which had been established and supported by the Lords of Lorne. No doubt Robert was pleased by the choice of the site, since it would be a smack at his enemies.

If you have any questions or comments about the history contained in my story, you can contact me at terri@terribrisbin.com. I like nothing more than to discuss brawny, powerful Scottish heroes and their heroines with readers!

* * * * *

If you enjoyed what you just read,
then we've got an offer you can't resist!

Take 2 bestselling love stories FREE!

Plus get a FREE surprise gift!

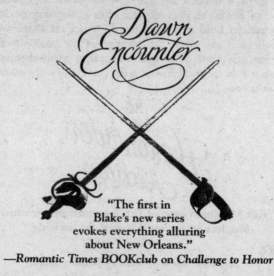